MW00908391

PRAISE FOR

ORCHID BLOOMING

"Tension and compelling chemistry that will leave you breathless."

—Barbara Conrey, *USA Today* bestselling author of
Nowhere Near Goodbye

"A love story for our times, *Orchid Blooming* reminds us of the power of empathy and will stay with you long after the last page."

—Lainey Cameron, award-winning author and host of
The Best of Women's Fiction podcast

"Precise and alluring command of language. *Orchid Blooming's* compelling imagery kept me reading. Another gold medal is on the horizon!"

—SSGT Aaron Michael Grant, author of *Taking Baghdad: Victory in Iraq with the US Marines*

"Rich with strong characters and a powerful sense of place, Orchid and Phoenix's story is also an important message about the serious nature of post-traumatic stress disorder, the importance of honesty in a relationship, and the enduring power of love and forgiveness."

—Susan Cushman, author of eight books, including
Pilgrim Interrupted and *John and Mary Margaret*

"Five-stars for *Orchid Blooming*! This page-turning novel is modern, ambitious, tempestuous, and ultimately gut wrenching. Torn between two conflicting worlds, Orchid must find the courage to forge her own path, even as she fears losing everything she holds dear."

—Rebecca Rosenburg, award-winning author of
Champagne Widows

Orchid Blooming
by Carol Van Den Hende

© Copyright 2022 Carol Van Den Hende

ISBN 978-1-958223-01-7

All rights reserved. No part of this publication may be reproduced, stored in a retrieval system, or transmitted in any form or by any means—electronic, mechanical, photocopy, recording, or any other—except for brief quotations in printed reviews, without the prior written permission of the author.

This is a work of fiction. The characters are both actual and fictitious. With the exception of verified historical events and persons, all incidents, descriptions, dialogue and opinions expressed are the products of the author's imagination and are not to be construed as real.

REBBL® Elixirs is a trademark of REBBL Inc. and used with permission of the company

Published by
Azine Press™

DEDICATION

To the best mother-in-law…
who brightens the world with her art, and
lights up our lives with love

Empathy is
seeing with the eyes of another,
listening with the ears of another,
and feeling with the heart of another.

—Alfred Adler

CHAPTER 1
WILD ORCHIDS

Orchid

SPRING, NEW YORK CITY

Fifteen years ago, Orchid Paige could've never imagined a world without her mother.

Today, April rain swept away the thought, blurring her view of Manhattan skyscrapers outside the conference room windows.

She straightened in her seat, surrounded by her Estee Lauder co-workers. Her cobalt-highlighted hair shone in the window's reflection. If the black strands of her Asian heritage could transform, what else could change?

Her boss, Joan, commanded the front of the room. She wore a structured suit and heavy earrings. Her mouth barely creased as she shared company news. "International experience is essential for the next level up. Here's a rare opportunity…"

The atmosphere became electrified.

Princeton, an Ivy League-educated coworker, leaned closer. His nostrils widened, like a racehorse chomping at the starting gate. He was named after the university that his parents believed he was destined to attend.

"Lauder China wants someone for six-weeks in Beijing. It'll be a high visibility assignment," Joan said.

Orchid's pulse quickened. Her imagination tipped halfway around the world, to a place where terra cotta soldiers guarded a long-dead emperor, where the age of dynasties was measured in millennia, and the scale of The Great Wall made it visible from the skies. *Visible from my mother's vantage point in heaven,* she thought, as an image danced in her imagination.

Beautiful, dark-haired Mom was the artist in the family, the woman who amused young Orchid with drawings of dogs in tutus, and cat soirees. When she was little, Orchid thought her Chinese half was connected to her creative side. Her analytical brain was from her dad's side, his long English ancestry stamped with stories of tradesmen and entrepreneurs.

Memories of her mother were faded. She pictured her, still young, unmarred by the accident that took her life, gliding carefree through the grounds of an Oriental palace. "You should visit China someday," her mom had said.

She realized that Joan was still speaking.

"If you're interested, let me know by–"

"*Song wo,*" Princeton trilled in Mandarin. *Send him? His grin telegraphed his assumption that privileged schooling and language skills would assure him the coveted assignment.*

Chinese warriors from her mother's ancestry beckoned… *your opportunity! Not his!*

She stifled an urge to nudge Princeton, to cuff him the way he'd snubbed her non-Ivy schooling. With his proud pedigree, his fat nostrils would likely drip blue blood, marring the silk of his pocket handkerchief. "Where did you attend uni?" he'd asked her by way of introduction, then sniffed at the response.

Princeton's smugness sparked her competitiveness. She'd earned everything in her life: every scholarship, every opportunity. This would be no different. The challenges from childhood had strengthened her for this battle. She would test her savvy against her colleague's arrogance. To give herself a chance.

After the meeting, she closed her notebook and walked out of the room with her boss. "I could add value to the team," she said. "Can we set up some time to discuss the assignment?"

Joan tilted her head at Orchid's blue locks; her expression was unreadable. "I'm free tomorrow. Schedule some time on my calendar." Her Christian Louboutin heels clicked down the hall.

Orchid hurried to her desk, opened her computer, and sent an invitation to Joan to meet her in the morning. Then she tapped open a new window to search for information about expatriate assignments. She lost herself in photos. Pictures of smog and crowded highways competed with images of cherry blossoms and temples. She knew that her mother's nostalgia was for China's ancient history rather than its present-day complications. Still, she nearly forgot to breathe as she sought her mother's features in the faces of pedestrians.

At the end of the workday, she exited her office building. The rain had stopped, leaving the evening air humid. Her phone buzzed with a baby picture from her best friend Mandy. The infant's halo of hair glowed in the sunshine.

Orchid was eager to share this China goal with Mandy. As she crossed the street towards her subway station, she decided to call, rather than send a text.

"Hey, hon," Mandy greeted her.

"Miss you, honey. How's my favorite godson?"

"There's a study that shows smarter babies sleep less. So, your godson must be a genius."

"Ha. Sleep-deprived parents everywhere will be wishing for less intellect."

She paused at the top of the steps leading down to her subway stop. Phone reception was always a problem two flights down.

"Speaking of intellect, how's the glamorous life of a beauty executive?"

"I'm going to burst your bubble. Glamorous and executive aren't part of my everyday vocabulary. There is news, though."

"Tell me! I need something more than eco-friendly diapers to spice up my week."

"Sustainable diapers are exciting," she said. "But let me fill you in in-person. Are you free tonight? To get a drink?"

"Did you forget that I'm breastfeeding? No alcohol for me, but I'm up for a night out."

"Cool, 'cause I figured out what I want... but chances are not looking good."

"I'm dying to know. Text me a time and place."

"Will do. Can't wait!"

That evening, Orchid hurried along the avenue. With few commuters, she made good time to the Pyramid nightclub. Sitting at the curb was an idling cab, its windows reflecting her slender figure in a post-punk black minidress with silver-toothed zippers.

She paid the bouncer and pushed through the doors into the black-painted dance club. Ever since the childhood trauma of witnessing her parents' accident, she needed to calm her nerves in busy places. It was a quiet night in this dive. She stilled her trembling hands, and checked for the exit, her escape route. This was an automatic response she had adopted as a teen.

One red sign shone at the hallway leading to the bathrooms. EXIT. *Good.*

Orchid spotted Mandy, who had secured a spot at the edge of the room and loped across the sticky floor to join her. Mandy wasn't only her best friend; she was her confidante.

"Sorry, I got lost in research," Orchid apologized, and hugged her friend.

Mandy raised her voice over the percussion notes. "As long as you made it. Now spill the beans. Your call has me on the edge of my seat!"

Even though Orchid's ebony-lined eyes and edgy attire telegraphed an effortless cool, she knew that Mandy could see through that.

"You told me you figured out something. Tell!"

"Chances are, like, nil that I'll get it," Orchid said.

Mandy pushed a ruby-shaded cocktail towards her. Orchid clinked her tumbler against her friend's glass of Perrier. "Thank you," she said, and sipped the cool drink.

Mandy straightened on her bar stool, ready to dig into what Orchid recognized as her favorite problem-solving mode. "Let's see. What do you want more than anything? I know. Tickets to Fashion Week. Or that thrifted Dolce & Gabbana peony-print dress."

"Better peonies than orchids." Orchid said. It wasn't just her pet peeve over orchid everything; it was the memory of her mother's dress, the one decorated with peonies. "Good guess, but no."

"Girls' night with your bestie?" Mandy stirred her sparkling water with a paper straw.

Nothing like Mandy's optimism to buoy spirits. "Love you. Okay, second best."

"A tattooed god who eats calculus for breakfast and gets into every club in the city?" Mandy gave her an impish grin, swinging her blonde bob.

"That sounds awesome, except you know I can't trust anyone. Dating's not in my future."

"Aww c'mon," said Mandy. "I need to live vicariously through my single friends." She tilted her head towards the end of the bar.

She glanced in the direction of Mandy's gaze. She saw a burly fellow with snake tattoos that ran along his thick neck. He seemed to be glowering at the ground. Counter-culture level: a near-perfect six. Not high enough to trigger cultish fears, and not low enough to scream *wannabe*.

The two friends became immersed in their conversation. The increased hum in the place made it harder to hear each other speak.

Hang on. Next to tatt-guy, a young David Beckham

lookalike curved long fingers around a bottle of beer. Eyes thick with lashes met her gaze, and her chest thumped with something akin to recognition. Impossible. They'd never met. Yet his eyebrows lifted, as if she had sparked something in him, too.

Orchid tossed the split-second connection into her brain's dustbin, along with today's forgotten dry cleaning.

She downed her drink and refocused on Mandy. "Get your mind off guys. What I want more than anything has to do with work."

"Work?"

"My boss said we need international experience for any shot at a promotion. And, oh, by the way, they're recruiting a Lauder marketer for an assignment to China."

"China? You know you can't leave me!"

"It's a temporary assignment, six weeks. And there's no way they're going to pick me."

"Who better than you?"

"Someone with more experience. The Princeton pedigree in my office, for one. He started speaking Mandarin during the meeting, for crying out loud."

Mandy nearly spit the mouthful she'd just taken. "Mandarin? But you can too, right?"

"I have the vocabulary of a two-year old." She inhaled, the truth spilling out. "The weird thing is, with this Princeton wretch vying for the spot, it makes me want it even more. If I get this, leave baby Matty with hubby and come with me!"

Mandy faced her phone screen towards Orchid. "I cannot leave this munchkin."

Cherub cheeks, ruddy with sleep, topped with a bunny-soft tuft of blond hair.

"Aww, he's the cutest."

Without prompting, Mandy swiped and paused on another photo of her son, his fists pumping in excitement over a spoon headed for his round mouth. "His favorite is barley."

"Neigh," Orchid whinnied.

Mandy snorted. "Back to you. Do you have family there?"

"None that I know of. But this is a fast track to promotion." Thinking in terms of her future with the company made more sense than talking about the growing urge she had to visit her mother's home country. She figured that her features were mirrored somewhere in the faces of those billion people. Just like her mom's.

"So, what's the plan?" Mandy asked, getting the bartender's attention and pointing to her glass.

"I've set up time with my boss, and I'm going to let her know I'll do anything. Study, learn the language, whatever it takes."

Mandy gave her a broad smile. "You go, girl! There's research about guys going for an opportunity even if they have only half the qualifications, but women feel they need a hundred percent to even apply."

"Don't worry, I'm going for it. It's perfect for me. It's the only way to a promotion, and I can't stand the thought of Princeton winning."

"I'd pick you," said Mandy.

Orchid gave Mandy's arm a gentle squeeze. "You're the sweetest. I'd pick you too. Now, I need the bathroom." She slid off the seat and straightened her minidress. In Hell's Kitchen, rocking an attitude was essential.

David Beckham was gone. Snake-tatt guy was still slumped on the bar stool. His slouch emanated an angst that Orchid could relate to.

The DJ seated on the far side of the bar transitioned to a driving bass line that urged Orchid towards the dance floor. The restrooms were situated down a corridor, somewhere on the other side of the writhing bodies.

The tacky floor tugged at the soles of her platform boots as she bopped along to the beat. A hiss accompanied a familiar scent. Faux smoke shrouded the space. Like she needed additional obstacles to finding the loo. That is, besides her buzz.

Orchid's bladder moved her toward the hallway and then the bathroom. The little symbol with the arrow was the women's room, right? How quaint that this throwback place didn't have gender neutral washrooms.

The handle turned easily, so she pushed through the door, flimsy like the card house of her life.

"Aiya!" came a deep voice. A tall figure jumped back from the sink. The door barely missed his athletic form. Orchid almost tumbled into him.

"What are you doing in here?" she cried out.

His azure eyes reflected kindness, and his full lips widening in a field of stubble caused her breath to hitch. The David Beckham doppelganger! His baritone rumbled with good humor. "I don't know about you...but I'M in the men's room."

She felt her cheeks warm. *Oops.* Before she walked out, she commented on his Chinese expression. "I speak English, you know, even if I look Chinese."

His eyes widened. Did cobalt blaze that bright? "Of course, you do. It's not you. *Aiya* just spills out. I keep forgetting. I'm just back from Beijing."

"Beijing!" she exclaimed. "That's where I want to go. How was it?" The connection of a faraway land made this stranger feel familiar.

Long fingers swung the spigot closed, then swiped a paper towel. He dried between each digit. "Hai keyi."

She couldn't help herself, air expelled at his use of the phrase that roughly translated to *pretty good.* "You sound like a native," she said.

"Hardly. Do you speak Mandarin?"

Her vision adjusted to the brightness. Light surfed his wavy hair. His blue eyes crinkled. "Bu hui." She shook her head *no.*

Humor erupted from him. "You could've fooled me, since you answered in Chinese."

Despite her bladder's protests, he'd made her chuckle again. "I need to learn more, if I want a shot at this overseas assignment. I'm too old for the kids' TV series *Ni Hao, Kai Lan*, and I don't have enough time for a semester at NYU." *Why am I babbling to this stranger?*

He chuckled again, balled up his paper towel, and lobbed it towards the garbage can. It sailed like a swan dive, as if refusing to mess with this guy's perfection. "The key is getting the accent right. In Beijing, they add an 'r' sound at the end of certain words."

"Then I'm completely screwed."

"If you're smart enough for an overseas assignment, I'm sure you could learn Chinese. Do you need the bathroom?" he asked. "I think the lock's broken. I'll stand guard for you, like this is Mao's tomb."

She guffawed. This guy was a riot.

He left the bathroom and stood just outside the door.

She finished using the bathroom and regarded her reflection as she washed her hands. Blue-streaked locks were swept to one side. She had figured that the drama of kohl-rimmed eyes for an evening out would deter most ordinary men. The darker she could amplify her appearance, perhaps the safer she could keep herself. Self-protection came first.

She refocused on what really mattered. *Now that I've told Mandy, I really need to make this assignment happen.* Internally armored, she stepped out. There was Beckham, protecting the broken door. Someone who kept promises.

"Mao's safe," she shouted over the deafening beat.

His lips widened over ultra-white teeth, brightened by the club's blacklight. His easy charm could belong on a men's fashion shoot.

"That was embarrassing," she admitted.

"Not really. It's dark in here."

The bar's partygoers grooved across the dance floor. Orchid paused, and saw that he had noticed her hesitation at the crowd.

One deft move, and he parted a clearing through the dancers. He beckoned for her to follow. Looking after her again.

Away from the density of bodies, Beckham looked back to check on her. Seeing her a few steps behind, he grinned and busted a move.

She couldn't help her mirth. How had she left for a simple trip to the loo and returned with a bilingual Adonis?

As they neared Mandy and her pace slowed. Her friend looked back and forth between them.

"You were gone forever. I almost called the National Guard," Mandy yelled over the music.

"Speaking of guard, this is..." Orchid ogled her kind protector.

He saved her. "Phoenix. Nice to meet you," he raised a hand in greeting. Mandy's mouth parted and nothing came out. He really was drop-dead gorgeous. Stop.

"Thanks again." Orchid waved and turned to speak with her friend.

"Bye...um," he paused, waiting for Orchid to fill in the blank.

"Kai Lan," she deadpanned.

He threw his head back in appreciation and then made his way through the crowd to the burly fellow. The tattooed guy's dour mood had faded. He said something, and Phoenix's glance alighted on her.

"I need to skedaddle," said Mandy. But before we go, do you have something you want to tell me?"

"Not a thing. I ended up in the wrong bathroom."

"That's an interesting approach. I thought the tattooed one was more your type."

"I have no type, because I'm staying single."

Orchid refocused on her goal. Tomorrow, she'd meet with her boss. *Goodbye, New York.*

CHAPTER 2
DREAMS OF THE LONELY

FIFTEEN YEARS EARLIER

Orchid was twelve. At her insistence, she was home without a babysitter. The early evening hours alone were fine, filled with verboten snacks and colored pencil drawings she'd made for her parents. Then, the last wisps of dusk fell behind the thick woods that towered over their house. The sky was dotted with thick snowflakes. As temperatures plunged, the snow twisted into glistening streaks of ice.

She turned on the television. "A sudden squall. Stay off the roads," the TV newscaster warned. This filled her with trepidation.

After midnight, she turned on the hall lights and crept up to her bedroom, where she huddled in a ball beneath frigid sheets. She pulled the comforter over her ears, over her pigtails, warming the stale air in her little curled space. Her mom had plaited her hair into two neat braids before leaving.

Walls creaked. The hot water heater pipes moaned. Ice drummed against the roof. The house's hollow stillness confirmed the absence of other living creatures. She had never felt so alone… or afraid.

She must've dozed. The shrill phone woke her. Her room was so dark that she was reminded of the time a squirrel had chewed through some wires and they lost all electricity.

Her sleep-thick legs stumbled down the hall to her parents'

bedroom and she picked up the receiver. "Hello?" she said. Her throat felt froggy. Outside, there was no light coming from their porch lantern, and the halogen light above the driveway was lost in the foggy night. Clouds misted over the moon, casting a ghostly glow across the sky. The wind shrieked.

"Orchid, it's Mom."

Relief washed over her. "Are you coming home?" She fumbled for the clock on the nightstand. Its blank screen stared back, lifeless. They'd lost power.

"Soon," her mom said.

Orchid heard ice drumming on the slate roof. It made her think of demons trying to hack their way in, one shingle at a time.

"We're almost there, honey. The roads are worse than we thought."

"I'll put salt out," said Orchid.

When the call ended, she headed downstairs.

In the foyer, she pulled on her puffy coat and boots, and tucked the phone into her pocket. She yanked open door and ice whipped her face. She trudged across the yard, to dig through their chaotic garage and find rock salt. A handful of minerals seemed useless against tonight's winter storm gods.

Wild waving beams of light caught her attention. The headlights to her parents' beater car pointed down the long steep driveway.

Suddenly, a piercing screech jolted her eardrums. It took a moment to realize that the screaming sound was coming down the winding driveway. The car's brakes. keened and wailed. Then...an exploding crunch. Impact reverberated through the trees.

Cold fear shot through her.

She raced up the driveway, slipping on ice, into the darkness.

"I'm coming!" she screamed out.

And then she stopped running. The car was crumpled against a tree. No sounds emerged.

She felt goosebumps on her arms. Her scalp stiffened with something primordial.

Help! We need help.

She pulled the phone from her pocket and punched in 9-1-1. Her limbs trembled. When she heard a woman's voice, she begged between hyperventilating breaths. "My parents," she said. "There was a crash. The car…"

The dispatch operator confirmed the address. "Stay on the line with me," she told Orchid. "Emergency services should be there in minutes."

She drew closer, desperate to do something.

The woods echoed their silence. The only sound was the spattering sleet that covered everything around her.

Shards of ice pelted her face and her nightgown, now a sheet of ice, clung to her legs. She suddenly remembered how her parents had joked that the steep descent from the road to their house was their insurance to keep trick-or-treaters away, and they were left with all those Halloween sweets for themselves.

As she neared, hazard lights flickered, momentarily illuminating crumpled blue metal, and then plunging the toothless grille into darkness. She tried to make sense of googly-eyed headlights. One angled up to illuminate gnarled limbs of trees, their branches grasping towards the wreckage like twisted fingers. The other pointed down, an oblong light marking the spot for a grave.

Then the smell reached her. She gagged as oil and gas and brake fluid stung her nose. The smoking engine cautioned her with a hiss. It was quiet except for tiny daggers of ice hitting ice. Too quiet. "Mom? Dad!" She moaned, slipping up the icy surface. The car crumpled around a felled tree at the hairpin turn that always seemed like murder on her bike.

This is the place she should've stopped. Heeded the warnings of the spitting hoses, grasping branches and the wandering eye of a mangled headlight. If she had paused, she could've saved herself seeing the red spray. The driver's door yawed open. Her dad usually insisted on driving, even if he'd been the one to drink.

The front of the car was compressed as if the engine had been chopped off. The hood folded like a tin lid. Her father's torso ejected from the front windshield to lie on the hood as if a crash test dummy. The hazards strobed a pale gleam, lighting the space where his thighs bent like a puppeteer's, crimson streaks creeping over their limp surface.

Orchid screamed and slipped nearer, then circled away in terror. What to do? CPR? Apply pressure to wounds? Sirens sounded in the distance. She reeled in panic, unable to either snatch air or expel it.

FIFTEEN YEARS LATER

Tonight's nightmare twisted. Her father lifted his mangled head to turn towards her, one eye bulbous and purple, crimson creeping below both nostrils. His neck snapped at an improbable angle at his Adam's apple, he barked at her. "Your fault."

Orchid suddenly awake, her chest constricted, her cheeks wet. Reality returned to her consciousness. She was not twelve. She was twenty-seven, forged by struggles, determination, and triumphs.

She sat up in bed.

She could still remember her aunt's spotted hand on her shoulder when she brought her home to pack her things.

Using Orchid's Chinese name, she said, "Take what you need, Lan Hua."

She couldn't help it. She had to unload the worst of it. "I'm really sorry, auntie. It was me. I was on the phone with them, right before they were driving down the scary part. I didn't even have time to put down salt."

"Just an accident," her aunt said.

Her mother's sister's mouth was pursed tight. Orchid understood her expression of blame. Her aunt hadn't disagreed with her self-indictment.

During her teenage years, she found that being pretty hid her blight. She grew into her oversized hazel eyes, and her long legs were an attraction. Her skirts got shorter, her heels higher, her look more daring. When she blackened her lash line and straightened her hair, she looked mature enough to slip into clubs with her older, leather-clad boyfriends.

And then college, where she met Mandy in her assigned dorm room. She opened the door to find a pretty blond unpacking neatly folded underwear into one of the dressers. When she pushed back her perky bob turned to face Orchid, everything about her was soft. Her rounded cheeks, button nose, smooth forehead and curvy body looked as though a potter had smoothed away every sharp angle. Cotton candy to her sour sucker.

That moment was when Orchid's new life, her new world, began.

"You must be Orchid!" she said. Orchid dumped her duffle bags onto the industrial carpeting, then swung the door shut behind her. "Yup, and you must be Mandy." They shook hands and Orchid started to unpack. Mandy handed her a box of wet wipes. "I haven't had a chance to clean the shelves—who knows how dusty they are!" She wrinkled her nose. Mandy looked like the type who'd brought pearls.

"Worse, maybe guys lived here last. You know, freshmen guys, the ones who smoke weed instead of going to class, and pee into Pringles cans when they're too lazy to go down the hall to the urinal."

Mandy grabbed a wet wipe and scrubbed the surface of her dresser. "Ugh, I hope not. Aren't Pringles cans cardboard?

Wouldn't they disintegrate? I'm kind of a neat freak," she said.

Orchid joined her and wiped the closet shelf. "I like things clean too." She hung the rest of her things, pushing them to one side to leave half the space empty for Mandy.

During the years they roomed together, Mandy bolstered Orchid each time she dated another unreliable type.

"It's me," Orchid groaned.

"It's not you. It's definitely him. He's a jerk," Mandy said.

Orchid wondered how she could trust, when almost no one ever stayed. Maybe guys could sense the void where her family used to be. Who wanted to deal with filling that? Like an adept seamstress, Orchid carefully stitched over that need. A temporary patch over a wound that was sure to reopen.

CHAPTER 3
RESILIENT ORCHID

Orchid

In those moments of post-slumber and consciousness, the boundaries loosened between Orchid's past and her possible futures. She floated from a primal state of fear into reality. On this particular morning, sunlight blanketed her comforter, twisted from another night of terror.

Outside, the sound of horns oriented her and told her she was not alone. The city was always there. The sight of her phone was an anchor, securing her to the present, her life in New York, her apartment, her workday. Eight a.m. Past the time she'd intended to rise. There was just enough time to make the meeting she'd requested with her boss.

Her feet hit the floor. She hurried through her morning routine, skipping coffee in case her commute was delayed.

She dashed through her living room, vaguely noting how sunshine spilled over her furniture. Her favorite one-armed fainting couch beckoned. There was no time for chilling.

At the door, she unhinged the security bar and twisted the deadbolt. Outside, she heard the bolt lock with a satisfying clunk.

She peeled down the hallway to the elevator, then slowed her pace in the lobby. "Morning! How's your daughter feeling today?" she greeted her doorman.

"Better, her fever broke last night. Have a good day!"

She headed to the subway, glad that his daughter was doing better. She'd remember to buy their favorite crescent-rolled rugelach pastries on the way home from work.

In the station, she hung back from the edge of the platform. Standing too close to a speeding train always seemed like an unnecessary risk.

She squeezed into the least-packed subway car. Her thoughts swayed along with the click-clack of two-ton wheels screeching along bare metal, and she told herself to focus on the day ahead. She wanted this assignment almost as much as she had wanted to join the excitement of the beauty industry following her MBA.

But this was different. China had always seemed a place of mystery, even though her mother's ancestry gave her a direct link to the country. Her mother rarely spoke about her parents' turmoil of leaving behind family, property, and wealth when they fled the Communist regime in 1948. When stories did emerge, they were relayed in whispered tones that alerted Orchid to secrets and shadowy unknowns. Since no one spoke of it openly, China had formed in her imagination as an unreachable and mystical place.

And now? She sensed that this might be the one place where she could feel most connected to her mother. Maybe even find forgiveness?

From the subway station, it was a brisk walk to the GM building, taking her past the Apple logo suspended from a two-story-high glass cube.

Inside her building, it was forty floors up to the Estee Lauder offices.

Orchid loved the allure of the ads lining sage-shaded walls. This company was the one place where her efforts had a chance of yielding results. Work hard enough, and a career could be her ticket to financial freedom. Because she sure wasn't going to get that from any inheritance.

The front desk receptionist greeted her. "Happy Friday!"

"You too. I love your hair," Orchid said.

"You do?" she asked, primping her highlights. "Wish I could pull off your wild colors."

Orchid thanked her and headed towards her desk, while wondering if her blue-tinted hair harmed her chances for this assignment. She made a mental note to schedule a salon appointment. *I'm taking no chances.*

She grabbed a mug of coffee and hurried to the media room. Her boss, Joan, was already there sporting a no-nonsense, square-necked suit and more rings than fingers.

"Good morning, Orchid," Joan greeted her, phone in hand. "We'll talk later," she said into the mouthpiece, then turned to focus on Orchid.

Orchid smiled. "Thanks for this meeting. How are you?" She sank into a chair and placed her computer on the table.

"Great. Your friend Princeton was just presenting team training ideas to me. How are you?"

Orchid felt her nose wrinkle at the mention of Princeton. He was no *friend*, this guy who lorded his Ivy League background over her. Instead, he'd leveraged his privileged background to catapult himself into leadership thinking of him as top talent.

She pried open her laptop and switched to a topic she knew her boss would find interesting. "I'm good, thanks. We finished consumer interviews for the new men's skin care line, and have a lot of insights. First, there's a segment of males who don't care; they'll wash their face with the same soap they're slathering everywhere else. Then there's a growing group who wants to age well, or at least show up well on dating apps, but they don't want to follow any more than a step or two. We call them one-and-done."

"Convenience has been a long-time insight," Joan said.

Orchid regrouped. "True. The target I'm most interested in, though, are the ones who want to set their own standards of beauty. I love this, because it fits with the zeitgeist of plus-size models, disability, inclusion and diversity."

Joan put her phone down and leaned closer.

"And I have the best idea for taking all of this to action."

"I'm all ears."

"Lauder China wants to learn from us. With these new insights, I could do a great job recommending how they'd want to launch in Asia."

Joan tapped the table. In the silence, Orchid's scalp prickled with hope. I need this.

"And the China assignment would be the perfect opportunity for me to immerse in how Asia is thinking about male beauty," she added.

"Oh. Well." Joan's flat tone matched her unmoving forehead. Her speech was measured. "This assignment is tricky. The Chinese market isn't the same as ours. Different channels, different influencers, different platforms. You'd need strong strategic and creative expertise. You'd have to be ready to navigate politics at a whole new level. Last time I was there, they spoke Chinese right in front of me whenever they had something to say that wasn't flattering."

"I agree with you. The assignment is three months away. I'm sure I could learn about the Chinese channels, platforms, and influencers. I could even sign up for Chinese classes and get my language skills up to par. You've always appreciated my team-building skills, and work ethic. I'd do a great job." She couldn't prevent the memory of Princeton bursting into Mandarin when Joan had announced the opening.

"Honestly, the China leadership team will be looking for strategic advertising experience as a sign of seasoned talent."

Orchid racked her mind. She hadn't worked in advertising but she was capable. Her competitive spirit sparked. "Advertising experience? Can I work on a Lauder campaign?"

Joan pursed her lips. The unlined "o" shined smooth like a plastic flotation ring. "I can't think of any brands at that stage right now, can you?"

Orchid persisted. "Okay, how about if I find a volunteer opportunity? Like for a non-profit?"

Her boss leaned back. "They're not easy to find, but you're welcome to look. There's time before I need to let the China team know who I'm recommending. Probably until July."

July gave her a few months. Still, Orchid would need to act fast. An idea struck her.

"How about this? Let's ask ad agencies to come talk about their non-profit work. For team training."

Joan's forehead raised a few millimeters. "I like the idea. You know what, I have agency contacts. I just had a boutique firm call me. They'd be perfect."

"I'd be happy to help." Orchid meant it. Work gave her life purpose. Filled her with energy. She wanted this assignment.

Joan stood. Their time was up. "Thanks. Time for my next call. Good luck building your creative chops."

The woman blew out of the room, and Orchid exhaled. She'd persevered and was clear on her mission. And it was true: more than anything, she needed to build creative chops. Or at least convince her boss that she had the right experience. She hoped one of the agencies could provide that opportunity.

CHAPTER 4

COMBAT WOUNDS

Orchid

Her plan was in motion. Since their meeting two weeks ago, her boss had scheduled three external agency sessions. After one of them, she'd sidled over to her account executive friend. "Hey there, great job," Orchid had said.

Her friend smiled wide. "You, too. I've heard you're working on a top-secret launch."

"Not so top secret, it seems!"

They both had laughed.

Orchid had a request, and she framed it carefully. "I'd love your help. Joan wants me to gain advertising experience. I'd like a chance to wow her with work on an ad campaign."

"Oh, cool. You've got great brands here. There must be opportunities."

"I'm surrounded by strivers. Every last one would eat their co-workers for lunch to get ahead. So, any opportunity would be surrounded by a gang of piranhas. Plus, there's nothing right now."

She chuckled. "Ah, I had no idea. I mean, our agency has different campaigns kicking off, but they're fully staffed. I'm not sure how I could help."

"Keep me in mind?"

"As long you don't tell the other piranhas."

"No chance," she confirmed.

Today, Orchid was cheered by the sunny walk to her office. She texted Mandy a photo of a billboard that dazzled with colors and space, swirling around the angelic face of a cherub baby. Advertising as art.

Orchid checked her notes. She wanted to be prepared for this morning's meeting with one of Joan's smaller ad agencies from a past role. Orchid wondered if any opportunities might present themselves. Orchid had donned an outfit that reflected her optimistic outlook, a white dress layered with shimmery platinum feathers and leather cuffs. Sweet with an edge of badass.

Orchid entered the conference room. Joan was standing to one side and conversing with a well-built man dressed right out of GQ. "How's my favorite creative genius doing?" Joan asked the man, whose back faced the door.

"Dex? He's doing well. You know our pro bono military ad campaign? The one designed to encourage hiring our service-injured troops?" His pride was evident in the squared stance of his broad shoulders.

Joan nodded.

"It was nominated for an Effie."

"Oh, congratulations!"

Orchid was barely listening to their chatter about marketing awards. The only free spot among her coworkers was across from posh Princeton, attired in his typical starched suit and pocket kerchief. She considered introducing herself to Joan's visitor, but there was no sense calling attention to the fact that she was the last to arrive, even though she was right on time.

"Hey," said her friend Violet.

Orchid waved and slid into the open chair, then placed her coffee onto the gleaming white tabletop.

Joan turned to face her team. "Now that we're all here," she said, glancing at Orchid, "I'll turn over the meeting to Mr. Walker, the head of counterAgency."

Orchid shifted towards the fit gentleman, then froze.

"You can call me Phoenix," he was saying to the group.

The angular cheekbones, the strong jaw, the intensity of his azure eyes. Every line, every twitch of a tendon told a story, one that raised her curiosity to a new level.

Orchid caught Phoenix's attention and proffered a little shake of her head. That tiny motion requested discretion. He composed his expression as Joan waved a farewell.

"I can't stay," Joan said, already at the doorway. "You're in good hands, and you've already been through introductions. Mostly. Tata!"

Damn! She had arrived on time, but had missed something.

Phoenix took the few steps to the front of the room, chatting as he walked. "It's great to meet Joan's team. I'm impressed by the work you're doing."

A clean soap scent wafted over Orchid as he passed near her, a light touch of something alluring. She locked into his familiar cobalt gaze framed by thick lashes. His full lips, straight nose and masculine brow were impossibly perfect, even by daylight. The faint stubble indicated he hadn't shaved this morning. She couldn't tear herself away long enough to see Violet's reaction.

"I'm Orchid, by the way, Orchid Paige," she blurted, to make up for her missed opportunity.

"Nice to see you," he said. One side of his mouth twitched up.

The whole night came flooding back. The sticky floor, her hand on that bathroom doorknob for an eternity as they volleyed Chinese phrases. How his proximity had brightened the bar's beer smell to something light and clean. *This was the guy who guarded the bathroom door and didn't even hit on me afterwards. Do gentlemen still exist?* Her ears buzzed with possibility.

Princeton looked from Orchid to Phoenix, probably upset over being left out of this tête-à-tête. "Go tigers," he said, and tugged at a deep orange cloth peeking out from his breast pocket.

"Princeton fan?" Phoenix asked. He must've recognized the school colors.

"More than that, my parents named me after the school I was destined to attend. I graduated cum laude." His precise diction tapped out a familiar line.

"Congrats," Phoenix said. Coupled with a suit that looked like it cost more than Orchid's weekly pay, the exchange chilled her estimation of this agency guru. Another privileged education snob who probably knew nothing of loss, she judged.

"Joan said you'd share some case studies with us," Princeton enunciated. "We've just seen some amazing work from one of the big four agencies. With some real data science behind the results."

Phoenix paused, as if this Princeton pest were an unwelcome insect buzzing in an otherwise perfect moment. He straightened to his full six feet, his presence filling the room. Leadership isn't universal. Its presence is ephemeral. Orchid's assessment shifted. She wanted to capture this mental image of Phoenix demonstrating his earned power, in contrast to her coworker whose mouth was agape.

"Analytics are table stakes," Phoenix said. "Joan wanted me to share some work where purpose is at the center." He tapped one finger to wake his laptop. The screen on the front wall lit up. It showed an understated logo on a clean white background. The design aesthetic was pleasing. "My business partner, Dex, and I formed counterAgency four years ago. I'm not going to apologize for being a young company. We have experience across industries, and being young means we bring a fresh perspective," he said.

"What about the name?" Orchid asked. "What does counterAgency mean? I like that it sounds underground and vaguely dangerous."

Phoenix grinned, apparently amused by her candor. "It is. The 'counter' part definitely means counter cultural. Don't worry, we're not overthrowing governments or anything. We just think a little differently."

"About the creative concept? Or the media placement?"

"All of it. Let me show you some case studies."

Phoenix clicked to a page showcasing military logos.

"We're proud of the work we do to raise money for combat-wounded veterans. These soldiers train until they're in top-notch shape, yet when they're injured, that can be a long way to fall. We help them find their footing through tough times. It's the work I'm proudest of."

Phoenix moved to a page with a collage of print ads. The black and white pictures were beautifully shot. They contained images of fit men and women proudly exhibiting missing limbs or gapped teeth, with drops of sweat visible from the intensity of physical exertion. The contrast of the high-resolution grays with the injured bodies elevated the ads to art.

"It's really impressive what people can achieve, just through sheer grit and determination," he said. "My partner Dex and I feel especially close to this message. This is part of our pro bono work."

One image differed from the rest. A soldier lay in a hospital bed, the truncated ends of his limbs weeping ochre liquid through black stitches.

Orchid stared at the scarred skin and twisted muscle. Without wanting to, she pictured the trauma that must have caused those wounds. The possibilities unspooled memories from when she was a little girl. Locked wheels skidding over ice. The explosion of metal. *My fault. My secret.*

Orchid cupped her hand over her forehead, hoping it looked as if she were deep in thought. Her skin felt clammy. She pressed her other hand into her lap to stifle a tremor.

Phoenix seemed to notice Orchid's reaction; his voice faltered. He skimmed ahead several pages, until the presentation stopped on a page of familiar logos. "Enough about the military. Maybe you want to hear about our work on a beauty brand?"

Orchid nodded weakly. When would she be able to get through a presentation without recalling her parents' accident? It had been fifteen years. When was she going to be a normal human being? She felt angry with herself.

"This is a well-known example of our unique branding approach." Phoenix said, passion in his voice.

Orchid couldn't listen. She focused on breathing. Inhale, exhale. A little deeper, a little slower. She told herself she was going to be okay. She raised her head, hoping she looked better than she felt.

"I remember when those ads launched," Violet said, commenting on Phoenix's final slides.

"What questions do you have?" he asked, turning to the group. He avoided looking directly at Orchid.

"No questions, we have another meeting," Princeton said, getting up.

"Thank you. That was amazing," Violet added. and they traipsed out, leaving Orchid and Phoenix alone in the conference room. Phoenix slipped his MacBook into a slim black case.

Orchid stood and sipped her cooling coffee.

His cobalt eyes found hers. His proximity sent an electrical charge between them. "Ni hao, Kai Lan," he said, as if uttering the secret code between them.

She nearly spewed the liquid in her mouth. "And to think I was about to thank you for not blowing my cover," she said, stilling her desire to smack his arm.

"Joan would've never believed me anyway," his mouth widened.

"I can barely believe it myself," she said.

"From dancing queen to beauty maven," he mused aloud.

"How about you? From door guard to CEO. Tell me you're not a spy, hired to follow me."

"I'm not about to be tiptoeing around corners," he said, glancing down at his feet. His polished shoes were considerably bigger than her stilettos.

"Good, because I have a meeting now. I can walk you out first."

She led the way out of the conference room. He scooped up his bag and followed.

"They're probably used to you being late," he teased.

She returned his grin. "I wasn't late; you guys were all early."

"Just kidding. You're right: a bunch of go-getters."

Her chest buzzed with the feeling that he was on her side. "By the way, your purpose-driven mission is impressive. I wanted to ask you something."

"Thanks. I wanted to ask you something too, because I'm sorry if the work upset you. Are you okay?"

Her ears warmed. His caring gaze reminded her of his kindness.

They arrived at the elevator. The dim overhead light almost made it safe for her to divulge the truth. She prattled on for a moment, as if hoping to divert him from recognizing her Achilles heel. "Yeah, I'm okay. I'm just worked up about getting this assignment. I've never even been to China. Which probably means Sir Princeton is going to get it."

He threw his head back and laughed. "Sir Princeton," he repeated.

"Plus, Joan says I'm lacking creative chops," she added, trying to refocus on her mission: to get this assignment.

"Creative chops?" He angled his gaze towards her.

"I don't have any major campaigns to my name, or awards."

"So, go work on one."

"At my level? It's a catch-22. You need the experience to move up, but they don't want to risk giving you the experience until you're more senior."

"Except Sir Princeton?" he asked with a guessing tone.

"Yeah, he's got creative medals up the wazoo from his last company. Which leads to what I wanted to ask you. I'd appreciate your advice on where I could get more advertising experience. I've worked on ad production, so I could add a lot of perspective. You know how tough Joan is, right? She says I'm strategic." Even though she'd practiced a more polished pitch, the words emerged sincere.

As the elevator door opened, she felt him studying her earnest expression, then pulled out a simple business card.

"You know what?" he said, holding open the elevator door. "I might be able to use talent like yours for our non-profit ad work. Reach out if you'd like to discuss it."

Hopefulness rose. Talent like hers? His initials P.W. were embossed in the azure side of the square card, with his email address and phone number on the other side.

Phoenix stepped into the elevator, joining a food delivery guy who was holding boxes emanating savory odors.

She aimed for snarky before she could make a fool of herself. "You mean my talent for finding the men's room?"

The doors glided shut on his grin.

She exhaled. How had this damned stranger managed to worm his way into her head?

His business card seemed to hold answers. The crisp edges of the cardstock felt like the ticket to another world, one in which advertising wizards granted wishes with the snap of slender fingers. She swallowed. *Business, all business.*

Mandy's sweet voice took on a teasing tone as she answered her phone. "A phone call instead of a text? Did you win the lottery or something?"

"More like a lottery ticket," Orchid said.

"Spill the beans, 'cause I'm up to my elbows in diapers over here."

"Ha! Hug Matty for me."

"Only if you want to smell like poo. So, what happened?"

"You remember that guy from the club a few weeks ago?"

"Oh, you mean Mr. Chivalry who doesn't mind you practically falling over him in the bathroom? Or do you mean his sidekick, the guy who would take out your knees with a crowbar in the back alley? Or did I miss someone?"

"You are hysterical… but you're on the right track. So, it's the one who looks like a GQ model. His name's Phoenix Walker, and he's the hotshot founder of a boutique ad agency. They're doing pro bono work with military vets and, even though they've only been around for four years, they're winning all kinds of awards."

"How do you know all this? Are you stalking the men you meet in bathrooms?"

"You're never going to believe this. He showed up at my office today."

"No way. Fate."

"I've told you, I'm not in the market at all. I'm off dating. But get this. His agency is doing just the kind of work to prove I'm the one for the China assignment."

"I am so confused."

"He knows my boss, Joan. She invited him to give us a presentation today. I walked him out afterwards, and he said he might be able to use me on his pro bono ad work."

"I've never heard you sound so excited."

"This is just the break I need. To shore up my experience. But wait, if Sir Princeton finds out, he's going to call foul. If I can even convince Phoenix I'm the right person for the job."

"First name basis, huh?"

"Quit it, it's just business. My intuition says I should get the experience, hit it out of the park, but not let even Joan know how the opportunity came about. Princeton might already be suspicious, because when I introduced myself, Phoenix said 'nice to see you' as if he already knew me."

"Cool. So, what's the plan?"

"Guess I'll call the guy, sell my experience. And if he agrees to take me on, I'll ask him to keep it confidential between us."

"More power to you."

"And to you. I'm coming over with wine later this week, before you drown in diapers."

"Sparkling water until I'm done nursing, but bring some for you." Mandy made a kissing sound before saying goodbye.

Now all Orchid had to do was maintain her composure with this advertising whiz. After a lifetime of shattered dreams, having to make do with whatever life handed her, and generating every opportunity out of her own ingenuity, she tried to quell her expectations. That didn't stop her from dreaming up ways to encourage this agency grandmaster to grant her most ardent desire.

CHAPTER 5
JUDGING GOOD WORKS

Phoenix

Phoenix Walker never believed he could live up to his father's legacy as a respected judge. It had occurred to him on too many occasions that he might die trying.

Floor-to-ceiling windows hushed the traffic din from below. He leaned into his marble desk while penning an awards acceptance speech. Gleaming chrome placards and golden lion statues winked encouragement from within the glass case lining one wall of his office. He recalled Dex's suggestion that he replace the fragile crystalline surface with tempered glass. Phoenix had grinned with his customary wry humor. "You know what would be easier? Let's not break it."

He refocused and began to revise the text. "This Effie nomination is dedicated to my dad, Judge John Walker," he said aloud.

Wind buffeted the windows. Rain wept rivulets, smudging the view of the elegant high rises. Easter had fallen early in the calendar this year. It was their first without the patriarch of the family. Grief rumbled like a forgotten animal inside his stomach, mixed with loss, and more complicated stirrings of love and respect. Longing, regret.

The lone photo on his desk showcased his parents with their sons, all of them puffy with ski gear, three of them with their teeth bared through reddened cheeks. Except his twin. As always, he wore his taciturn glower. The brothers had inherited their dad's height, his good looks and dark hair.

There, the similarities ended. Phoenix's blue gaze shone bright against pale skin and a field of stubble, whereas his sibling's dark intensity and massive physicality seemed to fill the frame with fury.

By the age of thirty, Phoenix had lost the chance to tip the scales of pride. Three quarters of a year ago, his dad had collapsed, been rushed to the hospital in cardiac arrest, and never recovered.

The secret letter provided one final chance to prove himself. He pulled the envelope from his top desk drawer, his dad's familiar handwriting on its surface. Nostalgia swept through Phoenix like a second pulse. On the envelope was written: *Confidential for Phoenix only. To be opened six months after my death. Read in private.*

My death. Phoenix's view fogged. *Forever more, forever never.*

He skimmed the familiar entreaty he'd studied multiple times.

Phoenix, as you were growing up, I never fully shared how much it weighed on me, the gap between your privileged life and those who came through my court with so little. You'd think a judge could do more to right those scales, but the inequity was stark. If you're reading this, it's six months after my death, and I have one last favor.

During the frenzy of those days in court, I couldn't help everyone. Who knows, maybe I couldn't help anyone. I always wondered if I could have done more. Perhaps this burden is too big to ask of you, but it would ease my soul if you could sprinkle one more good deed into the world on my behalf. Tip the scales in a way that I wasn't allowed to.

With complete discretion, and without revealing the source of the request, could you please find and

bestow a good Samaritan deed on one of my long-ago cases? It would give me peace to think of this girl doing well. And if there's anything she needs, that you provide a little nudge in the right direction. Writing this, I'm imagining that your act of kindness for her will be emblematic of the good I hoped for all the people who stood before me.

The depth in her eyes haunts me still. She was a teen when you were, so it struck me hard. Her name is unforgettable. I hope you can find her. Thank you for granting me this one last wish. Perhaps I'll rest easy, knowing that you might be able to help this girl, and knowing that you'll keep this confidential. Please don't tell even your brother or mom. You know I'm breaking privacy rules. Her name is Orchid Paige.

God bless you in this endeavor. Dad

When he'd first read the letter, his dad's request seemed out of character. Who was this Orchid Paige to him? Then again, how could he say no to his deceased parent?

An online search revealed that Orchid Paige was a unique name, and easily findable in the city. Her LinkedIn profile reflected a successful businesswoman. Google wasn't enough to uncover what she needed. He thought of ignoring the request. If it was important to his dad, he wouldn't be so easily deterred. He was busy, so he contacted a trusted private investigator. To her credit, she grilled him about his motivations before being willing to take on the case.

Then she'd called one day to say she'd overheard Orchid say she was going to meet her friend to divulge what she needed. The investigator was unavailable that night, so could Phoenix go? He considered his options, and seeing no downside, agreed to swing by. His plan was to see if she seemed okay, and maybe overhear some good deed he could impart. He hoped the answer would be as straightforward as a check to charity.

When they'd met, everything changed.

He thought he understood why her case had haunted his father. Grace, bravado and strength shone from Orchid like a beacon. It was there in the luminous bright amber of her pupils, in the swish of her sheath of hair.

During their childhood, his dad often shared heart-wrenching stories at the dinner table. The tapestry of their collective sorrow had scored indelible marks on Phoenix's psyche, making him aware that his own blessings were capricious… and could be snatched at any instant.

He pulled himself out of his reverie.

He had discovered what Orchid wanted: creative experience to improve her qualifications for the assignment to China.

How ironic that one of the obstacles she couldn't scale was the easiest for him to resolve. So, he'd offered to discuss the pro bono ad work with her. Still, he wanted to make sure the work was right for her, and that she'd be right for his client.

Which might be complicated, since she'd looked like she was sensitive to images of injured people that the ad campaign would feature. Although, it would be satisfying to protect her from that annoying Princeton guy. And it couldn't hurt to deposit goodwill with Estee Lauder. Whether this would lead her to China, he had no idea, but he would be willing to give her a chance.

There was something he was reluctant to admit to himself: the biggest truth. Just looking into her charcoal-shadowed eyes sent a shock through him like the spark of a brilliant advertising idea.

Or maybe she wouldn't contact him at all.

Either way, his fealty to his dad meant he couldn't reveal the reason he'd agreed to consider her. Even if he could help, he needed to do so with a light touch and duck out as soon as the good deed was done.

Phoenix looked up from his desk to see Dex striding through the door and headed straight for him.

"Liv," he called to his assistant, loud enough for Dex to hear. "You're supposed to keep the riff-raff out."

"She knows to ignore you," the burly exec boomed.

Phoenix indicated one of the swirly white chairs situated in front of him. Dex was already plunking into it, the cushion gasping as all air compressed out.

"Hey, what's up?" asked Phoenix, pushing aside his dad's letter.

"*Fiona* wants to know who you're bringing to the Effies," he said, invoking the name of his wife as if it were a weapon.

Pain in the ass: another awards event. "You and Fiona, of course."

"Yup, the whole team who's up for an award will be there, which leaves one empty spot."

"Empty spots don't bother me." He glared at his friend and business partner, trying to send a silent signal: *my personal life is none of your business.*

Dex grinned through his beard, rounded cheeks pushing up towards his glasses. "Fiona doesn't think it's safe for an eligible bachelor like you to go out on your own."

"Then it's a good thing I'll have her to protect me. If some dangerous bachelorette approaches me, Fiona can fake-kiss me," he snarked.

"I wouldn't offer that. She may take you up on it," Dex answered, unperturbed. "No one since Tish?"

"Here and there," he answered vaguely. He pulled a contract from a pile of papers and began flipping through marked-up terms and conditions. "If you're here to discuss my dating, the conversation will be short."

Dex eyed him for a long moment. "Listen," he finally said. "Business was nonstop during our start-up years, but now we can relax a little. We've got some great clients, we're winning awards, and getting our name out there. You're allowed to have a life again."

Phoenix looked up. Yeah, a life sounded good. He'd forgotten how to have one. For a while, the agency and staying fit was everything, to the point where his ex-girlfriend, Tish, couldn't wait and left.

"You break women until there's nothing left," she'd said tearfully. Later, she admitted that she'd been overly dramatic, and forgave him. Yet even after they broke up, the accusation haunted him.

"Bruh, think of someone, anyone," urged Dex. "Whirl through your contacts and just call someone. C'mon, if I threatened you with thirty hours of bad commercials, who would you pick?"

"Orchid Paige," Phoenix answered without thinking.

"Who?"

Damn, where'd that come from? "Orchid. She works at Estee Lauder." Was it Orchid's vulnerability, beauty or smarts that made him unable to stop thinking about her? Whatever it was, she was different. Something about her had captured his imagination.

"Great, call her. You've only got a week. Give her time to buy a dress."

"I doubt she'd need to buy a thing," he said, thinking of the funky, flirtatious, and outrageous pieces that suited her uniquely.

"Even better," Dex said, standing, his job done.

"I'm not calling," he said, looking down at the contract's red lines without seeing them. He'd taken on his dad's wish as his own. He wanted to grant Orchid something good. His growing feelings of care for her would complicate the purity of that intention.

Dex sighed. "Why for God's sake not? I don't care if she's an alien, or mom to sextuplets."

Phoenix felt one eyebrow rise in amusement. "Oh, am I *your* cause now?"

"It'd be good to see you happy," Dex admitted.

Friends who cared. "I'm agency head; I'm not supposed to date clients. I know her boss. I'm not even supposed to think of her, other than to drum up business."

Dex brightened. "Perfect, invite her, and drum up business with Lauder." He left the office whistling.

What had prompted the thought of Orchid? He pictured her punked-out beauty at the club. Then, her surprised expression when she'd slipped into the room for their agency presentation. He assessed the way his pulse thumped at the thought.

Phoenix was still grumbling to himself when Liv popped her head in his door. His petite assistant's gaze pierced through angled glasses.

"Liv, how are you doing? How are things going with your developmental assignment?"

That relaxed her tiny shoulders. "Thank you for the opportunity. You were right that learning the production side of the business would be eye-opening."

"It always comes down to execution," he said.

She adjusted her glasses on the bridge of her nose. "I didn't come here about my work. I wanted to pass along some messages."

All business, as usual. It'd only been seven months since she had joined the agency. Give her latitude. He'd intuited her loyalty and wanted to fulfill his promise to develop her potential. Some people needed more than months to settle in and warm up. Time was a great healer.

Like the stray pup who'd stumbled into his college fraternity house late one night. Phoenix had read the dog's skittish nature, reassured her with proper distance, and patiently nursed her back to health. When the school explained they disallowed pets, he'd found her a country home with one of his fraternity brother's parents.

Liv glanced down at her steno pad and recited the reasons

for her visit. "Sam called to cancel. His dad passed. I've already placed a bouquet order."

Phoenix sucked a breath. "How sad. I knew he'd been sick. Flowers are a good idea, thank you. I'll give him a call later."

He shook his head. What comfort could he offer? His own life was haunted by reminders of the day his father had collapsed and never recovered. One of their last conversations filled him with shame. "Really, Phoenix? All that education and you just want to hawk antacids?" This judgment of his hard work and his passion cut him deeply.

"Not everyone can be a saint," he told his father. "Maybe we can't all live up to you."

"Aw c'mon, I don't mean it that way," his dad had answered gruffly.

Too late.

The words stuck with Phoenix.

From his afterlife, his dad had offered a way to heal the rift. Phoenix wondered, *Are you suggesting Orchid as a way to make up for hawking antacids?*

Liv kept talking, seemingly unaware of Phoenix's buried grief. "Orchid Paige called to ask for time. I told her I'd check with you." Her nose wrinkled, a sign of disapproval over anything of questionable productivity.

"I met her at a presentation yesterday. We're going to talk about counterAgency's non-profit work." This straightforward explanation skirted the deeper emotions brewing.

Liv swiped through her phone screen. "Looks like you have thirty minutes free two weeks out. Does that work?"

Phoenix lifted his head with an idea. "Listen, it's a damn shame about Sam's dad. I can imagine how gutted he must be. I'm going to message him. Since I'm free tomorrow, would you please check if Orchid has time to meet then? Say, at the Starbucks a block down from her office? The one that's on my way to the subway."

Liv gave a single nod, her efficient assent, and let his glass door swing shut behind her.

No surprise that Orchid had called; Joan had said she was a go-getter.

Phoenix picked up his phone to tap a text. *I'm so sorry to hear the news, Sam.* Hopefully his friend wouldn't be dogged by the same demons that haunted Phoenix.

He knew that counterAgency's awards and accolades paled next to his dad's ability to right lives and shape futures. In his dad's estimation, shilling laundry detergent couldn't stack up to being a judge.

Still, Phoenix tried to do good. Helping to fulfill Orchid's dream might be his next opportunity. Ostensibly, the effort would pay homage to his father.

Deeper in his heart, he hoped that his altruism might help her.

CHAPTER 6
GROUND RULES

Orchid

Orchid watched Phoenix approach the café. Even though they'd only seen each other the day before, the sight of him made her breath catch.

Heads turned as he pushed through the café door. His white shirt was impeccable, and his hair waved as if ad ideas livened every follicle. Tucked under one arm, he carried a book. *A guy who reads.*

Orchid remained seated and silently recited her mantra. *Creative opportunities. Business, all business.*

Then, Phoenix spotted Orchid and the joy in his crinkled gaze nearly undid her resolve.

This China assignment was a stepping-stone to her next promotion. Someday, she hoped, it would lead to the kind of financial wherewithal she needed to finally feel secure. So, what was it about this athletic man striding towards her that made her forget security, and simply want to know what he was thinking?

His eyes shone with kindness.

When he reached her little table nestled against the wall, his smile widened. "Three times in two weeks. Lucky me," he said. Like he was reading her own thoughts. He rested the paperback beside her.

"Double espresso, it's doubly your lucky day," she said, indicating the miniature mug across from the whipped cream concoction in front of her.

"Thank you. How did you know my coffee?" he asked, slipping into the empty seat.

Pride rose in her chest, for getting something right with this guy whose life seemed glossy-magazine perfect. "Online research about your personal life, which turned up almost nothing personal. But you did have one article last year where the interviewer mentioned a double espresso, so I gave it a shot, so to speak."

He puffed air in appreciation of her pun. "Well done. What's your beverage, so I know for next time?"

Next time. "It's a Caramel Frappuccino to sweeten my bitter life," she laughed, hoping the truth sounded like a joke. "But don't bother memorizing it, because I can be fickle." She aimed for a dark edge to her tone.

Like a laser, he honed into the truest part of her statement. "Bitter life? Is Joan that much of a tough boss? Or you have something else going on?" Blue eyes studied her over the rim of his beverage.

His selfless curiosity had the effect of a truth serum. She fought the urge to tell him everything. Her dead parents. Her own culpability. The burden of having your future wholly dependent on yourself. Not knowing how life would turn out. He'd already seen her anxiety over photos of injured veterans. How could this anointed Golden Boy relate?

"You two know each other. I'm not going to talk smack about my boss." She stirred her coffee and reminded herself to tread lightly. Phoenix and Joan had worked together. They weren't friends, but Joan spoke of him with respect.

She waved a hand over her leggings. "I'm trying a new dance class."

"Dance? What kind of dance?"

"Would it be embarrassing to admit that my gym has this hip-hop class that they strobe-light like a club?" She sipped her drink, wondering why she was discussing dance rather than non-profit work.

"Not if you're trying to be the next TikTok influencer."

Orchid burbled into her beverage, trying to decide whether she could swallow before laughter made her spit. The coffee made it down safely.

"You know TikTok? Because I couldn't find you online, except interviews about your business." Her face warmed wondering what he would think about her surfing the web to learn about his life.

"You don't need firsthand experience to understand something. Which you know, since aren't you launching a men's beauty brand?"

She could feel her eyebrows lift over this unexpected detail. The launch hadn't even hit the trade rags yet. "How did you know?"

"Joan mentioned it. Probably when you were late," he teased.

"I wasn't late."

"Or maybe you were in the men's room."

"I'm never going to live that down."

"It'll be a great 'how we met' story for the kids," he said, then dipped his chin as if he hadn't expected to say that. *Where had that come from?*

She chuckled.

The surface of the table, the people around them, all seemed to evaporate. Reflected in his irises, she envisioned blue-eyed, quarter-Asian toddlers on a grassy field. Giggling cherubs rolling with Phoenix, who was dressed in track pants and a well-fitted t-shirt. A white-shingled house sprawled behind their cavorting. The crisp fall colors were so clear, it was more a premonition than imagination.

Wait, no. He was the third serving of candied yams. They had seemed like a good idea, until her Thanksgiving pants no longer fit. She needed to back away. She'd only cast ruin onto his perfect life. She warned herself against indulging.

Orchid shifted until her ramrod back said all business.

"Speaking of us, I asked for time to express interest in your non-profit work, if you're still interested in me. For work, that is." *Heart, do not betray me.*

She watched him regard the pivot in her posture. "Honestly, I'm down a strategic planner and could use the help. Do you have experience writing briefs?"

He wanted someone to write the briefing document that would guide the ad agency's creative teams to craft advertising ideas. That'd be the ideal experience to prove her creative chops to Joan. "As a marketer, I've written other types of briefs: naming briefs, product briefs. I'm sure I could add good perspective to your ad brief. Will you be conducting research as input?"

"The client's planning some focus groups."

Her attention perked. "I'd be happy to join. What's the product?"

He hesitated, and softened his tone. "I can't put you on an account that needs ongoing support so I'm thinking of our pro bono work. It's the ad campaign to help military vets. How would you feel about that?"

His demeanor was gentle, yet she felt a prickle behind her lids. *Those broken bodies.* This was her burden. Forever the orphan who couldn't bear human suffering. She needed this chance, so she did what she always did: submerge her pain. Stuff it down with the hurt little girl inside. "I'm fine with that. I'm sorry about my reaction. The pictures took me by surprise."

Phoenix opened his mouth, then paused, as if he didn't want to hurt her. His aura of care made him look wiser than his years. "There's no need to apologize. But I want to make sure this ad campaign is right for you. I'd give you something different but there's nothing else right now…"

He was giving her a chance. She wasn't about to let him down. "I don't have anything against the military."

He waited, swilling his now cool espresso.

"I'm not so great with seeing people hurt," she finally said. She swallowed the bitter dregs at the bottom of her Frappuccino. She felt a wisp of something on the edge of her lip and wiped away a dollop of whipped cream.

He nodded. "I can't promise that won't be the case. You might want to think about it, if this is what you want to work on."

"I do. Really badly. I hope you'll mentor me. I should be okay, as long as you don't send me to help out in operating rooms or something," she joked.

She noted how his expression cleared from concern to humor.

"I think you could add unique perspective. Plus, the work would be a good experience that Joan would appreciate."

"I do have a few requests, though," she said, emboldened by his seeming acceptance of her.

One corner of his mouth quirked. Being direct worked.

She soldiered on. "First, it's complicated with work. Joan knows you. I appreciate you haven't said anything to her, because it might not look professional if she finds out how we really met."

Phoenix considered her. "You know what, your recommendation's going to come right from the client. Let's not complicate things. There's no need to tell anyone at your office about us at all."

Her chest relaxed. He was on her side. "Exactly. Especially not Princeton."

"Wait, didn't I tell you he's working with you on this?"

Horror welled up, as she pictured him stealing her credit, presenting their work as his own. Then, she read the mischief in the fine lines around Phoenix's lips and she felt the corner of her mouth twitch. Finally, they both gave in to laughter.

He straightened his face. "Sorry, too tempting to resist. Keep going, what else?"

"Maybe no jokes at my expense?" She winked.

He chortled like they were in cahoots. "Got it. You won't be the butt of any jokes. You want to be mentored, but don't tell Joan." he said, counting the points on his fingers.

Orchid nodded. Note to self: *never* underestimate this guy.

"Anything else?"

She swallowed. Could she ask him to be less handsome, kind, or appealing? She shook her head.

He studied her, emotions flickering that she couldn't quite read. He swilled the rest of his espresso, and his expression grew earnest. "Sounds like we have a deal," he said.

Orchid measured the depths of his eyes. Phoenix, who could be trusted to guard her at the club. Phoenix, who kept her cover at work. Yes bubbled to her lips.

"A couple of things you should know, too," he said.

She held her breath. *Uh-oh?*

"I don't have much time during the day. So, if you need my advice, it'll probably be after hours. Just the reality of my life."

"Sure," she agreed.

"I don't consider this a one-way mentorship. I can learn as much from you as you can from me."

"I doubt it," slipped out.

He continued. "There may be learning assignments that I'd recommend."

"I'd love that. And please invite me if you're having an agency training… or something."

"I wasn't thinking anything that fancy. More like reading. I brought a book you might like. This one's my favorite guide to cultural differences between the east and west."

"Oh, that's so thoughtful! That'll be useful if I go to China."

"You seem like the type to achieve your goals. You'll go," he said.

The most successful ad entrepreneur in the business just expressed belief in her. His confidence in her sparked a brainstorm. Wait, what event did he mention during his Lauder visit…

"What about the Effies?" The idea popped right from her mind to her lips, and it was too late to pull it back.

"You want to attend the Effies?" The space between his eyebrows scrunched.

She could feel heat rising in her cheeks. "Only if you have space, of course. I was just thinking, since the Effies measure marketing effectiveness, that maybe it'd be good to learn from the case studies."

He raked his fingers through his wavy brown hair, then lifted his gaze to meet hers.

Christ, now I'm asking for too much. He'd just agreed to mentor her, after all. "I'm being too presumptuous." She lifted both hands in apology.

"No, I'd actually like you to come."

She released a puff of air.

"To be totally honest, my business partner, Dex, wanted me to bring someone for the event. So come… for the professional experience."

"Count me in." Her voice sang bright.

They stood. She cupped the book to her bosom. The slender volume felt like more than the sum of its pages. It represented his thoughtfulness towards her.

Phoenix stuffed generous bills into the tip jar and accompanied Orchid out into the night air.

"By the way, you may want to try this place." He handed her a business card and bade her farewell.

"Thanks." She fought the urge to peek over her shoulder as they parted ways. In her mind's eye, he was back on the dance floor, busting a move to coax humor from her. When she looked down at the cardstock printed with pictograms, her jaw slacked. He'd given her a card for a Mandarin school.

He'd remembered.

Next up, a celebration text to Mandy. And dance class.

Afterwards, she'd be back to her one-bedroom, where she'd

finish a single-serving of Thai leftovers straight from the icebox.

Her high from the evening wobbled like jelly knees after a double workout.

CHAPTER 7
MIDTOWN MANDARIN

Orchid

Who hasn't experienced that gap between how we feel on the inside and how others judge us from the outside? Orchid couldn't change the hint of Asian in her silky strands, the smooth planes of her forehead, or the gentle sweep down to her button nose, all of this leading strangers to ask, "Where are you from?"

Her response was that she was from suburban New Jersey, although the pace and smells of New York City now ran through her veins.

If she went deeper, she sometimes felt she was forged from the painful markers of her life. Other times, she floated above it all, as if spun of steel from her Chinese warrior ancestors, and then merged with the beauty of fairy sprites.

Today, she wouldn't have to face that rude question that suggested she was *other*, *foreign*, or *exotic*. She was about to start her first lesson at Midtown Mandarin, a language school where everyone would have either some link to Chinese, or an interest in learning to speak it.

She was aware that Princeton had been launching an effective PR campaign to tout his qualifications. Even Orchid could rattle off his accomplishments. How not, since he'd been following the adage that says people need to hear the same thing up to seven times before it was firmly in their brain! *We're noticing!* He had studied Chinese in college, had spent a semester abroad in Beijing. He'd also led creative campaigns as part of his volunteer work.

On the other hand, Orchid's work managing brands and leading teams shone as her strengths. If she could add conversational Mandarin to those strengths, she'd have a real shot.

Phoenix was helping her to address the gap in creative experience. It was logical that her next investment in her future was expanding her language skills.

After he'd handed her the business card for Midtown Mandarin, she checked their website. It showcased young adult students enjoying goofy fun.

So, that's how she'd found herself walking into her first trial class on a Wednesday night. Late, because work had been a tornado of new commitments, and they blended with the old ones that were already weighty enough. She'd already contacted them, and arranged to start with a slightly more advanced cohort. She needed to accelerate her progress.

The place looked like so many schools. It was an open area featuring white tables, with each sporting a cup of crayons. The walls were lined with cubbies half filled with belongings, and sported brightly colored posters of everyday items, each one with an accompanying character pictogram.

Orchid imagined Phoenix striding in, his confidence flattening the everyday humans in his path.

Sissy, the owner whose photo Orchid had seen online, came over to greet her. "Welcome! Jian tian di yi ci lai ma?" she said.

Aw crap. Was this going to be one of those immersive experiences that would make her brain hurt. Luckily, the context helped her foggy memory unearth Sissy's meaning. "Yes, it's my first time here."

Sissy beamed and led her to a glass-walled conference room. A dozen students sat around a table, their faces angled towards an Asian woman whose round glasses echoed the shape of her cheeks.

"Tang lao shi," Sissy introduced the plump woman with a formal 'teacher' moniker.

The teacher came over and shook Orchid's hand. "Ni jiao shenme mingzi?"

"Orchid," she replied, glad that she understood the request for her name.

"Lan Hua, qing zuo," teacher Tang instructed. Orchid hadn't heard her Chinese name in many years.

As requested, Orchid looked for a place to sit. A guy with long hair scooched over to make space on the long bench. Orchid slipped onto the edge, leaving space between them. A young professional-looking woman on the other side nodded at her.

"Xie xie," she managed to say, thanking them, while still absorbing the foreign feeling of hearing her name in Chinese. Lan hua was a literal translation of the flower.

Teacher Tang, full of enthusiasm for Orchid's apparent understanding of Mandarin, started by asking her questions. "Ni de gongzi zai nali?"

Orchid tried to puzzle through the unfamiliar sounds. "Uncle?" she muttered under her breath, having some vague memory of having to call distant Chinese relatives *gong gong.*

Long-haired guy whispered to her. "Work."

"Wo de gonzi shi Lauder." She managed to say the name of her company, and the teacher moved to another unwitting student.

"Thanks," she whispered to her bench partner.

"Bu ke qi." He responded with a simple "You're welcome."

At the end of the hour, a mish-mosh of words floated through Orchid's brain, a jumble of English, Chinese, and business acronyms that had kept her busy during the work day.

She stood and stretched. "Want to grab drinks with us?" the professional woman on the other side asked. She'd been introduced as Lee-da, which she now explained was actually Linda.

Orchid had no brain power left for the emails that awaited her if she went home, so she agreed. "Drinks sound great, thanks."

The three of them—Orchid, Linda, and the long-haired fellow named Peter—walked the few blocks to a noisy neighborhood bar. It felt like good fortune to score a high-top table by the open-air windows. The waitress asked to see IDs, then jotted down their beer and cocktail orders.

"So, how'd you like your first lesson?" Peter asked.

She tossed up both hands. "I was a hot mess!"

Peter cackled. He had a way of laughing—it started from his belly and erupted out of his nostrils—that told Orchid that his humor was genuine. "You should've seen my first class."

"What happened?" Orchid really wanted to know, to help her burn off the shame of misunderstanding, guessing wrong, and generally being humiliated in front of a dozen strangers.

"Ni shi shei?" Peter mimicked their teacher's nasal tone when she asked who he was. "So, I said *wo shi Peter*."

Linda began to snicker.

"Okay, then what happened?"

Peter feigned indignation. "I had to defend myself after she called me Pee-duh."

Linda chuckled louder.

"I told her I didn't need the bathroom."

"Well, duh," Linda chimed in.

"Except that's your Chinese name," Orchid guessed.

"Which makes me never want to go to China," he said.

"It's the number one place I want to visit," Orchid confessed.

Peter gave her a long look. "Is that why you're in this class?"

"One hundred percent," she affirmed.

His face lit up "Then you should go, Lan Hua."

"Okay, Pee-duh," she replied.

They were still chortling when their drinks arrived. As the three of them clinked glasses and bottles, Linda's phone lit with a call.

She frowned at the screen then leaned forward to apologize. "I have to take this. I'll be right back." She hopped off the stool to find a quiet spot.

"So, what do you do?" Orchid asked Peter.

"Guitar."

"Play? Build?"

"Lessons, mostly."

He looked like he was at least twenty-five, though Asians sometimes looked younger than they were. "Can you make a living off guitar lessons?"

He laughed at her skeptical expression. "Wealthy Manhattan moms only want the best, and kids love me."

"Because you're a kid yourself?"

His good nature wasn't put off. "Look who's talking, what are you, twenty-three?"

"Twenty-seven." She didn't tell him that she had a birthday coming up. No sense up-aging herself.

"See? We're the same age."

"No way. I'm pretty sure the only reason the waitress carded us was because of you."

"I was going to say the same thing about you," he said. "What's your gig?"

"I'm a brand exec in beauty."

"Corporate, I thought so." He gestured with one dismissive hand towards the flowy silk blouse and business slacks Orchid had drudged up from a secondhand shop. It had been part of her attempt to look professional enough for the Lauder China assignment.

His pronouncement struck her in a visceral way.

"Actually, I'm kind of not corporate. I feel like I'm wearing a costume. Ever since my teen years, I've been pretty counter-cultural."

"Cool. Then maybe you'd like to learn guitar."

Orchid swilled the rest of her brew. "You know what, I'd love that."

CHAPTER 8
EFFIN' BEAUTY

Phoenix

What was wrong with him? How had Orchid wormed her way into his brain? Phoenix did not need another mentee, or a protégée. Dad requested this favor, he reminded himself.

Then, she showed up. Snaked her way through the four-story-high hall thronged with guests and servers. It was as if the columns, arches and myriad fabrics were a backdrop for her graceful entry. The purple and blue lighting chosen to match her dyed locks.

He noticed her glancing at the number woven into the table's centerpiece, then checking the card in her hand.

Phoenix stood. When she spotted him, she flashed white teeth like sunshine after an eclipse. A metallic minidress shimmered over her slender frame.

"You're a living Effie statue," he said, feeling his face split over the lightness in his chest. Even compared to the oversized gold, silver and bronze statues decorating the space, nothing shone as bright as Orchid's elegance.

"And you're an Oscar?" she asked, eying his suit.

He looked down at himself. "You do know that Oscar statuettes are naked knights holding swords, right?"

Her laugh tinkled like the golden hoops around her wrist. "Oops."

"Let me introduce you." Phoenix waved a hand towards the people seated at his table.

His business partner had already popped out of his seat.

"Dex," said the burly guy, shaking Orchid's hand. His girth was busting out of a tan vest, matching bowtie and khaki pants. "You've met the suit," he said, directing his bushy eyebrows towards Phoenix, "I'm the creative. And this is my wife, Fiona." He cupped a brunette's elbow.

"Finally," Fiona said, which caused a confused expression to flit across Orchid's face.

Before Orchid could follow up on Fiona's proclamation, the rest of the guests stood or gestured hello. "Good to meet you," she said to each person, waving at those across the linen expanse.

Like a Hollywood gala, the peal of music trumpeted the start of the program. An emcee began to announce the first category.

Phoenix pulled out the chair beside his. "Sorry if I'm late. I got caught up at work." Orchid slid into her seat. He'd saved her the best view.

"Your timing is perfect," Phoenix reassured her. "Would you like white or red?" he asked, indicating the curved bottles in front of them.

"White, please. I haven't had lunch, so wine will be a good appetizer."

"Haven't had lunch?" He poured for her, then fetched a basket of warm bread. Why did concern about her day suddenly wash over him?

"You're the best." She scooped a mini loaf onto her plate and broke off a piece with slender fingers. "Manna from heaven," she declared.

"What's with skipping meals?" he admonished.

Orchid polished off the roll and washed it down with the remaining wine. "What a day."

"Anything I can do?"

"More vino?"

Phoenix refilled her glass as she speared a pile of greens onto her salad plate.

"You're as hungry as a baby bird."

Orchid's fork paused mid-air. When she began to speak, Phoenix drew closer to hear her over the din of the show.

"My mom used to call me *hungry bird,*" she said.

Used to.

Questions swirled around his head like a thousand moths aloft in a moonlit field. "That sounds like a sweet endearment," he said. "Do you like being called that?" He was testing the water, which seemed like a deep ocean dive.

"I guess it'd be okay. It's a happy memory."

Her wistful expression unlocked part of the puzzle. *Used to. Memory.* He felt sad about the loss of her parents. He'd ask her more another time, when they weren't in the midst of an overloud gala.

"Thanks for having me," she said. "You're up for an award?"

Dex leaned closer to her, as if eager to delve into his favorite topic. "Yup, our work with wounded warriors was nominated."

Orchid picked up one of the programs scattered around the table and read a little of the blurb. "*counterAgency's work with military veterans is dedicated to Judge John Walker...*" His dad's presence loomed large.

"Congratulations," she said, looking away from photos of injured servicemen in the brochure.

"This work's really meaningful," said Phoenix. "I love advertising, but it can be trite. Here?" he said, pointing to the photos. "This is real. We can make a difference in soldiers' lives."

"I hope you win," she told him.

"Tough call, since we're up against Missing Children."

Servers removed the small plates and replaced them with larger plates of filet mignon and potatoes.

"I'm a vegetarian," Orchid explained to the waiter, putting up a hand before he could place the beef in front of her.

"It'll be a few minutes," the waiter said, and left to exchange her meal.

Despite hundreds of people crowded into the massive hall, and an announcer naming brands and companies over the speaker system, their proximity created a sense of intimacy.

"Have you always been a vegetarian?" he asked, leaving his food untouched.

"Since I was twelve," she said.

"So young. How'd you decide to do that?"

She paused. "It started because I couldn't stand seeing the blood in my steak. And then I found I couldn't look at meat at all."

"You were pretty sensitive for a twelve-year-old."

"You should eat before your food gets cold," she said, as if hoping they could move away from this subject.

He looked at his plate and felt his lips twitch. "I'm not sure I can eat my bloody steak now."

She opened her mouth, as if to protest, then smiled back. "Well, *I'm* not taking it off your hands."

"Maybe I should get a vegetarian meal, too."

The server placed a plate of mashed potatoes and vegetables in front of her.

"I'd highly recommend it," she said, sampling a tender carrot.

With a deft slice, he cleaved the center of his filet.

Orchid flinched and faced away.

He noticed her reaction and switched to the spuds. Then, he put down his flatware. "I'm sorry. I wish I'd known," he said, apology in his tone.

She rolled her eyes, as if this would be an antidote to his guilt. "You've found my kryptonite."

"Kryptonite. Well, you do have a superhero vibe going tonight." He waved towards the sheen of her dress.

Fiona called to Phoenix, "Your category's coming up."

The emcee stood at the podium and smiled out at the crowd.

"And the winner is...the Center for Missing and Exploited Children campaign by..."

"Ugh," Dex complained, head in his hands.

"Told you," Phoenix said, holding out the palm of his hand.

Dex handed over a twenty.

"You bet against yourself?" Orchid asked with shock.

"A guy's gotta know his limitations," Phoenix said.

"And yours would be...?"

"I have plenty, I just don't want to 'fess up to them."

"Are you sure? I googled your pedigree. Agency start-up by the age of twenty-seven, AdAge's 'Small Agency to Watch.' What's next? Is NASA recruiting? Need someone to second your Nobel Prize nomination?" Her voice lifted as she took a poke at him.

"Very clever. I'm sure you're just as accomplished. Marketing manager for a top company? Now you're working on a global launch... that's a huge accolade."

She nodded. "And thanks to you, maybe I have a shot at the China assignment."

"If you get it, it's your doing, not mine."

Orchid nodded, as if acknowledging that what he said just might be true. "Speaking of China, I started those Mandarin classes. Thanks for the suggestion! They put me up a level because I grew up knowing some Chinese."

"Is your teacher Tang Laoshi?"

Orchid practically spun in her seat. "Yes! And I feel like I'm always one sentence away from making a fool of myself."

"Everyone does. One time, I asked for a pen, and she informed me that the way I'd pronounced it sounded like the word for a part of female...um, anatomy." He felt his face warm. He hadn't meant to skirt into sexual territory. It was as if his subconscious wasn't able to remain platonic.

"How are we supposed to remember four tones?" she asked. "Shoe sounds like write, Soup like hot. And apparently, pen like...." Her lips seemed to cycle through surprise, indecision, and then halted on embarrassment.

Phoenix's humor bubbled up, in complete sympathy for the position his anecdote had created for them both.

Her resolve seemed to break and she joined him.

They looked at each other like confidants in a bank heist.

Fiona jabbed a thumb upwards as she left the table, giving the two of them a sign of approval before heading in the direction of the bathrooms.

Orchid swilled some wine, calming her hiccupped laughter.

Phoenix nodded towards her plate. "How's your dinner?"

She looked at her half-eaten meal. "It's fine, but the haricots verts could use some shaved asiago, and I would've blended parsnips with potatoes."

"I'm impressed!" he said. "I can eat, but I can't cook."

"Don't be impressed. When I was a kid, if I wanted to eat, I had to cook it myself." And then she turned away, cheeks growing flushed, as if she'd said too much.

Phoenix wondered if these were more pieces of Orchid's puzzle that she did not want to reveal. He was certain that under her gold sheath lay layers of complexity. He recognized her pain because he'd also lost a parent. Yet, Orchid also suffered in a way that was foreign to him. Beyond that, she effused joy, warmth, humor...and an edge. Her professional drive was apparent; the trait that had earned her the non-profit assignment.

Phoenix pulled them both onto safer ground. "This next category is about positive changes in sustainability."

She peered at the portion of the program he indicated. "Seems like they should have no page for that category. Save some trees."

"Ha. You make a decent point. Live your brand purpose."

"Right. Like this campaign, *Shut the Door*. She pointed to the adjacent image of a storefront with an open door. "I love their work; I've seen it all over the city. Save energy by making those thoughtless stores running their heat and A/C shut their doors."

They sang in unison, their voices lilting just like the ad's jingle.

"You chose well." Dex said, winking at Phoenix, one bushy brow taking a bow.

Phoenix read his friend's intimation. Dex's good humor reflected the two of them, their heads together, gazes locked, Phoenix laughing like he hadn't since his dad had died. It hit him. He shouldn't have agreed to be Orchid's mentor. They should've stayed at arms' length, especially after she'd been explicit about keeping their relationship professional. And he could never cross that line, not if he ever wanted to work with Lauder.

She gestured at the brochure. "Dex, shouldn't every Shut the Door account person in this room be petitioning to seal this place? Pointing out the wasted heat pouring out their open doors? Maybe their whole creative team should walk out in protest!"

"Damn, you're onto something." Dex regarded Orchid with what looked like renewed appreciation.

"Don't get me started," she said. "I'm like a lie detector for hypocrisy. Which doesn't keep me out of trouble."

"You're perfect for Phoenix's campaign," Dex said. "You'll be his human BS meter."

Phoenix tried to catch Dex's eye. *Abort mission.*

"Actually–" Phoenix began.

No one heard Phoenix over Dex's booming voice. "Oh my god, I've got it. This is brilliance. Aren't you meeting Tammy at the tri next weekend?" Dex flicked a gaze at Phoenix. He didn't wait for an answer; he turned to Orchid. "You need to go, too!"

"Who's Tammy?" Her forehead puckered. "And what's a tri? Do you mean a triathlon? I'm impressed!"

Dex smiled. "Yeah, Phoenix here is our superhero! As for

Tammy, she's the new talent for your work. The one you're going to be writing the strategy documents for. You can't lose this opportunity. You're free, right?"

"Yeah but–what the what?" She flipped her shiny locks over one shoulder.

"As long as you're free, you have to say yes. Say yes."

"Okay, sure. Yes. Okay, yes," she said, laughing at Dex's machine-gunned pleas.

And then she shifted to look at Phoenix and her eyes widened. "Unless you don't want...I mean, I don't have to."

If his expression revealed even half the devastation he felt on the inside, his horror could send the most stalwart person fleeing. Based on his promise to his dad, he had committed to mentor Orchid, to say nothing to Joan, and that they would be all business. *Just business.* The auditorium's blue light swept over Orchid's luminescent skin, highlighting the lamé draped over one delicate collar bone, the other shoulder bare. Honey sweet. Whip-smart.

He was falling for her. He shouldn't be spending time with her.

If nothing else, Phoenix was a man of his word.

"You should come. It's an early start though. We leave the city at six." His voice emerged husky.

Even if this was an error in judgment, he wasn't about to let his dad down.

Their evening together had illuminated raw truths about his feelings.. Whatever joy Orchid sparked in him, he wouldn't cross their professional line. Not only was this the most ethical position to take, it was also what she'd said she wanted.

Now, thanks to Dex, he would have her company driving down the shore to compete in the triathlon.

Phoenix tossed in bed that night, trying not to think about

Orchid, the smudge of Frappuccino cream in the corner of her mouth while she'd negotiated the hell out of him; her willingness to point out hypocrisy; and the way she seemed to be able to free him to be his most authentic self.

He woke at dawn and Googled vegetarian restaurants at the shore.

Business, all business. He needed to steel himself. They would get through this one day, and then limit their time together to the office.

The Pixies were blaring from the sound system in his car when Orchid bounded out from her building. He climbed out of the car and ran around to the passenger side.

She paused at the car door he'd opened for her and then climbed inside. When he reached out to lower the volume, she commanded "Don't turn it down!"

He looked at her. She was breathless from whatever fashion marathon had clothed her in form-fitting yoga pants and a zip-up hoodie. She tucked a knapsack at her feet. "Do you like—"

"Pixies, Surfer Rosa," she answered, waving a hand, as if nonchalant about knowing the group *and* the album name.

Good thing Manhattan streets were empty at six on a Saturday morning. Phoenix couldn't help swiveling his attention from the road to this woman. "Are you an old person in a young body? They're way before your time."

She laughed. "My parents loved them. What about you? You're only four years older."

Twenty-seven. Her parents. He'd known the bare facts about her but her sharing them felt like escape-room clues. To unlock the mystery of Orchid. "My twin brother, Caleb. He's really into underground subcultures. He says there was this golden period from the Sex Pistols to Nirvana that paved the way for Gaga and Taylor Swift, even if people don't realize it."

"Twin brother! Lucky you. I'm an only child."

"Yeah, he's alright. I told him about the race today, but it's not really his thing." Two syllables, *brother,* seemed inadequate to represent decades of memories. Caleb was his best friend and competitor. As a teen, Caleb was the rebel who wanted to uncover underground everything, as if seeking answers in songwriters' dark lyrics.

In the car's enclosed space, he could detect Orchid's faint scent of roses and something sweet. The speakers quieted to percussive instrumentals.

"Renegade Soundwave," she sang out the name of the obscure band.

"Are you always this chipper? Do you even need the coffee I bought you?" He gestured towards the lidded cup nestled in the console between them.

"Thank you," she said, lifting the beverage and taking a sip. "Caramel Frappuccino, you remembered!"

"As long as fickle you didn't want something different."

"This is perfect." For a moment, her glance at his profile seemed to indicate she meant more than the brew.

Today, Orchid was fresh-faced, her voluminous hair trussed up in a hurried ponytail. This assignment was important to her, and he reminded himself that his dad would be proud that Phoenix was mentoring her.

The most honest insight rattled him. If she learned that they hadn't met by accident, would she still be happy to see him? Would she believe that his motives were pure, that he'd only intended to meet his father's last wishes? That he hadn't meant to fall for her?

They entered the mouth of the Lincoln Tunnel; yellowed lights dimly lit the interior of the car. Their tires keened against the grooved pavement.

"When I was a kid," said Orchid, "these tunnels always seemed like a portal to another world. Ten minutes and you'd be in another state. I used to dream of flying through the Holland tunnel." She looked wistful.

"Freud would have a field day with that one." He decelerated for a slow-moving garbage truck.

"It wasn't something that needed to be analyzed. More like I was so free, and I might burst out the other side, and into the Milky Way."

"That kind of dream would make a great ad."

"Speaking of dreams, thank you for helping me with my dream to get to China."

John Walker would be proud. "You're helping me, too," he reminded her.

They popped out of the tunnel and into the sunshine, then curved past New Jersey billboards and a sign for Weehawken.

He glanced over and saw that she was taking in all of it, from the landscape to the traffic. He was coming to the conclusion that the grace with which she carried herself conveyed more wisdom than her twenty-something years should be able to produce.

She turned towards him. "Have I properly thanked you for the book on Asian culture?"

"Do you like it?" he asked.

"I'm halfway through. It's super cool. I knew about culture shock, but I never thought about *reverse* culture shock."

"Coming back is harder than going," he said, recalling the message in the book.

"After they explained it, it made sense. You change even if your friends haven't, so suddenly you don't fit in."

"You're going for only six weeks, so you might not get reverse culture shock."

"I love how you're talking as if I'm getting the job."

"Talk as if; act as if," he advised. "I think it's interesting how America and China are polar opposite cultures," she said.

"We're egalitarian, China is hierarchical. Your company culture might override some of that at the office, though."

"I've been reading up on the difference in values. Like we

think it's unethical to steal someone else's intellectual property."

"But they see it as efficiency to build on an existing idea," he said.

"Right."

"You're a fast study."

"Thanks."

They navigated from Interstate 95 to the Garden State Parkway.

She paused to hum along with another obscure song. Sunlight brightened her face, deepening the blush of her lips.

Green expanses and mile markers whizzed by.

"Tell me everything about the assignment," she said.

"This next set of ads is going to raise awareness for veterans, so they know where to turn for services. We'll assign it to multiple creative teams. The agency is down a strategic planner—she's on maternity leave—so your job will be writing the brief."

"Sounds awesome. I already started looking at the earlier work online."

"You've done your homework, excellent. The talent we're meeting is amazing. She was in an explosion in Iraq, suffered a debilitating concussion. Now, she's healed physically, but her invisible injuries are almost worse than visible ones. People around her don't realize what might be going on inside. She'd find herself lashing out, or jumping at any little noise. And then, bit by bit, she found strategies that worked for her. All she wants to do now is tell her story to people like her, so they can find help, too."

"What kind of strategies?"

"It's what you'd expect: breathing exercises, meditation, therapy."

"Unconditional love," she added. "That's my theory for what heals all."

Phoenix glanced over at her bowed head. She appeared to be studying her nails.

Her emotions were killing him.

He was falling so hard.

"Yeah, try and see," he responded.

CHAPTER 9
A SHORE THING

Orchid

The work week had given Orchid the opportunity to reset her expectations.

With a belly full of wine, agreeing to the triathlon had seemed like a good idea. Now, she wasn't so sure.

They pulled into a parking spot facing the beach. Racers in wetsuits milled about, along with spectators and athletes. A starting line along the street was marked with a white banner between two poles.

Phoenix unloaded his bicycle and deposited it with the others.

"Let me introduce you." He led the way towards the beach, where groups of racers and onlookers chatted.

A gorgeous redhead, her body thick with strength, gave a wave. She wore a wetsuit, and she paused chewing her gum to grin at them.

Phoenix's long strides closed the gap between them in a few paces.

"Orchid, this is Tammy. Tammy, Orchid will be working on our campaign."

Tammy stopped working her jaw long enough to give a nod. "Hiya."

Orchid stuck out a hand to Tammy. "Great to meet you."

Phoenix gestured towards the water's edge where racers gathered. "I'm up next. You both good?" He turned to head toward the starting area.

"Break a leg," Tammy called.

"Don't drown," Orchid added, with a half-smile.

"Stay out of trouble," he called over his shoulder.

The guy on the bull horn announced his age group.

Tammy balanced on one leg and stretched the opposite hamstring.

"Dex and Phoenix think highly of you," Orchid said.

Tammy paused her flexibility exercises to grin. "They said the same 'bout you, when they texted me that you'd be coming. Somethin' about bein' a strategy hotshot?"

"Uh-oh, you think they're snowing us with compliments?" Orchid joined her good humor.

"Nope. Can't blame them for havin' good taste."

"I'm impressed with the cause you're representing; glad to be part of it."

"No sense having people suffer when they don't gotta," Tammy proclaimed.

Orchid intuitively trusted this straight-talking stranger. She turned to face her.

"Maybe Phoenix sensed I'd connect with this work. I saw something bad as a kid; I still have issues with it."

Tammy studied her. "You know, somethin' as simple as breathin' helps me."

"My aunt sent me to a counselor. I did group therapy."

"The Navy Seals came up with box breathing. You know it?"

"Nope." Orchid was intrigued.

"It's easy. Try it with me. We're going 'round the four sides of a box. Just breathe in deep through your nose for four counts. Then hold for four, but not a tense hold. Real loose. Now exhale through your mouth for four counts. Until your belly is empty, then hold again for four."

Orchid followed along, envisioning her breaths scaling a square.

"Yeah, good."

"That's it?"

Tammy guffawed. "Try it whenever you need it. My shrink taught me, this guy named Todd Head."

"Okay, thanks. I'll try it when I'm writing your brief."

Tammy chuckled. "I like you," she said.

"Same with you," Orchid said.

A megaphoned voice bombarded the air.

"It's my age group next," Tammy said, then turned and walked towards the shoreline.

Orchid moved to a spot near the water's edge, among other onlookers. She saw Phoenix wading into the chill sea with dozens of triathletes. At the starter's sound, he took several long strides, transitioned into a neat dive, and then plunged with swift strokes into the roiling surface. He moved fluidly. Within minutes, his white cap and black tri-suit blended with the others, and she lost track of him.

She stood facing the water, shielding her eyes from the sun. Then, the phrase *"risk of drowning"* infiltrated her imagination. The undertow dragging him deep. His leg seizing into a cramp, unable to kick his way to the surface. Avid racers churning the water above him. Damn her over-active imagination! She executed the box breath Tammy had taught her, imagining the equal sides of a box with the number four on each side.

The first swimmers rounded the buoy and headed back towards shore. The early wave of swimmers emerged from the water, dripping, stripping off wetsuits and dashing to their waiting bikes. Phoenix sprinted by in the melee.

As she turned towards the bike path, she saw a hulking, dark-clothed figure approaching her. Something familiar in his appearance shivered goose bumps over her arms. His gait hunched forward, as if fighting a storm only visible to him.

The man vaguely reminded her of Phoenix. Except his straight nose flared at the bottom, his jaw clenched in a straight line, his hair waved coarser. A faded Harley tee shirt was shoved into black jeans, which fell in one dark line over boots the size of feral cats.

When he reached her spot in the shade, he slowed and pointed a meaty chin towards her.

Without meaning to, Orchid took a step back. Instead of warm blue eyes, inky black ones pierced hers.

"Phoenix in the water?" His voice emitted like a low growl.

"Um. No." She felt like a slip of light in her Keds and hoodie against his darkness.

He stuck out a hand tattooed with a snake's unhinged mandible. Serpents wound up both arms growing as wide as the circumference of his biceps until they disappeared under his short sleeves, and there were sharp tails emerging on either side of his neck. They slithered like twin protectorates.

"I'm Caleb." He took her slender palm in his callused one.

"Oh, Phoenix's brother! How'd you know who I was?"

"I saw you at the Pyramid Club."

"For like two seconds. In the dark."

He cast her a side eye. "True. Phoenix told me he was bringing you."

The thought of being a conversation topic deepened her inhale. Validation by a darling of the advertising world. She tried to pay it back with the scant information she had on this taciturn brother. "Phoenix wasn't expecting you here. He said triathlons aren't your thing."

He snorted and waved a humorless hand over his black-on-black get-up, down to his motorcycle boots. "I'm not exactly the tri type."

It wasn't just self-deprecation, or even judgment on the diverse athletes competing. Orchid sensed an edge of self-loathing. "I don't know that there's any one type. I'm sure– "

He cut her off. "I'm only here because our mom made me promise. Walkers stick together." He high-pitched his voice in imitation of their mother.

Orchid pictured what must be a close-knit relationship... or not. "How nice to have family that cares. I'm an only child," she added as evidence. Even though she knew her hurt bled darker than missing a sibling.

Caleb turned to study her shift in her tone.

"Do you have any tattoos?" he asked.

Her head swiveled. The snake tattoos on either side of his neck craned with their owner. "No. Why?"

"It's usually the things that cause great angst or pride that drive people to tattoo."

In that instant, she understood that feelings ran deep in this tough-looking guy. Below the faded fabric and armor of ink lay tenderness and insight. "Then your brother should have awards imprinted all over him."

Caleb's lips twitched.

She wondered if it was too late to take back her inane statement.

After a moment, he answered her. "If you knew him, you'd know it's not about winning, but making people feel something."

It reminded her that she couldn't assume anything about either of these men. "What do you do?" she asked.

"As in work? I own tattoo studios, two of them."

She felt that he was almost daring her to snub his profession. "Then you're an entrepreneur, too," she said.

He studied her face. "Guess I am," he said. Then his expression softened. He was as good-looking as Phoenix, only in a dark, scowling way.

"Takes a lot to run your own business. How big's your staff?"

He assessed her. "I've got a couple of artists in each place."

"Much competition?"

"My locations are good. My guys are the best. Not much to worry about."

Three sentences in a row. She nodded. Progress.

"He's really proud of his work for the military," she offered, thinking that he'd trusted her, bringing her here to meet Tammy.

"He was up for some award."

"He didn't win." She recalled the conversation between Phoenix and Dex and felt that two months of her spirits could be buoyed by that one evening alone.

"Oh, were you there?"

"Yeah. I saw that the work was in honor of your dad. I'm sorry for your loss."

Caleb's face shadowed, surprising her that his scowl could grow any deeper. "Thanks."

Around the corner of the makeshift finish line, Phoenix came into sight. Dark hair damp. He looked strong, pumping his legs and angling into the spot for the bikes. He hopped off and swerved towards his brother and Orchid, his grin widening at the sight of the couple. "You found each other." He slowed just long enough to high-five Caleb and offer Orchid a fist bump.

"You didn't drown," Orchid shouted.

"There's still time to keel over," he tossed over his shoulder with a grin. His back receded as he passed other runners.

Orchid's mouth split wide like a fool when she sensed Caleb observing her.

"You have it bad, huh?" he observed.

"What? Uh, no. He's my mentor. We're just working together."

"On what?"

"His pro bono ad campaign."

"On a Saturday?"

"We're meeting the talent."

Was it that obvious, even for someone who'd seen them together for mere seconds?

Tammy flew by. "Go Tammy!" Orchid cheered and she waved.

Caleb walked towards the finish line and Orchid kept pace

with his long strides. Phoenix had mentioned that he wanted to beat two hours, which meant they had less than twenty minutes left.

"When he said he was bringing someone, at first I thought he might be getting back together with Tish," he grunted, as they sauntered past spectators.

An alarm sounded in her head. "Tish?"

"His ex, didn't he tell you?"

"I don't know why he'd tell me about his dating life. We're working on ad campaigns."

He ignored her attempt to deny an attraction that was evident in less time than it took for a NASCAR pit crew to change a tire.

"He was with Tish forever, and then… he lost interest. He dumped her. She said it was like she suddenly didn't exist. And here I thought they'd get married. My brother can be a bit mercurial."

Caleb was warning her. *Mercurial.* She felt a pang, having no right, yet imagining Phoenix's attention shining on her, and then withdrawing. "I'm just lucky to get this assignment. Hopefully, it's my ticket to China."

"China. Why would you want to go there?"

"I've never been. If my mom were around, I think she would've wanted me to see her home country." Her voice caught over a memory of her mom teaching her to count in Mandarin. She breathed deep and ticked off four beats silently in Chinese. *Yi, er, san, si.*

A little of Caleb's hard edge softened. The coiled hold of his muscles practically melted to human levels. "Sounds like it's my turn to be sorry."

She waved off the pity she usually detested. "Just so you know, I'm not taking advantage of your brother. I want to do good work for him. And hopefully learn from him too."

Caleb watched the racers with hands on his hips. "Learn from him. It's what everyone always wanted from him. In school, I could tell which kids were really his friends and which just wanted to cheat off him."

Orchid felt her nose wrinkle. "That must have sucked. Like I said, I don't want anything from him."

"Just more time. To learn."

"And go to China," she said, hoping that the consistency of her story could convince herself as well as his brother, who was reading her too easily.

"Well then, you should come to our family thing over Fourth of July."

"I told you, this is just a work thing…" Her voice trailed off as she perceived him sweeping a gaze over her outfit, reminding her they were at a competition. On a Saturday.

"Exactly. There's a parade with military personnel. Dad used to take us kids. It's probably where my bro first started caring about veterans. Perfect place to research your ads."

"I guess if he asks. And he's not going to. It almost killed him to bring me today."

"Why's that?"

"His business partner made him."

Caleb snorted.

"What about you?" she asked, eager to change the subject. "Are you married?"

Caleb ejected air, full of disdain. "Marriage isn't for me."

"No?"

"Girls seem to think it leads to kids."

"And?"

"And there aren't any ankle-biters in my future."

Caleb ambled towards a pylon with a digital clock that timed the racers.

Orchid followed, stopping with him in the shade of a grove of trees where the finish line was visible.

"How about you?" he asked. "You want kids?"

"I don't know," she said softly, thinking how she'd been the curse that had snuffed her parents' lives. She turned the focus back to him. "Why don't you?"

"I'm too fucked up, I guess."

Taken aback, she wondered how Phoenix and Caleb had come from the same family, much less shared a childhood.

Pounding feet foretold the winners streaking towards the finish line. Cheers erupted as the first runners broke the ribbon and volunteers marked race times.

Phoenix rounded the final corner. Orchid bounced on the balls of her feet, filled with excitement. Waving and jumping up and down, her own heart pounded as he flew through the finish line.

"The hero as always," Caleb declared.

Phoenix slowed his strides dozens of feet beyond the end of the race. He was panting, hands on hips. And then he turned to join them.

"That was great!" Orchid cheered.

Phoenix rewarded her with a grin. His legs had just pounded three miles of pavement, yet hers wobbled. "Did you two keep out of trouble?" he asked.

"Whatever. I'm heading out." Caleb said.

"Already? You want to meet Tammy? Or at least see if I placed?"

"Nope."

"Alright, I'll see you on the Fourth."

"Right, I invited Orchid there, too."

Phoenix opened his mouth, then compressed his lips.

"It was just an idea," she quickly added. "I don't need to come. Really." She had known not to hope. Her bones had predicted his reaction.

"I thought the military parade would be good for research, but whatever... your call." Caleb shrugged. "I'm headin' out. Bye." He turned and loped towards the motorcycles stationed nearby, and straddled an elongated dark Harley painted with snakes matching his arm tattoos.

With Caleb gone, Orchid absorbed Phoenix's stricken expression.

Tammy bounded by them. She crossed the finish line and pumped a fist in the air.

They drew towards Tammy, their steps in unison. To anyone else, they'd appear a young, trim couple, out for a sports day. Orchid knew better. She was becoming his regret.

"You made impressive time," Phoenix noted when they reached Tammy.

"I look more tired after carrying groceries up to my apartment," Orchid quipped.

"Military's top-notch training," Tammy responded. She was still breathing hard. "Walk with me along the beach, while I cool down."

"How come you're not winded?" Orchid asked Phoenix as they headed towards the Atlantic. The sun shone overhead. Orchid stopped and slipped off her Keds, so she could feel the sand squish under her bare feet.

"My heart rate's still elevated," he said.

Mine, too, she wanted to say.

Other than a sheen of sweat and a blush of ruddiness across his cheeks, he didn't look like he'd just swum, pedaled and pumped more than fifteen miles.

The trio angled towards the magical place between land and sea, walking along the firm wet sand. Orchid held close to the water's edge. The waves licked her bare soles like kitten's tongues.

Tammy, between the two of them, turned her attention to Orchid and chuckled. "You're blue like the ocean." She waved towards Orchid's hair, and then indicated her feet.

Orchid followed the path of her gesture from her cerulean hoodie down to her shimmering toenails. "Aqua Attack," she said, naming the nail polish shade she'd picked to complement her superhero dress from the night before.

Phoenix turned and snickered into his hand.

"Quit it. Anyway, I'm changing my look."

"Branching out? I've got it. Add some purple and gold and call it peacock. Start a new trend."

"Peacock already exists. And you missed green. Good thing you don't work in beauty."

Phoenix's chuckle turned into a full-blown snort.

"I like your look," Tammy pronounced. "I couldn't pull it off."

"I do, too," Phoenix concurred. "Why are you changing?"

"My job." Orchid raised her voice over the wind that ruffled her azure hair. "I need to look professional. I'm going back to my natural color, to give me a better chance at that China assignment."

"If hair color's enough to make you lose an assignment, sneak some tennis-ball green onto Sir Princeton's pillowcase," Phoenix said.

The image of Princeton's proper 'do shot through with chartreuse filled Orchid with glee. "Hair color probably has nothing to do with it. I just don't want to regret anything later, when Princeton gets the job."

"Who's this Princeton dude? I'll take him out," Tammy offered.

"My nemesis at work. He gets everything. Knowing my luck, I'll be working for him next."

"Except, you have a secret weapon," Phoenix offered in his low rumble.

Tammy looked from Phoenix to Orchid. "Sure is hot out here." She grinned.

Orchid blushed. Was her attraction to Phoenix that visible? She moved closer to the lapping waves, taking a minute to regroup. Froth swirled around her ankles. She tossed her Keds onto a dry spot on the beach and shivered with delight. The crisp blue of the sky reminded her of a cobalt gaze that jolted her alive. Salt air misted her face. "The water's cold," she called out.

"You should feel it a half mile out," Tammy shared. She and Phoenix paused to watch Orchid wade into the surf.

Orchid's steps sank into the silty, soft sand. No matter that Phoenix felt obligated to bring her. She was going to relish this beautiful day. She loved Tammy's military cool. She was going to absorb everything she could and earn that assignment.

Deeper and cooler here, her toes perceived larger granules. She tugged her cropped leggings over her knees. Mixed with murky water, the sand sucked her down. "Come join me!" she called out. Tammy bent to remove her running shoes. Phoenix had already discarded his onto the bright sand. Even his squared off feet were long and elegant.

The next step sank deep. Pain shot through her. A piercing like a knife breached the arch of her foot. She shrieked and recoiled from whatever had attacked her in the swirling water. Stumbling, she would've fallen if it weren't for the strong arms that surrounded her. She turned towards Phoenix's warmth. The worry on his face mirrored the horror she felt.

"Jellyfish? Or are you just seeking attention?" he asked, his tone low and calm.

His humor and proximity eased her nervous system. Her brain slowed from alarm to assessing herself. "I stepped on something. Be careful. Don't come any closer. There's something sharp here."

His lips spread with mirth. "Any closer?" He glanced down at the two of them in an embrace.

She felt the roundness of her breast pressed against his muscular chest. There could be no closer. Well, maybe, but she wasn't about to let her imagination roam there.

Tammy waded up to them. "You two love birds need help?"

"Be careful, don't come any closer," Phoenix deadpanned, and Orchid cracked up. A miracle, considering her foot was now throbbing.

"Sounds like you're okay." Tammy grinned and kept the distance between them.

"Can you walk?" Phoenix asked, his gaze of concern sweeping over Orchid.

She tiptoed a ginger step and nearly crumpled from the stabbing sensation traveling up her leg. Good thing his whole body kept hers upright.

Tammy came over and positioned herself on the other side of her. Orchid's arms wrapped over the shoulders of one athlete, and around the waist of the other. She hobbled the dozen hops to emerge from the water.

"I'm ridiculous," she said self-assessing how she must look.

"You're kind of adorable," Tammy assured her.

Phoenix tilted his head. "A wounded blue bird is kind of adorable."

Orchid attempted to dismiss her heart's traitorous thud with the wave of a hand. Too late. Her chin lowered, her lips resisted a smile, revealing her heart. She felt seen.

They arrived onto the dry sand, their shadows like a five-footed monstrosity.

"Can I take a look?" Phoenix asked.

Orchid bobbed her chin and held onto Tammy for support, while Phoenix kneeled and probed her fleshy instep.

"Ouch," she said.

He looked up, his blue eyes checking hers. "Nasty gash, but I don't see glass or anything."

Orchid lifted her leg to peek at the damage. Red, glistening streaks formed erratic lines around her pale flesh. She stared at Phoenix's concerned expression, feeling her eyelids frozen open. She shouldn't have looked. *Accident. Blood.*

"How about we get you to an ER and see if you need stitches?" he said.

"E-R?" Orchid's panic lengthened her syllables. "No hospitals."

"Maybe I can find a clinic then."

"No, no doctors."

He studied her expression. "Tammy and I can get you to my

car. My aunt and uncle have a place not far from here. How about we get you bandaged up there?" The tightness in his voice meant he'd noticed her fear. He motioned to Tammy to grasp her around the waist, checking her expression.

Orchid nodded. Her cheek wanted to rest against his chest, the safest place she could imagine in this moment.

Tammy scooped up Orchid's tennis shoes and shoved her feet into her own sneakers. "Try breathing," she said.

Orchid took several deep breaths as the three of them hobbled towards the parking lot.

"How are you feeling?" Phoenix was checking on her.

"Sheepish."

"Baa," Tammy offered.

At the car, Phoenix unlocked the passenger side and helped Orchid settle into the leather seat. Her sense of smell was heightened, and she noticed a faint odor of gasoline. She breathed through her mouth and refocused on Phoenix.

He pulled his tee-shirt over his head and snugged it around her arch, allowing her foot to rest on the elevated fabric instead of the sandy floor mat. His breath warmed her cheek as he leaned down to check on her. "You okay?"

The sight of his well-defined musculature evaporated her coworker status and awakened the *woman*. "Just, sorry to ruin your day." She looked away.

"Nothing could ruin this day," he said, and brushed a hand over her arm before standing. The connection left a trail of sparks in its wake.

Phoenix turned towards Tammy, while Orchid was still marveling at his words. *Nothing could ruin this day.* What could cause him to utter such a generous sentiment?

"Their house isn't far from here," he said to Tammy. "Do you want to join us? We can order take out."

"Thanks, but I need to run."

"How about I call you in the morning about the campaign?"

"I guess." Tammy frowned.

Orchid realized that this injury had sucked all the time Phoenix and Tammy were going to use to pitch their ideas.

"I'll be right back," he said, and headed to the back of the car.

Tammy deposited Orchid's shoes on the mat in the front passenger seat. "I probably should've told you guys earlier. I'm not sure about being in any ads. Feels like a sell-out," she said.

"It's not selling out," said Orchid. "This is non-profit work. It's finding the people who need help and showing them a better way."

"Do I get to work with you?" asked Tammy.

"Kind of, and I promise that my strategic abilities are better than my beach-walking ones."

Orchid's humor eked out a half smile from Tammy. One side of her mouth quirked up. "In that case, I'll think about it," Tammy said, then waved goodbye.

Phoenix accompanied her to fetch their equipment. He had pulled a fresh tee over his torso.

Orchid almost muttered, "Thank goodness." It didn't seem safe for him to operate the car shirtless. Not safe for her, anyway. She pictured him slinging a bare arm over the back of her seat as he backed up the car, his stomach muscles engaging as he shifted gears.

Stop already. She observed the two triathletes stride towards their waiting bicycles. They collected helmets, water bottles, and equipment from designated spaces, talking along the way.

What was she to do with this kind man, someone whose cobalt eyes seemed to glean her true spirit, remembered her coffee, and knew the decades-old bands that prompted her parents to dance around their kitchen? The tips of her ears warmed. He fit like he'd been made for her.

No, this was a ruse. The devil's work. She needed one thing from him. Award-winning creative as a proof point for her boss. She hated using someone who seemed genuine. Yet the world hadn't served her many good fortunes. She'd do as she'd always done, look out for herself first.

She heard the trunk pop open and turned to see Phoenix hoist his lightweight racing bike into the back and circle to the driver's side. He flicked his key fob and the tail end of the car closed with a quiet thud.

"How's your cut doing?" he asked, and tilted his head towards her.

"It's throbbing. Like a mantra saying 'you fool' over and over." She risked a glance at the reddening fabric and decided that checking it out was a bad idea.

He reversed and pulled onto the street. "I don't know. You're being chauffeured to a mansion for personalized medical care. Maybe not such a fool."

Orchid's laugh erupted, then paused. "Wait. Mansion?"

"Well, at least a very nice house. With a view. And five bedrooms. Eight if you count the ground floor."

Orchid ran fingers through her blue locks. "I don't care how nice the house is. I'm in no shape to meet your family."

"They're not there. This is their second home. It's empty until summertime."

Orchid sighed relief as they passed lifeguard stands, a series of jagged pier posts jutting into the skyline, and eateries closed during low season.

"I messaged my aunt. We can stay as long as we want. She said she hopes you feel better."

"This is like a storybook. Your uber wealthy family says I can bleed all over their mansion as long as I want?"

"I didn't actually mention the bleeding. Since half the rooms are upholstered pure white."

Orchid groaned.

She felt like a princess in a dream, cocooned in this beautiful car, beside this sweaty yet elegant man.

They eased along a street of elegant homes, and then pulled

up to a pale grey three-story. A wall of windows opened onto the panoramic view of the ocean.

"Very nice house, all right."

"I have a lot of happy memories here."

She wondered if he was thinking of his dad.

Phoenix maneuvered into the driveway and came around to her side, but she'd already pushed the passenger door open.

"Do you want me to carry you inside?"

"This is humiliating enough. I can manage." But when he moved closer, she took his hand, and then slung an arm around his waist, staggering the dozen steps up to the front porch. His tee smelled freshly laundered.

He pressed buttons on a keypad while he held her, and the door's lock clicked open.

The living room reminded her of a shoot for French Vogue, all distressed wood and robin's egg blue walls. She peered down at the bloodied rag snug around her foot and shuddered. "Please tell me we're going to a non-white room."

She limped into an adjacent room, well-furnished in soothing navy tones, and settled onto a sectional. Phoenix propped her foot, dirty rag and all, onto a cushion atop a glass coffee table.

"That fabric probably costs a hundred dollars a yard," she warned, wondering if his aunt would appreciate them using her silk pillows for triage.

"No doubt," he answered, unfazed. "I'm going to get some supplies. You okay here for a minute?"

She absorbed the color-blocked spines and photos lining floor-to- ceiling bookcases, the subdued dark video screen, and the sand below a blue sky visible through one of the floor-to-ceiling windows. "More than okay."

He pushed buttons on a remote control and soft music emerged from the ceiling. He brushed her bare calf. "Anything you need, you say the word." The warmth of his touch lingered even after he'd left.

Family snapshots and books filled the room's built-in cabinetry. She studied framed pictures on the table next to her. A younger Phoenix and Caleb, posed in navy jackets on a cruise liner stood with two other teenaged boys. Tanned adults bared teeth in big smiles, behind them a backdrop of palm trees. There was another photo of Phoenix and his family as they slalomed down a ski run, with "Walker" imprinted onto his race cap. The last was Phoenix diving into a large swimming pool, his grace frozen midair for eternity.

His world was opposite hers. Privilege. Money. Vacations to exotic locales. Most of all, a family to share in all that joy.

Phoenix padded in barefoot carrying a metal bowl. Inside were folded cloths and a first aid kit. He also toted a tall tumbler. He placed everything on the table. "This place is stocked for a nuclear war," he declared, sounding jovial compared to her sudden sorrow.

He glanced at her, and his humor aborted. "What's wrong? Are you in pain?" He tore open a small white packet. "Ibuprofen," he explained.

She took the tablets and swallowed them.

"We should've gone to the hospital," he said. "Who am I to play doctor?" He knelt and began to unravel the makeshift bandage.

She tried to upend her grief. He'd been wholly kind. She had no right to fill him with guilt. "It's not that. It's just, you grew up with so much. I'm not jealous. But honestly, I had nothing." She waved toward the books and memorabilia, soft pink seashells and earth-blue pillows. Her throat surprised her by tightening. She was not one to indulge in self-pity.

He studied her. Their gazes connected, more than man to woman, certainly more than colleagues. At an elemental level. "Don't let the outside fool you. I see you, Orchid Paige. You have heart and talent and smarts that are rare. That is not nothing."

Warmth flushed below her cheekbones, and her eyelids pricked with a feeling that wasn't related to her physical pain.

Phoenix turned his attention to her injury. The tee-shirt bandage, now crimson, had peeled away in a crusted mass and she cringed at the sight. Phoenix laid a clean dishcloth over her plush footrest, which reduced Orchid's worry for the pillow. "This will be warm," he said and wrung a thick wet handcloth above the stainless-steel bowl.

His words, generous and offered with no expectation of a response, soothed the ragged edges of her defenses. She was exhausted from too many years of battles with a world that yielded nothing, and yet required her to work for every last crumb. It was her penitence for her parents' accident. *My fault.*

She refocused on his gentle care. Could it heal a touch of the little girl buried deep? She studied the whorls of his hair as he worked. That amount of empathy had to be hard-won. He'd grown up without material need, yet he'd also suffered. She observed it in the way he intuited her pain, and the despair in his expression when he spoke of his father.

I see you, too.

She suddenly raised her foot. "You'll never get stains out of snow white," she objected.

"In this house, the linens are white."

"Your aunt's going to kill you."

"Nope. She's going to kill you." His eyes crinkled with mischief, and

he cradled her foot. She arched it back for him to examine. The warm terry felt comforting against her skin, as he wiped away sand and dried blood. He dipped the fabric in the warm water and went back to work.

"Looks good. I googled it. If it kept bleeding, we'd have to get it checked out. Have you had a tetanus shot in the last ten years?"

"Yes," she said, even though she was unsure of the answer. If she'd admitted her doubt, he'd probably make her promise a trip to the doctor.

His care reminded her of the time she'd suffered a

nosebleed. Both of her parents had crowded into the bathroom with her, her mom demonstrating how to hold the napkin against her nostrils. She was eight then, but the memory was still fresh.

She distracted herself with talk. "Why are you being so nice to me? I ruined your chance to talk with Tammy."

"Quite the opposite. Tammy said she'd only consider the campaign if you're working on it."

"What? Does she know I'm playing strategist? That I'll write a brief, maybe attend research and, at best, give feedback at the creative presentations?"

"Nope."

Orchid returned his sly grin. "Maybe you're not so nice after all."

"There," he said, "all cleaned up." He lifted her foot for her to admire his handiwork.

She twisted her knee to see, then regretted the move. Fresh droplets oozed from the gash and her stomach clenched. She squeezed her eyes shut. "I'll take your word for it."

Behind shut lids, she could feel strong hands snugging gauze around her foot. One final tug, and then his weight settled on the cushion next to her.

"I'm sorry I forgot about your kryptonite," he said.

She opened her eyes and saw him studying her. "Ridiculous, as usual." She aimed for joking self-deprecation. Her undertone sounded sad instead.

"Only during hip-hop class."

"Which won't be any time soon," she said, the realization hitting her as the words sprang from her mouth.

"We can fatten you up meanwhile. Can I order vegetarian takeout for us? Indian? Thai? Italian?"

He kept surprising her. "How'd you become an expert in vegetarian cuisines? Actually, I could use a bathroom," she said.

"Of course. The men's room is right this way." He waved towards a closed door behind the sofa.

"Will you ever let me forget that mistake?"

"I think that inside joke's good for a few decades, at least."

Orchid groaned as Phoenix helped her stand. She placed her weight on her left heel and limped towards the direction he'd indicated. A few decades? They'd known each other less than a month and he was talking about a lifetime.

"Take your time. I'm going to grab a quick shower. Unless you want sweaty me in the car with you."

"Go shower. Or else you won't live down *sweaty you* for a good few decades."

Phoenix laughed as he sauntered out of the room.

The powder room was immaculately outfitted in gray-veined marble and brushed gold hardware. The mirror surprised her with good news: her windblown hair had survived the day. Plus, she'd been a help with Tammy after all. She washed her hands and returned feeling refreshed.

The room was empty. Water drummed overhead. Bandaged now, she could manage her uneven gait, so she carried the cloths and bowl to a sunny oversized kitchen. She pictured him on the second floor, in a rainfall shower for two. She shook her head at the image as she rinsed the fabric in cold water.

By the time the water ran clear, she'd concluded that her imagination was wandering into unhealthy territory. She turned off the tap, then wrung out the washcloth and left everything neatly piled in the sink. In the cabinet underneath, she located a plastic bag.

She limped back to clean up the wrappers and ruined tee-shirt. She packed up the first aid kit. The photo-shoot ready room looked exactly as when they'd arrived.

Along the bookshelf, framed images showcased smiling faces. In one photo, a plump woman, burly gentleman and tousle-haired boys posed together with a young Phoenix and Caleb. Another picture revealed a grown-up Phoenix peering up at a tomboyish woman. *Was this Tish?* Orchid's button nose and rounded cheeks seemed soft compared to the woman's angled features.

Phoenix cleared his throat behind her, and she nearly jumped.

"I was just admiring the peonies. They're my favorite." Orchid pointed at the vase of silk flowers on the shelf beside the family pictures.

"Not orchids?" he asked.

She wrinkled her nose. "Orchids are fine, as long as they're not a gift for me."

"Too obvious?" he guessed.

"It wasn't easy growing up a half-Asian orphan with a quirky name. It's enough to make you avoid orchids," she tossed back lightly.

His nostrils flared in sympathy. "I can relate. Try running for class president when your opponents are burning effigies of birds and challenging you to rise from ashes."

Orchid nearly snorted. "That's kind of hysterical."

"I'll give them credit for creativity."

"Did you win?"

He nodded. "In the end, I did rise from the ashes."

"Why am I not surprised? Your life looks pretty nice in these pictures."

He glanced at the smiling family in the silver frames and pointed to a group shot. "That's Aunt Betsy, Uncle George and my cousins, Harry and Stew with Caleb and me." No mention of the other photo, the one with the woman.

Orchid detected a scent of coconut shampoo. She restrained herself from leaning in for a deeper inhale. He looked as alluring as he smelled. Wet hair dripped onto his cheeks. She resisted the urge to sweep away the droplets.

"By the way, I cleaned up," she said, and waved around the room, an excuse to break their magnetism.

"Thank you. Me too." He shook his head like a pup, spattering her with drops of clean water.

She laughed and stepped back to avoid the mini shower. "We should go, right?"

"You kidding? This is just the start. Want to hang out for a while?"

She pointed at the playing cards she'd noticed in a crystal case. "I challenge thee to a game of Egyptian Ratscrew."

He threw his head back. "Are we in grade school?"

She was embarrassed by whatever childish impulse had come over her. "I'm kidding. I've taken up enough of your day. Like I said, we should go, right?"

He paused and she tried to read his expression. Relief? He shrugged and it almost seemed like disappointment. "Sure, we can go." He scooped up the trash bag and offered her his other arm. At the front door, he indicated her white Keds, neatly lined up as if assuring her spot in his world.

"I thought you might want these."

How kind that he'd fetched her tennis shoes.

She slipped into them, aware that something had shifted in their relationship in the short time since they'd arrived at the house. She saw herself as Phoenix's words and actions had reflected, a woman who embodied rare talent and heart and smarts. It wasn't that he created this truth. Instead, he was mirroring what he saw, and the care he was showing her was evidence.

His arm flexed with muscles as he supported her, as they inched down the front stairs.

"You're more patient than I ever could be," she laughed, embarrassed by her slow progress.

"Then let's never trade places," he said easily.

"Promise?" she teased.

"Here's what I'll promise. Next time, when you're steady on both feet, you'll get a better tour."

Next time. Beautiful words. Like a fairy tale.

On the final step, an ocean gust pushed her slightly. That nudge reminded her of her real world.

Before they reached his car, she recalled the Lauder conference room and his presentation. *Mentor. Ticket to China.* An admonishment rose up to snatch her from this this suspended reality. She recommitted her own demands from the first time they'd met. *Nothing more than business.*

As they drove, Orchid realized she'd become accustomed to his scent, the masculine undertone beneath his showered cleanliness.

With this little crisis behind them, she was finally able to relax. It felt as if they'd known each other longer than four weeks. They'd spent enough time together that she recognized the way fingers through his hair helped him think, or indicated an emotion; that he owned his space in the world with easy grace; and he thought of others before he thought of himself. His handsome features reminded her of his brother.

"Caleb seems like a real character," she said.

"We're fraternal twins."

She thought of Caleb's demeanor, his similar yet not identical features. "Fraternal twins? I wasn't even wondering about the physical differences. I was actually thinking he's more of a loner."

"He's not had the easiest life," he explained.

"I thought you both had a cushy life, went to the best schools."

"I did. He's the dark twin. Went the GED, community-service route."

She noted his pained expression.

"My dad was an elected judge," he said. "He couldn't allow the appearance of special treatment."

Dad. She heard the wistful note in his voice. "You know, I'm no shrink, but I might be able to relate to what you're going through. If you ever want to talk…" Her voice trailed off, the intensity of his gaze evaporating her next thought.

"I appreciate that. It's really easy to talk with you," he said.

"You too. I feel like you don't judge me for my issues," she said, returning his honesty.

"I don't. I think you've been through a lot."

"You, too."

She watched his fingers tapping the steering wheel.

"The thing with my dad is that he's impossible to live up to," Phoenix said. It sounded like a confession.

"Uh… have you looked in the mirror lately?"

"Ha! I hope that's not me. But seriously, he was like this warrior of justice. This upright citizen in our community. He joked that what I do is hawk antacids."

Orchid turned to face him. "That's unfair."

"Yeah, 'cause I work on packaged beverages, and laundry detergent too."

"Not that there's anything wrong with all that. But what about your charity work?"

"And why do you think I do that?"

Understanding sunk in. "You know what sucks? Once your parents are gone, you never know what they would've thought of all your accomplishments."

"I didn't know them, but I think your parents would be proud of you. Any parents would."

"Same with you."

"Thank you."

"Can I ask what happened? To your dad?"

He shot a glance at her.

That spark of a connection made her wonder if she shouldn't have crossed into personal territory. *Too late to be worried about that.*

"Heart attack. It happened at work. If he'd been in a public area, they could've gotten him help sooner. They found him in his chambers. The suddenness of it…"

She nodded in sympathy. "There's no time to adjust. No warning." Here, with Phoenix, she wanted to return his vulnerability. "My parents died in a car crash. I witnessed it," she said.

"Oh, Jesus, I'm sorry."

"When I was twelve. I'd begged them to let me stay home without a babysitter. They went out to a party and the weather turned bad. From snow to ice. If someone had been with me, they would've stayed wherever they were. But they came home because of me, even though the roads were murder." She coughed as she recalled her culpability, a cold sound without humor.

"I hope you're not saying it's your fault."

"They called me right before it happened. They told me how bad the roads were."

"You were twelve. Just a kid." Phoenix wiped at his eyes. "Orchid, be kind to yourself. Your parents made a tragic judgement call. It's not your fault."

Coming from Phoenix, the words landed. Like no one else, he saw her. "Thank you."

Yet, she didn't let anyone into this particular space.

Her vulnerability erected a fortress. An absence of emotion followed. Nothingness wasn't even relief. Her view of the highway shrank to a narrow band. Phoenix's lips moved. She heard no sound. His actions were detached from hers. She was alone, as she had been that night. Except, instead of screaming and tearing at her pajamas, she was in a car with a kind man and incapable of speaking. And this man by her side was trying to soothe her through her emotional fog. She stared at the unending pavement, refusing to cry. Refusing sentimentality. It was what it was. Her cross to bear.

There were physical scars. Those were bad enough, the puckered skin and twisted flesh telling a permanent story of action gone awry. At least, those rips heal.

Then, there were the invisible hurts. Deep injustices, daggers flung by those closest, or offhand remarks from near-strangers that continued to burrow into an unexpectedly tender place. Emotional wounds, she had long ago discovered, could be far worse than physical wounds.

Phoenix cupped a hand over hers, the warmth of his palm like a connection to all their memories: sun on her face at the beach, the scent of a coffee shop, music echoing through an awards hall, the familiarity of her office, his family's beach house. And now, the intimacy of this moment, ensconced in the leather of his sports car. *Love you,* she thought. *Oh no.* Orchid refuted the idea.

"You okay?" he asked.

His presence was comforting.

"I'm okay. You drive." She squeezed his hand and then removed hers. "Christ, you've been through a lot." He gripped the steering wheel with both hands.

"You, too. We all have our hardships."

"Not like that, Orchid. Not at that age."

"There's always worse. I refuse to feel sorry for myself."

"Do you know the concept of self-compassion? Researchers like Kristin Neff say this is more important than self-esteem. Think what you'd say if this happened to your good friend. What would you say to Mandy?"

She thought of her best friend's cheeks pulled down by loss. "I'd say that it's terrible, what happened. And that it's actually made her a more empathetic person." The tightness in her chest loosened.

"There we go," Phoenix said, his voice low and kind as he nodded in her direction.

There *we* go, Orchid noted. His nod felt encouraging, as if confirming that what she'd been through was terrible, that it forged empathy into her every fiber, and that he was right there with her.

It was such a relief to be no longer alone. Despite her ground rules, she was falling for this handsome, big-hearted entrepreneur.

CHAPTER 10
DEAR INTERIOR

Orchid

Courage. Encourage. In courage.

Bolstered by Tammy, and strengthened by the ghosts of a thousand Chinese ancestors, Orchid vowed to try the practitioner Tammy had recommended.

His office's waiting area soothed with sienna walls and brown pillows lining velvet sofas. A gentleman appeared in the waiting room who matched the photo Orchid had seen on the therapy website. As his lips lifted, the droop at the corners of his eyes became more pronounced. Did this lead to him being a therapist, the fact that he naturally looked sad?

"I'm Todd," he said, and offered a soft grip. They shook hands.

"Dr. Todd, I'm Orchid."

He chuckled, a melancholy sound to accompany his drooping lids. "I'm a licensed clinical social worker, not an MD."

She mirrored his jovial demeanor. "If it's okay, I like how it makes you sound official." She needed to believe his credentialed skills could help her.

He cracked a downcast smile. "Okey dokey. Sure, you can call me Dr. Todd."

Orchid followed him into his office. He gestured towards the sofa and swiveled his desk chair towards her.

Once they were facing one another, Todd rested a pad of paper on his knees and arranged his mournful expression.

Tammy said he was the best for trauma, she reminded herself.

"What brings you here today?" he asked.

"I'm working on an ad campaign for wounded veterans, and for the first time in a while, I opened up that I saw something as a kid. I'm having nightmares, flashbacks. And I'm easily startled."

"Do you know the source of your trauma?"

Orchid looked down. Images arose. The smell of gas and oil clogged her nose. "I saw my parents die in a car crash. When I was twelve."

"I'm very sorry," he said. His voice sounded sincere.

Memories washed over her. She shared what had happened. "I lived with my aunt after that, and she sent me to therapy. I'm doing better now, in a lot of ways. I can't complain, I have good friends, and a job I love. But sometimes, I'm still kind of a wreck…" The word's double meaning struck her.

"Are there certain triggers?"

She counted on her fingers. "The sight of blood; the sight of doctors; anything medical; seeing people hurt; or anything that reminds me of accidents."

He nodded. "You know to be gentle with yourself?"

"Not my strong suit."

"First of all, it's not your fault."

She paused, stuck on his conclusion. "You know, other people have told me that but when you said it, I believed you."

"Good."

"What about me getting triggered?"

"Trauma changes the brain. Especially when it happens at a young age. Your brain is trying to protect you from danger. But even when that danger is no longer there, it's searching for it."

"So, what do I do? I've lived with this for a long time, and sort of accepted it. But then, I've just met someone who has it altogether. Something about him makes me want to be a better person. So, when this wounded veteran recommended you, it struck me as a good time to work on these fears." She stopped and smiled at the memory. "She taught me box breathing."

He nodded. "Breathing exercises are great. Meditation can help, or mantras. Some clients respond to somatic methods, to address the trauma that's remembered in your body. And there are newer techniques, like neurofeedback, brain spotting or EMDR. Today is for intake, Orchid, and then we'll discuss a treatment plan. How does that sound?"

She tilted her head. "Brain spotting? EMDR?"

He smiled. "It means Eye Movement Desensitization and Reprocessing. It's where you walk through the event, and we track where in the brain the trauma is, based on your eye movements. I know it sounds far-fetched, but the reason these mind-body techniques work—especially when other approaches like traditional talk therapy might not—is because trauma impacts the emotional centers of the brain which are most directly healed through connection with the body alongside emotional experiences. The typical talk therapy approach can be helpful, but it doesn't process through the underlying trauma as effectively as these more somatic approaches."

"That's the first time I've heard any of this described in a way that makes sense."

"It can be very confusing. We'll try different approaches and find what works for you."

Orchid felt hopeful. Perhaps the next time she cut herself, she would be able to press the gauze on her oozing wound.

"I can get better," she said. It was a new idea.

"What we do is teach you techniques to soften the reactions when you're faced with a trigger. This will teach you to be less reactive overall. Would you like to work on that together?"

"I would," Orchid said.

He smiled again and leaned back into his chair. "You know, sometimes people think that only soldiers get PTSD, but a post traumatic response can affect anyone."

"PTSD. I thought that's what I've been having, but I didn't want to self-diagnose."

"Now you have a professional opinion." He offered a hopeful smile.

They talked through the forty-five-minute session. When her time was up, he took out his calendar and they booked the next appointment.

Orchid rose, feeling lighter than when she'd arrived. "Thank you," she said.

"You're welcome," he responded, opening the door leading into the reception area. "See you next week."

She breezed through the waiting area, out of the office, and into the night air. *I can get better.*

She thought that Phoenix might never fully know his impact on her. He'd not only given her the work credentials she thought she wanted more than anything, but he also inspired her to heal what she'd thought was permanently broken.

Several sessions in, Orchid continued to think of her therapist as Dr Todd. Even without a medical degree, he was helping her to heal, bit by bit, memory by memory.

They worked on a meditation regimen, and focused on breathing. At the next session, they delved even deeper.

"You talked about your trigger at the beach," he began.

"Yes, the cut on my foot."

"Have you heard of mantras?"

"Like ommm?" she asked.

"Right, that's one. There are many. You can even create your own."

"I'm game," she said.

"What's helped you in the past? When you're feeling panic come on?"

She thought about this for a moment. "Well, there was this

time at work. When that guy I told you about, Phoenix, showed photos of wounded veterans. I started to hyperventilate, so I kind of slowed my breath… and then told myself I was okay."

"Mmhmm. What would that sound like, telling yourself you're okay?"

"Like you'd talk to a child. You know. *It's okay, you're okay.*"

"What were you thinking at the time?"

"Honestly, I was thinking about the night of my parents' crash. How cold it was in my room. Being scared and alone, and then reminding myself that I'm not there. That I'm not that little girl anymore."

"Does that help?"

"I guess. I mean, when he stopped showing those photos, I felt better."

"The idea of a mantra is to codify getting yourself to that safe space. Like a shortcut. Can you think of something that would work as that reminder?"

Orchid pondered. "You mean, like: It's okay. You're not there anymore. You're here *now?*"

"How does that feel?" Dr Todd asked.

"It's maddening, your tendency to answer a question with a question."

He returned her candor with a doleful chuckle. "That's why we get paid the big bucks."

She thought about his initial question. "I like the idea of a mantra. A reminder in the moment. But it's probably better to have one that's not such a mouthful. How's *That was then, this is now.*"

"Try it," he suggested.

She experimented. "That was then, this is now. Not then, now. This is now, this is now."

"Play around with it. Pick one that feels right, stick with it for a while, see if you can get into the habit of using your mantra when you're feeling stressed."

"Okay," she agreed. She was motivated. She didn't want to

feel bad. She didn't want to be the Orchid who could be triggered by the sight of blood.

"Good. Now, homework for next week." He ignored her groan. "Have you ever tried journaling?"

"I kept a diary as a kid. I stopped after my parents died. I wonder why?"

"Why do you think?" he asked.

"Question with a question," she grumbled, and he shared another laugh. She thought for a moment, taking herself back to that time when she'd moved to her aunt's apartment. "My diary was a place to say what I was really feeling, and after they died, my thoughts were so terrible, it made me feel worse to write them down. I needed to move forward."

He dipped his chin. "If you decide to try it again, you don't have to write about their accident. Only if you want to. One of my clients writes the ending she *wishes* happened. As if her life were fiction. It gives her power. Would you like to try that?"

"I'm on it, doc," she promised.

That evening, Orchid opened her laptop and started a fresh document. She stared at the blank page, feeling the years melt away until she was twelve again. *As if your life were fiction,* Todd had said. Her story began to flow from her heart to her fingertips to her keyboard.

> "You look so pretty," I told Mommy. She was wearing a dress I loved.
>
> She leaned down to kiss me good night. Her feather earrings tickled my nose. I pulled my covers up to my chin. Extra layers of winter blankets pinned me like sandbags in a storm.
>
> "We won't be long. And if the weather turns, we'll

come home early," Mom promised. She'd always kept her promises.

Mom flipped off the bedroom light, and clacked down the wooden stairs. I heard the front door bolt click into place.

I must have dozed off. The sound of car tires crunching down the driveway woke me. The clock ticked past midnight.

I sacrificed my warm bed to peek out the window. Car lights shone at the top of their steep driveway. Two lit orbs inched down the winding path, careful to navigate the pavement that Dad had salted earlier that day.

I ran downstairs, turned on the porch lights, and unbolted the heavy front door.

Just in time, I watched Dad help Mom emerge from the passenger seat. The car's front hood steamed in the frigid air. Its smooth metal gleamed in the moonlight.

"Hi sweetie, you'll catch cold!" Mom called.

Her feather earrings whipped in the wind.

Ice pelted the layers of her colorful dress visible below her short coat.

The red splotches were peonies. Not blood.

Mom clung to Dad's elbow. They came inside and shed scarves, gloves, and layers of outerwear. I flung my arms around Mom.

"I was scared," I said. "I was scared something happened to you."

She was warm. Her feather earrings tickled my cheek.

"You're never alone, hungry bird. Even if something were to happen to us, we're with you always," Mommy said. Daddy joined us.

We rocked like we hadn't seen each other for a long time.

Their embrace filled me all the way up to the empty space into the sky.

"Love you forever and ever," I said, my face pressed into Mom's peony-printed dress. Like Mom, I always kept my promises.

Tears welled, and then spilled. The ending she'd wanted and never dared to dream now elbowed out the nightmare of reality. Her cheeks damp, she pictured that snowy night as beautiful, her parents' beater car as quirky.

Another thought struck her. Dr Todd's insight.

She took a deep breath and texted him. "You were right. I *can* get better."

Three dots appeared. "Yes you can," he responded.

Yes, I can.

Love you, Mommy.

CHAPTER 11
DIVING IN DEEP

Orchid

Fueled by the feeling that work in China would bring her closer to her mother, Orchid had spent all of May working on the pro bono ad campaign. Her job was to write the briefing document, a document that seemed deceptively simple. A brief is meant to be short, yet the most common pitfalls are either jamming the document full of barely related detail, or writing a piece of prose that didn't inspire.

On the surface, it didn't seem difficult to deliver a few pages of insights. Yet, professional strategic planners spend years honing their skills to be able to decide which focus areas would result in breakthrough ad campaigns. Those outside of the ad world might not recognize the strategy needed to craft a compelling brief. However, Orchid knew that her client would recognize the difference between an inspired brief versus a pedestrian one. Joan would know. And she had to admit, she cared that Phoenix considered her work well-delivered.

An associate from Phoenix's team had sent her research documents about the Post Traumatic Stress Disorder (PTSD) that some veterans suffered from serving in combat.

She attended video conferences with her client. "I'm a fainter," she explained with a light tone, whenever they flipped past images of injured soldiers. Together with the creative team, their job was to help soldiers recognize when they might be suffering from PTSD, and encourage them to seek mental health support.

For weeks, she toiled over different messages, weighing which ones would most motivate the military personnel they aimed to support. *Was it more compelling to depict the first step of awareness, or the assurance that the programs in place are effective?* She shared her work-in-progress with her boss. Joan supported the assignment, and knew about the work she was doing. What Joan didn't know was who initially recommended Orchid to this non-profit organization that combined media and creative talents to produce public service ads.

It was during a team meeting that Joan shared Orchid's project. "She's taken the initiative to address her development areas," Joan said. "Not only is she taking a Mandarin class, but she's also working on a non-profit campaign."

Orchid inwardly groaned when she saw Mr. Princeton's startled reaction. The privileged go-getter would probably have his family buy him his own agency, so he could run ten campaigns to her one.

After the meeting, her friend Violet caught up to her in the hall. "I like your hair," she said.

Orchid smoothed her newly dark mane, chemically returned to its natural hue. "Thanks. You've gone the opposite direction."

Violet laughed, and twirled an amethyst-dyed curl. "Have to match the name!" Then she switched topics. "By the way, I was impressed back there. I'm going to double down my money on you."

Orchid slowed her pace to look at her friend. They were alone in the hallway that led towards the ladies' room. "What do you mean, double down on me?"

"You know, for the pool. To see who's going to get the China assignment."

"There's a pool?"

"Oops, I thought you knew."

"Why aren't you betting on yourself?"

"Oh c'mon. Everyone knows it's between you and

Princeton. He'd been leading. But now, with this inside scoop, I think you have a shot."

"Oh, crap," said Orchid. "As if my own internal pressures aren't bad enough! Now, I have to worry about my friends losing money over me."

"Don't worry, not all your friends are betting on you."

Orchid nearly choked on the realization of how visible her failure would be. "Just great. What are you betting on, who gets the assignment?"

"Yeah, plus when Joan's going to announce it."

"What the–?"

"Some bullish ones think it'll get announced mid-June, others think you won't know 'til mid-July. I'm the only one going with the Fourth of July."

Orchid groaned, out loud this time. "What's going to happen to whoever loses?"

"There's a pool for that, too. The money's on whether the person who doesn't get the assignment will resign. And how quickly."

Funny to hear these dire predictions delivered in Violet's bubbly voice.

"Can you just call this whole thing off?"

Violet laughed. "No way! It's half the reason I get out of bed and come to work every day."

"Well, at least come to dance class one-night next week and fill me in on all the deets," said Orchid.

Violet pushed through the bathroom door. "Sure thing. Ta-ta," she called, as the door swung closed behind her.

Orchid searched her brain for a slam dunk to bolster her chances. Beyond her own personal reasons for pursuing the assignment, she did not need a public work humiliation.

Eschewing a bathroom break, she headed to her laptop to type out an urgent note to her mentor. "Phoenix, I'd love to show you the brief," she typed, and hit *Send* before she could change her mind.

Violet arrived at her desk, popping into her field of vision as purple poof and cheer. "I'm heading out. Are you staying late tonight?"

Orchid checked her phone. It was after five. "Yeah, I'm working on hacking the pool."

Violet's face split wide with glee. "No can do. The head of cybersecurity's administering this one."

Orchid tossed her phone onto her desk in surrender. "Is every last person in on this?"

Violet tilted her face towards the sound-deadening tiles of their office ceiling. "Nope. We had to keep Joan out. We didn't want to sway her decision." And then she waved and whirled out of Orchid's office. "Thanks for the entertainment!"

Orchid lacked the time, or the inclination, to formulate a snide comment.

Her phone screen lit with a call from a name that took her aback, even though she shouldn't have been surprised. "Phoenix?"

"How are you?" came his low baritone.

"Um, good. You're calling me. How are you?"

"In the middle of pitch hell. But you texted so, yeah, I'm calling. You good?"

"Yes and no. I can't wait to show you the brief. But then there's this office pool. My colleagues are betting against me getting the assignment."

Phoenix chuckled, sounding less like the agency head who'd initially called and more like the kindhearted caregiver she'd last seen at the beach. "Office pool?"

"It's awful. Just mortifying," Orchid complained.

"You just want to avoid being embarrassed? I would've hoped it'd be about the quality of work."

Phoenix and his standards. Growing up a judge's son would embed high morals. "Of course the work matters. Which is why I reached out to you."

"You want to email it to me? I'm working late anyway."

"Email? Let's video. I'd appreciate practicing presenting the work."

"Okay, I'm starving so just give me fifteen minutes to dredge up instant ramen or something from the kitchen, then I'll be back at my computer."

"Instant ramen? I'll tell you what. Let me come by with real food and I'll pitch you live."

"Deal."

Orchid could finally do something for this entrepreneur who'd given her so much.

CHAPTER 12
BRIEF BONDAGE

Phoenix

Two long weeks. Phoenix hadn't seen Orchid during that time. It wasn't that Phoenix hadn't thought about Orchid. Her demands had been clear the first time they'd discussed the ad work. *I'm her mentor.* Phoenix had played his part. Mentor. Mensch.

The call with Orchid finally broke the frozen glacier of their fortnight of silence.

She was coming to his office so they could work on her brief together. Suddenly, he couldn't concentrate on his emails. He surveyed the conference room where he was working as she might see it. The disarray of papers and half-drunk mugs needed to be banished. He straightened his notes, then carted the cold coffee to the kitchenette.

As he strode through the empty office, he recognized that he cared what she thought.

His dad's letter weighed on him. He'd wanted to tell her the truth about how they'd met. Yet if he did, he'd be breaching his father's final wish to keep the case confidential. Worse, her childhood trauma meant that she didn't trust easily. If she learned at this late date that their first encounter wasn't chance after all, would she lose all faith in him?

Something had shifted between them during that trip to the beach.

More than anything, she'd touched him deeply. Her tenacity to thrive despite her obstacles was admirable. Her charm, towards Dex and Tammy, and even Caleb, were evident. Life had buffeted her unfairly.

She'd been explicit about what she wanted from him. *Nothing but business.*

This was the one thing he could gift this sensitive woman who'd faced an unfairly hard life. He could help her achieve her dreams. His path would be the high road. Phoenix vowed he'd never add to her pain. He couldn't protect her from the world. He could promise that *he'd* never be the one to hurt her.

To do that, he'd help her with this assignment and then leave her alone. She never needed to learn about his dad's hand in their meeting. She was too proud to take that secret lightly.

His phone buzzed with a text. Four simple letters, each producing a thump in his heart. "Here!"

He swore. At his own human weakness. At their untenable circumstances. Then, he heaved to his feet and counted his steps to the elevator bank, a handful for every level she ascended. She'd be past three, building management's floor, and maybe past ten where their partner graphics agency resided. The elevator doors parted. Definitely past ten. Orchid's pale skin rouged with unmistakable pleasure, and she exited the paneled lift. She must be relieved to have help for the ornery brief.

"Ni hao," she sang hello, stepping into the vestibule.

"Kai Lan," he greeted her, his voice husky, as if he'd had no reason to speak in their time apart.

She threw her head back in appreciation. Dark black strands swirled in a chignon against one side of her long neck.

"I miss the blue," he said, honesty spilling out.

"It's a whole new me," she said, sweeping her hand to indicate the silk blouse and pencil skirt.

He reached for the blocky green bag she toted, and she relinquished it to him. "You actually own sensible heels?"

She kicked one ankle up and observed it like a foreign object. "I feel like I'm in costume."

"This way, Madame Executive." He executed a mock bow and swept a lavish gesture towards the agency entrance.

Orchid pretend-curtseyed and followed him. At the threshold to the open door, she paused. He turned to view the agency as she must be seeing it.

"Oh," she said, her eyes round with admiration. It was her first time here.

The area past the receptionist's desk opened into a waiting space with clean, angular tables and a coffee bar. Modern leather chairs were punctuated with electric-blue pillows that shimmered in the light.

"It's completely you," she said.

She followed him past white-brick walls decorated with oversized ads.

"Is your cut all better?" He gestured towards the pale arch of her foot.

"Yes, thanks Doc."

His cheeks hurt from their inability to stop smiling. He guided her into the conference room, feeling lighter than he had in weeks. He watched her survey the glass case filled with trophies, and his papers scattered around his laptop.

"Vegan, hope that's okay," she explained, pointing to the bag he was hefting onto the table.

"Hen hao." *Very good.*

"Would you like something to drink?" he asked, waving at the coffee machine near the mini fridge. Like a hotel, it was stocked with Pellegrino and sodas.

"Sparkling water would be great, thanks."

He twisted open a green bottle and poured a tumbler-full for her.

"What's keeping you here tonight?" she asked, rings glittering on her fingers as she unpacked containers of food.

"Our brash CEO agreed to a July pitch date." He pointed at himself and made Orchid chuckle.

"Want to show me the work?" She gestured towards the printed papers stacked on the table.

He picked up a colorful page and read aloud. "Get young millennials to video their brand experiences by engaging them through key opinion leaders."

Orchid fake yawned. "Bo-ring. Tell me one brand that isn't doing that. Are you trying to lose the pitch because you're too busy with other stuff?"

He opened his mouth to protest and then humor started to bubble up. It rumbled and she joined him, until they were both full-blown laughing.

"God, I've missed you," he said, the words slipping out.

Her hands stopped over a casserole dish. "It's good to see you, too. You've been well?"

He aimed for honesty. Because she deserved nothing less. "Better now."

"It's good you'll be with family."

It struck him that she was an only child. No siblings. Just her own resilience. No wonder she was so strong.

She looked at him like she was assessing his earnestness.

Phoenix's stomach growled like a wounded animal.

"Let's serve this before you faint," she said, and peeled lids off the containers.

He stared down at the steaming food. "Hey, are those reusable containers?"

She beamed. "Yup. I convinced some local restaurants to try these to reduce single-use plastics. Customers pay a deposit fee, then they get it back when they return them. After that, everything gets sterilized and reused. I branded it Circ."

He swept a hand through the air. "Angling for a Cirque du Soleil tie-in, huh?"

"Quit teasing. People totally get the circularity reference. I've got a dozen restaurants signed up, and we're tracking usage to see when it pays back."

"Any results yet?"

"Some of them are actually seeing foot traffic increase. Which makes complete sense. Lots of people have been feeling guilty about takeout waste, but they haven't known what to do about it."

"Honestly, you're brilliant. Do you know what you'd love?"

"Hanging out with you?" she blurted.

He glanced at her, startled.

Her expression clouded; her lids shuttered.

"I was thinking Cannes. Did you know that Cannes gives out a Grand Prix for Good?"

She looked as if she had recovered from her too-honest faux pas. "As in the Cannes Lions awards?"

"Yeah. They've partnered with the UN to give out Sustainable Development Goal Lions. You should come."

"You know," said Orchid, "you're giving me an idea. To build my creative chops. I'm going to ask Joan if she'll sponsor me to go to Cannes."

"Speaking of creative chops, do you want to pitch me your brief?"

"Let's eat first. You were starving." She offered him a ceramic plate.

"Real china *and* cutlery?"

"Serving spoons, too." She handed him a ladle. "This is eggplant parm with cashew cheese."

He cocked an eyebrow. "Bless you."

She cuffed his arm with the back of a lid she'd just removed. Her bracelets jangled against her slender wrists. "Cashew cheese is delicious. Don't judge until you try it. I also brought Caesar salad and bruschetta."

He offered her a scoop of eggplant. "Can I serve you? You're really thoughtful for bringing all this, you know that?"

"Well, thanks but I'm here for your brains."

He laughed and settled a rectangular serving onto her plate. The sauce scented the air with oregano and basil.

She dropped some greens and two crusty bread rounds

onto his. They stood close to each other. She smelled sweet, like something bright and clean. Making sure she had food filled him with satisfaction.

Then he looked up, remembering where he was, and who he was to this woman who'd come to him for career help. He circled the wide table and sat on the other side.

She carried her dinner to a spot near her bag and sank into one of the swivel chairs.

He waited for her to start her meal and then tried a bite. Then a second. "The eggplant is delicious."

"Yeah, this is vegan on training wheels. Something familiar, without too many substitutions." She polished off her salad.

He chuckled. "Maybe I can graduate to kindergarten next time."

"The ricotta is made from almonds and the parmesan is nutritional yeast."

"Yeast?" He paused mid-bite through the bruschetta.

"Nope. You're not ready for kindergarten yet," she said with a teasing tone.

He grinned. An idea struck him. "You'd be a great consultant on the business we want to win."

"Oh, yeah?" She chewed and swallowed.

"It's a beverage made with roots, extracts, berries, and botanicals."

"REBBL," she named the elixir brand. "Plus love. The l is for love." She lifted a hand to her neck, like the last word had taken her by surprise.

"You're exactly right," he said.

"That would be a cool brand to work on. A strong point of difference and hugely motivating." The rings on her fingers flashed with her gestures.

"I hope you're as excited about your campaign."

She pushed her empty plate aside and twisted one gold bangle around her slender wrist. "I can't wait to show you the work."

"Go for it," he encouraged.

She pried open her satchel. It was studded with silver grommets.

Phoenix felt humor percolate.

She narrowed her eyes at him. "What?"

"It's just you've revamped your whole look to be this prim businesswoman, and then your true self comes through in that kick-ass bag."

Orchid glanced from him to the dull spikes gleaming across its midnight-hued vegan leather, then she joined in his amusement. "Maybe I should give up the ruse. Do you know how hard it is to hoof it across town in a pencil skirt?"

"Harder than writing a brief?"

"Nope. But easier than pitching one."

"Try me," he encouraged.

"The project has been clear. We're trying to reach military personnel who are experiencing PTSD, so they learn to recognize the symptoms and seek help. Without stigma. Sometimes, when people hit rock bottom, they feel like they'll never get better, or nothing can help."

He got up. He couldn't stop himself. Her pain was evident in the scrunch of her forehead.

"You know how medical students think they have the disease they're studying?" she asked.

"Yeah." He drew closer until she was looking up at him, angst in the frozen angles of her face. In this moment, he wanted to hold her, make *her* feel better.

"PTSD symptoms are flashbacks, insomnia, nightmares, heightened reactions and avoidant behavior." Her words slowed. Emotion tinged her cheeks pink.

Intuition told him what the issue was. He wanted to comfort her. "You don't have to work on this." He pointed to the printed page. He could write the brief himself.

She shook her head. "I want to. It's my one chance to prove myself to Joan. To go to China, and make my mom proud."

Orchid was a warrior. Her life's inequity doubled his resolve to help her. He sank into the seat next to her. "I bet your mom was proud, is proud. And we can come up with some other project. Maybe REBBL."

"You're going to trust me with your plum project? I think you need a real strategic planner. Plus, there isn't enough time. Joan's going to be making her decision soon. Maybe even next week. I need at least one solid recommendation from this work to have a shot."

"I feel like an ass putting you on this campaign. Like I'm torturing you."

"It was my call, if you remember. You warned me that you couldn't guarantee there wouldn't be triggers. I just didn't know that it'd be like looking in a mirror."

"I'm sorry, Orchid. Do you want me to connect you with a specialist at the VA?"

"I didn't come to you for a shrink."

"What can I do then?"

"Help me to present this in the strongest way possible." She pushed the paper towards him and began to explain the rationale for the recommendations, as if she were taking their client through the brief.

He listened as she walked through familiar sections: background, objectives, target, single-minded message, mandatories. She stunned him with the depth of insight into the audience for this work. She spoke with conviction, backed by facts. "And the talent is perfect," she concluded. She turned her laptop towards him and played a video montage of Tammy's experiences.

During the final bars of the music bed, Phoenix looked at her with wonder. "You're hired," he said.

"Quit joking."

"I'm not. Your work's in great shape. Both the content and the delivery. I think you're onto something with how you're presenting Tammy. Did you make that video?"

"Yeah, I fooled around with some video editing software. I had a mood I wanted to capture."

"You have a really good eye."

"Thanks. I've always loved beautiful things. Maybe I got it from my mom, my sense of style and how I see things."

His gaze followed the curve of her collar, appreciating the soft shape of silk against her curves, and the way she chose a pattern over a texture that others might never think to pair. He'd already intuited that Orchid craved beauty. A second reason why the ugliness of her wound at the beach didn't fit her view of perfection. He tucked away another puzzle piece, along with her intellect, humor, kindness, and uncompromising values. How might he measure up against her high standards?

"You don't think there's any risk they would want different talent, right? Because Tammy's perfect," she said.

He considered this. "I don't think so, but it couldn't hurt to voice-over her bio first, to intro the video."

"I'm not sure if this is too much. but I was playing around with an idea for a manifesto for her. You want to hear it?"

"Absolutely."

She peered down at her screen and read aloud. Her voice grew stronger as she lost herself in the meaning of the words.

Life isn't easy. Who hasn't suffered injustice, misunderstanding or hurt on a schoolyard playground, been disappointed at work, or challenged as a parent?

That's what humans are built for. Brains are resilient. They make sense of the world. They seek solutions. But what happens when the injustice or challenge is too great for a single person to bear? When the brain itself is injured by its experiences? The wound may not be visible, but the pain is real.

Meet Tammy. Her three tours of duty yielded a Bronze Star of Valor. Her quick thinking saved many lives. Yet the cost of witnessing cruelty after cruelty, of being devastated by friends being blown up, was having every nerve tuned to imminent danger. When Tammy returned home, she suffered headaches, nightmares, sensitivity to noise, and triggers which left her ill-suited to function day-to-day. She wasn't the same. She learned the name for this insidious ailment that affects more people than you might guess: Post-traumatic stress disorder, PTSD.

Luckily, Tammy's story has a sunny ending. She found resources to help. She worked hard to get better. Today, she trains as a triathlete and counsels others. Now, she wants nothing more than to support others who need those same resources. Tammy's found her life's work. She wants to get the word out. There's hope.

Countless people can benefit from this message. Some say 6% of the population will be affected by PTSD at some point in their lives. Not only soldiers, but people all around us. Tammy knows she alone can't solve PTSD. She has one question for you. Who else can help? Are YOU in?

Orchid looked up from the lit screen. Her eyes shined. The manifesto was ostensibly about Tammy. Anyone listening would know that she connected to this work at a personal level.

Emotion roiled through him. Not an easy feat in a business sometimes characterized by cynicism. How much of these feelings were for her insight, and how much was because he cared about her? "Spectacular. You have to keep that." His voice was husky.

"Really?" Her face brightened.

He nodded. "Your work demonstrates real talent."

"Thank you so much. And… what can I do for you?" she asked.

He'd committed to his dead father's memory that he'd help her. Could he do so without letting his own feelings get in the way? The words came out before he could fully weigh the consequences. "You know, you're right that my ideas aren't fresh enough. Would you mind being a sounding board on our work-in-progress?"

"I'd love that!"

"We're on a tight deadline, so it might be last minute, like over a weekend."

He watched her cover the leftovers and pile the empty plates into the green tote.

"No problem," she said. "Can I leave some food for you?"

His appetite was completely gone. "Thanks, it's all yours."

"You're just scared of nutritional yeast," she joked, then slung both bags over her shoulder.

He walked her to the elevator, smiling when she began practicing her Mandarin.

"Wo jiao Lan Hua. Ni ji sui?" she asked.

He laughed. "How old am I? No more than five, from the phrase you used."

"Ni duo da?" She corrected herself.

He pressed the elevator button and the doors slid open.

She smelled like roses. Her hair shone like silk.

"See you later!" she waved and stepped into the lift. The doors slid shut before he could explain that his weekend work wouldn't be at the office.

CHAPTER 13
GUITAR HERO

Orchid

Their first guitar lesson was scheduled to take place at Orchid's apartment.

"My studio's big enough for two amps and not much else," Peter had explained.

So here he was, slipping off his shoes at her front door, his oversized jeans sagging below a Rolling Stones t-shirt. A mop of soft hair was falling over his eyes. Orchid thought how much his silky hair and smooth cheeks reminded her of a little boy, compared to the unruly waves and stippled beard of the agency head that she couldn't stop thinking about.

"Hey," she greeted Peter and waved him in. How would it feel to welcome Phoenix? And would he be dressed in such casual attire, his gym bag slung over a shoulder?

"I dig your place," Peter said, nodding his approval.

Orchid looked around her. It was a one-bedroom, neat and compact, small compared to Phoenix's luxuriousness. "It's home," she acknowledged. "Would you like a drink?"

"No, I'm cool." He loped with an easy stride into the living room.

"I looked up some chords online," she said, leaving out the part about most of her time spent researching PTSD symptoms and perusing counterAgency ad campaigns.

"Damn, girl." Peter whistled as he swung the stickered case off his shoulder and onto the floor next to her couch.

She indicated a spot on the sofa, and he joined her with a

relaxed slouch. "It wouldn't be the first time I've been accused of being an over-achiever," she said.

"I figured. The way you picked up real fast in Chinese class."

"Well, I knew some already from my family. I'm half-Chinese."

Peter pulled out his gleaming blond-wood guitar and rested it on his knees. "You always tune your instrument first." He plucked each string and tweaked the knobs, aiming for notes that sounded arbitrary to Orchid's untrained ear. "Half Chinese, huh? You should model." He looked at her as he sharpened or dulled each twang.

"Geez, thanks, but I'm pretty sure I'm too short and too old."

"You're taller than I am, and you got carded the other night."

She saw how he was taking her in from under his dark lashes. She catalogued his expression. Nope, she didn't want interest from this particular man. Best to avoid the bait of his compliment. In truth, she wished for that look of longing from someone else. If Phoenix offered that compliment, well...*Well, what?* She'd been clear with him. She needed work experience. That was her requirement. Her rules.

Which she could undo.

"How do you know when it's tuned?" she asked.

"My noggin knows, but you can buy a tuner gizmo."

He strummed the strings a few times. Satisfied, he placed the guitar on her knees.

"It's so big."

He pulled the strap over her head and helped her adjust the guitar until it was snug on her lap. "Now try an open strum."

She thrilled to feel the strings vibrate under her power. "I watched a video on the G chord," she said, demonstrating for him. He adjusted her fingers, making them stretch farther than felt comfortable. "The more you play, the broader your wingspan." Peter demonstrated by fanning his fingers wider than seemed possible. And then he added, "Hai keyi ma?"

Orchid laughed. "My brain is trying to learn to play and you want me to speak Chinese too?"

When he smiled at her, his face rounded. Under Peter's tutelage, the G chord began to sound heavenly. But there was only one person she hoped to impress with her newfound skills.

She thanked Peter, but not for the music lesson. Through his attention, she had realized how much Phoenix had come to mean to her.

CHAPTER 14
HOMELESS HEART

Orchid

Orchid had, in fact, agreed to help Phoenix with his pitch. He hadn't told her it would be *here*.

Errant moths high on psychedelics fluttered inside her chest as she stood in front of Phoenix's apartment, hand poised to knock. His doorman had been jovial, the elevator pristine. A few scuffs marred the molding, but she mainly noticed the framed art hanging along the carpeted corridor. The impressionistic strokes felt as watery as her emotions.

"It won't take long," Phoenix had rumbled on the phone when she'd called. "But I'm working from home. Are you free to swing by after four?" His address texted to her cell phone felt like the key to a new kingdom.

Before she could knock, the door swung open.

Phoenix looked happy to see her. "There you are."

"Help is here." She felt her shoulders relax and returned his lopsided grin, trying not to stare at the gray t-shirt stretched across his broad chest and shoulders.

"Please, come in. I've been in back-to-back calls and am just starting to catch up on emails." He closed the door behind them.

His apartment offered respite, the view stretching eleven stories above the sounds of street traffic. Somewhere, blocks away, was her little flat, its one bedroom just large enough for a double bed, which she had to mount while standing sideways.

His place flaunted unusually high ceilings for a newer Manhattan building. Tasteful furniture with a masculine touch of leather. The space was understated elegance, cool white tones with pops of blue. "I thought your office was you. This place...it's not that it looks like you, but it feels like you."

"I'll introduce you to my designer. My mom's the best." He smiled with what seemed like a fond memory.

Orchid imagined the woman who'd raised two strong men. In her mind, she must be tall as an oak, with a booming voice, able to flatten a foe with one shove of her massive shoulder.

She followed him through the large living room that sported a table for four, as well as several sofas intimately arranged around an oversized ottoman doubling as a coffee table. The adjacent kitchen was at least twice the size of her narrow galley. This one showcased gleaming appliances. "I bet you don't even cook," she grumbled.

He paused to admire his kitchen with her. "This is wasted on a bachelor."

"Which of these appliances can you even use?"

He accepted her joshing good-naturedly. "Listen, I can heat up a serious cup of coffee."

She pointed at a Kitchen-Aid mixer in cobalt metal. "Do you know how much those cost? And in designer colors. Have you even turned it on?"

"I thought it was for decoration only," he responded in mock surprise.

"I know a place that can give it a good home." She cocked her head and framed her chin with her palms.

He laughed. "I'll put you in my will." And then he pulled open the fridge. "Can I offer you a drink?" The cavernous space inside the large appliance yawned near-empty, like store shelves before a winter storm.

"A six-pack, Tabasco, a dozen eggs and milk. What do you live on?" she asked.

For a moment, his mouth downturned, as if he were suddenly crestfallen. "I bought you cheese and Pellegrino. Even wine, in case my work sucks." He waved at the extra items Orchid hadn't mentioned, as if that could justify his double-door Sub Zero.

"Thank you, I'd love a sparkling water." She fought the urge to cheer his expression with a spontaneous arm around his back. The muscles under his shirt warmed a spot deep in her belly. She dropped her gaze.

While he poured her beverage, she unzipped her bag and pulled out items she'd chosen at Zabar's, all while keeping what she felt was a safe distance from him. "I brought you rugelach and REBBL." She placed the paper pastry box next to the bottles. Her aesthetic sense had picked the turmeric variety for the metallic gold packaging.

"Ah, the perfect set-up for looking at the REBBL pitch."

She chuckled at the memory of their evening at his agency. "It better not be boring."

"That's exactly why you're here. The anti-boring police."

He brushed past her and he smelled clean. Was she hearing the thump-thump of his heart, deep and strong, or was she just imagining it?

"Want to see the rest of the place?" he asked.

She caught her breath and nodded.

They passed the little table set with two placemats and silverware, as if he were expecting company.

"You can leave your stuff here, if you want." He indicated the sofa that was littered with his papers, phone and laptop. Her grommet-studded bag looked at home next to his things. She pictured the two of them squeezed so closely on the couch that her hand could find his knee.

A paneled door merited a quick wave on the way to the back of the apartment. "Powder room, in case you need it. You should make yourself at home."

Home. Orchid knew from her teen years that she couldn't

take the concept of home for granted. Kind-hearted Phoenix was being generous, as usual.

At the end of the corridor, a doorway opened to a bedroom with a king-sized bed. It was flanked by side tables, both with stylish lamps, and matching bureaus. The hardwood floors were covered by a plush carpet. The room was so large that even the bed seemed small.

He showed her the adjoining bathroom, with its glass-enclosed shower and double sink. More than the marble, what caught her eye was a navy-colored tube of shaving gel on his countertop.

"Don't tell me you buy the competition!"

He grinned. "Not a Lauder brand, sorry."

"You don't sound sorry."

"I'll tell you what. When you launch yours, I'll try it."

"Good. Now we're working on naming the new line."

He led them back out to the bedroom. "That's fun. What ideas do you have?"

"There's functional names like One-Step, or ones that are playing up the masculine angle, like Fierce. The one I like best is based on my favorite insight."

"Oh yeah?" he looked intrigued.

"Acceptance, because the brand accepts wherever you are, and helps you to be the best you can be."

He paused and looked down at her. "It's elegant. It's insightful. I'm not surprised you love it."

"Oh thanks." The space around her eyes warmed with pleasure. His opinion meant a lot to her.

He waved around at the pale walls, indicating an end to the tour. "En suite. It's only a one-bedroom, so that's it."

"My place is 'only' a one-bedroom, but it's like a quarter the size of yours. If this is a one-bedroom, mine is a two-bit room," she mused aloud.

"I almost forgot," he said. "The realtor was excited about the walk-in." He flung open a door and revealed a closet bigger than Orchid's bedroom. Shelves and cubbies lined one wall.

On the opposite wall, there were neat rows of shoes. Hanging suits and shirts were ordered by shades of blue and gray. There were weights stacked on a shelf

Orchid released a loud sigh. "Damn, this closet is nicer than my whole place."

"The sublet's really affordable," he joked.

"You'd rent me your apartment?"

"Just my closet."

She blew out a chuckle. "Karma's going to get you for all your jokes at my expense."

"No doubt."

She followed him back to the living room.

They sat together on the sofa, his pile of stuff between them.

"We probably just need twenty minutes," he said. Does that work for you?"

"Honestly, I'm good all evening. After you're done with yours, I have a presentation to show you."

"You do?"

"I pitched Joan to send me to Cannes."

He looked genuinely impressed.

"But let me see your REBBL work first."

Phoenix pulled out an oversized sheet of paper. "You're going to love the sustainability angle."

Orchid could see from the colorful graphics that the work had progressed well.

As they sat together, he presented his logic, growing more and more animated.

Orchid weighed in, adding her ideas.

Phoenix was scribbling notes when his phone buzzed.

Orchid thought it sounded like a petulant child insisting on attention.

He looked at the screen and frowned.

"Do you need to get that?" she asked.

"Nah, I can call her back. We haven't looked at your presentation yet."

Orchid saw apology in his eyes. *Her*? she wondered. "It's fine if you want to grab it. I have my computer, so I can work."

"Thanks," he said. "Make yourself at home. There's wine."

"Can I rummage around the kitchen?"

"God, yes. It's wasted on me. Help yourself to whatever… open the wine."

She stood, then turned to him. "Take as long as you want."

He punched a button on his phone, picked up his Mac, and headed to his bedroom. "Hey, Tish, sorry I missed your call. How are you? I'm in the middle of something." He shut the door, and the sound became a muted version of his comforting rumble.

Tish?! THE Tish? The one who Caleb had used as a cautionary tale? "He's mercurial," Phoenix's twin had warned about his brother. She shook off the inner voice and pulled up her presentation deck, typed a few edits, undid the changes, then shut her laptop. She was filled with nervous energy. She had no right to wonder, yet she was filled with an itch to know what this mysterious woman wanted. Eavesdropping would be below her.

"Make yourself at home," he'd said. *Home*. That's why she'd yearned to travel to China. Still seeking a place to call home.

Orchid pushed the power button on the music system's remote. Music sprang to life, quiet and soothing. A female singer crooned over lost love and sacrifice. It not only suited her mood; it gave her energy to explore.

She shucked her shoes and padded barefoot to check his bookshelves. Tucked among business memoirs and titles touting stoicism were photos of Phoenix and older people she assumed were his parents. They laughed while they skied, swam, and hiked. This was what Orchid had missed: family experiences. Phoenix's relatives looked happy. They liked each other.

She grabbed her phone and crossed to the kitchen. A whimsical clock, with joggers to mark each hour, told her it was after five. *That must have been a kitschy gift. Maybe from Tish.* Jealousy was beneath her.

She found the opener and twisted the cork out of the chilled Sancerre. Wine glasses were on a high shelf. They were dusty as if they hadn't been used in a long while. She used a kitchen towel to clean them off, and then poured herself a glass. The first sip sparkled crisp over her tongue.

A low murmur of conversation hummed through the wall. Why did Orchid want to know what they were discussing? What business was it of hers?

She opened a cabinet door and discovered the mystery of his sustenance. There were energy bars and protein powder, as well as spices, oils, flour, crackers, even instant mashed potatoes. Inspired, she began to pull out ingredients and some crockery.

Phoenix finally emerged from the bedroom. "Are you okay? Did I keep you too long?". When he saw her with a spoon in hand and wearing his apron, he smiled. "Well, look at you! It smells amazing."

The proximity to the oven warmed her skin, but it was his smile that heated her from deep inside her belly.

"Wait'll you see what I can do outside the kitchen."

Phoenix paused, his quizzical quirk of one eyebrow making her laugh.

"I mean my presentation, of course."

He joined in her humor. "I wouldn't have expected anything else."

Orchid pulled the Sancerre from the fridge and poured him a glass. "Cheers," she offered.

They clinked stems.

"To the miracle maker," he said.

"Your dinner's on the table." She shooed him out of the cooking area and removed the apron.

He approached the table with awe. "Where'd you get these ingredients?"

"Your pantry. Let's try it before you get too impressed."

They sat across from each other, like a couple christening their new place. She touched her crystal glass to his, thinking that her cooking might bring him joy during this busy period.

"Bon Appetit," he said. He took one of the pastry bites that was smeared with soft cheese and topped with a dollop of fig jam. "I'm pretty sure I didn't have anything this gourmet in my pantry,"

"You're excited over an appetizer? You really don't know how to cook, do you?"

He threw his head back. His teeth shone white.

She'd never seen him this happy. Even more buoyed than he'd appeared in his family photos. Her savory nibbles were tasty. The joy on his face was intoxicating. "Have mine, I'm bringing more." She nudged the toasted rounds towards him and left the table, as if she were the hostess and owner of this beautiful flat.

The kitchen smelled like... home. She lifted a platter of sweets from the counter. Phoenix entered the kitchen, with the saucers in hand. He placed them in the sink. "Can I give you a hand?"

Like a mirage, she pictured strong fingers nestled in the indentation where her spine curved as it descended downward. She pushed the thought away. "Maybe just grab the wine." In this apartment, intimate with his cooking utensils, she needed to remind herself: *Business, all business.*

As he refilled their glasses, she put more food on clean plates and carried them into the room, where she settled into a chair. The temperature in her cheeks elevated from more than just wine.

"Was everything vegan?" he asked, while easing into the chair across from her.

"Puff pastry has butter, and I used Pecorino from your

fridge, so it's vegetarian but not vegan. You're out of nutritional yeast, in case you didn't know."

He rewarded her with a hearty laugh.

His perfect teeth, well-fitting garments, and air of Ivy League confidence drew her to him. He was accomplished, kind, and attractive. A feeling of care for him filled her. On the one hand, she didn't want to leave. On the other, she feared losing herself in the masculinity of him.

He sampled a bite. She'd drizzled honey onto the bakery goods, coaxing more sweetness from the pastries.

His expression mirrored what she'd known in her first taste; the concoction looked deceptively simple, yet left you wanting more.

"This is delicious; did you make it?"

"Nope, I just dressed what I'd brought."

"You're a miracle maker."

"I could teach you to cook. It's not hard."

"No doubt you could teach me lots."

"Speaking of teaching, you know how you mentioned Cannes?"

"Yeah."

She twirled her fork. "Well, I did it. I convinced my boss to let me go."

"You did? How?"

"Well, I kind of used your idea." When he looked confused, she added, "You know how you said there were awards for good works?"

"Related to sustainability," he said with a nod. "Yeah, so I said there'd be a learning opportunity, if Lauder would sponsor me."

"And she said yes?"

"She said it was a great idea."

"You're a genius."

"That was the presentation I was going to show you."

"Congratulations."

"Thanks. Will you be going too?"

"Wouldn't miss it. I leave in a week and a half."

She swilled the last of her wine.

He read her expression. "Thursday. It's one of the last direct flights with seats left. How about you?"

"Um, I need to book my trip. I've never been to France, so maybe we could...?" Orchid didn't want to have to spell out her request explicitly.

"If your timing matches up, do you want to travel together? Since you've never been," he offered.

Something hitched in her heart. "That'd be great." Through a wine-induced gaze, she met his eyes. *Business, just business,* she reminded herself, but the words buzzed with the dissonance of the lie.

"I'll ask Liv to send you my itinerary."

"Do you want to show me the rest of your work?" she asked.

As he pulled open his laptop, she went to fetch the sweets she'd brought.

Not that she needed baked goodies to top off the sweetness of this day.

CHAPTER 15
RIDING ON THE METRO

Orchid

Phoenix was waiting for Orchid at the entrance to the first-class lounge. A patch of sunlight brightened his smile at the sight of her. She was sure that was a smile of relief.

"Experienced travelers like cutting it close, so you must be a platinum pro," he said.

The lines above his brow smoothed when she neared. His clean smell, the scruff of his beard, made her want to lean in for a kiss. "I wasn't aiming for pro status. Just enjoying the free escalator rides," she said lightly, attempting to joke away the last half hour's anxiety hoofing it through JFK Airport.

Phoenix's dimple rewarded her humor.

He guided her to the reception desk. "She's my guest," he said, and flashed his phone to grant them access to a space crowded with leather seating and racks of newspapers. He paused at a buffet of snacks. "Hungry bird?" he asked.

"Maybe later," she said. She turned away and slipped a package of butterfly crackers into her bag. She herself felt like a chrysalis about to transform.

She hadn't been this excited about a trip since… well, maybe never.

Phoenix led her to a pod of four armchairs by the window, a welcome sanctuary away from the squalor of strollers and suitcases littering the gate area. She sank into the leather chaise he indicated, and he sat beside her.

A thought struck Orchid. "I've been studying Mandarin day

and night, and now I'm going to have to remember my high school French!"

"You polyglot."

"It's going to come out all jumbled: my own brand of Frandarin."

"Learned languages might get mixed up, but native tongues are stored in a different part of the brain."

"So, no worry about Frandarin?"

"Try to say something in French." He waved an elegant palm in encouragement.

Orchid blurted the first phrase that popped into her mind. "Voulez-vous couchez," she began, then covered her face in embarrassment. Perhaps starting with *would you like to sleep* was the wrong choice, especially when the complete phrase ended with *with me.*

"That sounds like high school French alright," he managed to say between chuckles.

"Mon dieu, merde, ça va," she muttered, her gaffe inspiring this flurry of phrases.

Phoenix shook his head as he tried to hold in his amusement.

His attempt to still his mirth made the matter funnier. She couldn't keep herself from joining in his laughter. "You can't take me anywhere," she concluded.

He wiped at his eyes. "You are so fun. I'm taking you everywhere."

She knew he was joking. Her chest expanded with hope anyway.

When the loudspeaker announced their flight, they wheeled their bags through the automatic doors and down the long corridor to their gate.

"I better sleep on the flight, since I have meetings tomorrow. Otherwise, Frandarin might slip out," she mused as they walked.

"Or worse, high school French," he replied.

They approached the ticket agent at the gate.

"You together?" he asked.

Phoenix nodded. An innocent question. Orchid wished for an answer that was less than innocent.

They were on the bridge, just before stepping onto the plane, when Phoenix handed Orchid his boarding pass. Then he held out his hand for hers.

She swapped with him, confused.

When he stopped in the fifth row, she raised a hand to wave goodbye.

"May I have your bag?" he asked, and then hefted it into the overhead bin with the easy grace of an athlete.

"I might need stuff from it," she said.

"Sure, you can pull it down if you need it," he said with a shrug.

"Wait," she said, understanding dawning. "This is your row."

"Now it's yours." He glanced at the document in his hand. "I'm in 35C. Center seat. My favorite."

She shook her head. "No, you are not giving me your first-class seat."

"Business class," he said, "and you need your rest. You have meetings tomorrow, right?"

He left her with a wave.

She sank into the plush leather. Never had someone pampered her like he did.

The stewardess offered her champagne, warmed nuts, an appetizer on a ceramic plate, and freshly baked rolls. After her vegetarian meal, dessert arrived. Orchid thanked the server, then took the lemon bar and rose from her seat. She walked back to where Phoenix was seated, his six-foot frame asleep between a portly grandfather-type bent over a crossword puzzle and a sullen teenager lit up by her phone. There was a tin of tomato-smeared pasta and an untouched roll left abandoned on Phoenix's tray. Gratitude swelled in her chest.

"May I borrow your pencil?" she asked the gentleman. He looked up at her blankly, so she tried again. "Votre stylo, s'il vous plait?" He handed over the pencil and she scribbled a message on this untouched beverage napkin, leaving it under the lemon treat.

Orchid swayed back to the front of the plane, passing through the curtain and into Business Class. Her steps were unsteady, as much from her emotions as turbulence.

She settled into her seat and stretched her stockinged feet onto the elevated leg rest, so flat that became a bed, then pulled a comforter over herself. She tucked the soft pillow under her cheek. It was like a caress that whispered, *He loves you.* No, that was impossible! Where had that come from? She didn't even want that, right?

A decade-old wish surfaced. For someone to know her. For her needs to be seen. To be cared for.

The hum of the fuselage soothed her. She felt such longing. When had she ever been attended to in this way?

The plane was preparing to land at Charles deGalle Airport. It was eight in the morning. Orchid stretched, depressed the seat button until she was upright, and slipped on her shoes.

The purser plucked her blanket from the floor and folded it into a neat square. "We still have time for a warm croissant, if you like."

"Non, merci." Orchid shook her head, and he left with a smile.

Outside the window, clouds wisped against a brilliant aqua backdrop.

"Trés belle, n'est pas?" noted her seatmate, glancing towards the view.

"Oui," Orchid agreed. And indeed, the bright sky was lovely. Yet again, she was warmed by Phoenix's thoughtfulness. She'd never flown in business class before.

A few mild bumps, and they were on the ground. It took nearly a half-hour to taxi to the terminal, and then another twenty minutes to deplane. Orchid retrieved her suitcase and laptop and left the plane. She waited in the gate for Phoenix. Each successive wave of passengers looked more haggard, as if the rear of the plane had bounced them into exhaustion.

Phoenix sauntered off the plane and into the terminal. His rumpled, button-down look was like studied elegance for a men's cologne ad. He was conversing with the elderly man who'd been his seatmate. When he spotted Orchid, he bid the gentleman goodbye with "Au revoir."

"You speak French, too?" she asked when he joined her.

They set off, traversing the cavernous terminal, passing through enormous glass tubes that carried them towards the passport control area.

"Bien sur," he replied.

"You might try to give us mere mortals a chance," she joked.

"Feisty. Sounds like you slept well."

"I did. That was nice of you. Really."

"I wasn't fishing for a thank you, but you're welcome."

They showed their passports, got them stamped, then followed the crowd heading toward the front of the terminal. After passing through Customs, they were met with a wall of drivers holding signs exhibiting the names of passengers.

Phoenix gave a small nod towards a placard revealing WALKER, nodded to the woman holding the sign, and she stepped forward to greet him. "Would you like a hand with your bag?" she offered in English, in a pretty lilt making her vowels soft and round.

"No, thank you," they both responded.

They wheeled their suitcases to the trunk of a sleek black car, then climbed into the back seat.

Orchid fastened her seat belt, aware that Phoenix's fingers rested on the smooth leather surface between them, just inches from hers. They pulled out of the airport and onto the motorway, heading south towards Paris.

"Do you want me to take your suitcase to the hotel, since you're going straight to your office?" he offered.

He was so thoughtful. "That'd be great, thank you. What will you do today?"

"Hmm. Locate some espresso. Work out. Check email."

"Mmm, espresso."

"Tonight, I might try to find the vixen who left me this." He pulled a folded napkin from his pocket and unfolded. On it was written, *You're a prince*.

"Are you sure she didn't mean frog?" said Orchid.

He lifted an eyebrow, which raked his handsome face with even more character. "I did compete on my high school swim team, but I've never been called an amphibian."

"More like a tadpole?"

"I seem to be falling down the evolutionary trail."

The car stopped in front of a white-washed office building. Phoenix handed her a card imprinted with the name of their hotel. It identified as being in the Marais, but Orchid had no idea what that meant. She dropped the card into her bag, pushed open the door and nudged one foot onto the curb. "Did you know in the original princess and the frog tale, the princess threw the frog against a wall?"

"Ouch."

Orchid stepped onto the curb, briefcase in hand. She turned to say goodbye and felt buoyed by his radiance. The image seared itself into her long-term memory like a perfectly captured beauty ad. Crap, she had it bad.

Inside the building, she traversed the vaulted three-story entranceway and took the elevator up to the conference room. All the while, including during and between meetings, and even between thoughts about ad campaigns, she had flashes of chestnut hair, eyes as blue as the ocean, and the gallant prince who had sacrificed his seat for her comfort.

By the time she returned to the hotel, jet lag was weighing heavily on her eyelids. She entered a cozy hotel room and was pleased to see that Housekeeping had hung her clothes in the armoire. She stripped off her outfit and dropped onto the bed.

The cool sheets warmed against her bare skin, and she slipped into a deep sleep.

With no sense of how much time had passed, she awoke to the trill of a foreign phone, the sharp ring jarring her memory, reminding her that she was in Europe.

"Bonjour," Phoenix said from the other end of the receiver.

"Oh, God," she murmured, barely able to speak through her slumber.

"That's an upgrade from amphibian," he said, sounding chipper.

"What, you slept all day?"

"Nope, and we should go out for a bit, to adjust to the local time."

"Spoil sport."

"Meet me downstairs in a half hour. You won't regret it, promise." He hung up before she could protest.

After a few minutes, she roused herself from the warm bed and began to rummage through the closet. Choosing an outfit, she dressed, checked her hair and make-up, then took the elevator down to the lobby. She was wearing spike-heeled booties and a fringed minidress.

Phoenix was standing in the foyer. When she looked at him, the rest of the hotel fell away, leaving a gallant gentleman in a black shirt and dark pants. He could fill any space with his presence.

She got close enough to smell spiced cologne and a hint of scotch. "Did you start on pre-dinner drinks without me?"

"Let's get you caught up," he said, and led her out the front door. Her heel wobbled on the cobblestoned road, but his steady hand caught her elbow.

"Damned cobblestones," he said.

She looked around before slipping into the waiting cab. Warm evening air bathed her face.

"They're hazardous but charming. Did you know that more than a third of Paris' cobblestones have been paved over? I wouldn't want to stay anywhere without them," she replied.

From the back of the taxi, her senses were awakened by the yellow headlights of passing cars, honking horns from frustrated drivers, even distant sirens, foreign though recognizable.

"Oh, my God," she declared. "We're actually in Paris!" The hum of the city around her struck her with waves of excitement.

"Yup. Want to go anywhere in particular?" he asked.

"Anywhere with good food and drinks."

"That narrows it down," he said with humor. "I know just the place."

Phoenix exchanged pleasantries with the driver as they traveled through narrow streets and onto a wide boulevard.

Again, his easy grace struck her. It was as if he belonged here, in this European summer evening, as much as he did in bustling Manhattan, or along a beach.

It struck her that Phoenix was the only person she knew in France. Rather than feeling trepidation, however, she was feeling something more dangerous, that somewhere along their mentor path, between advertising briefs and beaches, she'd grown to trust him. She trusted him with scenes from her past, ones that could be the subject of a horror flick. Yet... he was still here.

Orchid watched the city swim by, Paris lamps and car beams pooling strobes of light onto their faces. The shifting light on their skin cast a colored tinge more evocative than a fashion show, more beautiful than a movie.

Phoenix spoke. "How was your day?"

She told him about the dynamics of a managing director and junior staff, upcoming new launches, and how her eyelids were drooping by the end of the meeting.

"I don't think you'll be able to fall asleep where we're going," he predicted.

They passed dense blocks of buildings, many of them carved with statuesque detail, and then the Louvre Museum, with its magnificent glass pyramid casting a golden illumination across the square.

When they arrived at Les Halles, the driver opened the door and Phoenix helped Orchid from the car. She inhaled the warm air, filled with the pleasure of being in Paris.

They took the escalator down several levels of this underground mecca and joined a throng of locals and tourists, all moving in the same direction. Orchid thought of koi swimming frantically toward tossed crumbs.

Storefronts beckoned her with colors, scents and sounds. They passed places with orange block letters, the radiance of pure spa white, then a kaleidoscope of Bohemian layered fabrics, a Turkish flute melody, and incense.

"They'll be open until midnight," Phoenix explained. "The tourists never go home, and this is a central point for one of the city's major Metro stations."

They walked a good ten minutes before arriving at Musique de Nuit, the restaurant chosen by Phoenix. When they stepped inside, Orchid felt as if her senses were on overload. The aromas of many dishes were almost heady, while at the same time there was a rhythmic, low-level thumping coming from a separate room where people were dancing.

"What do you think?" Phoenix asked.

She looked around. "Let's eat!"

"*Deux*," he told the hostess.

The restaurant was full of couples and groups of friends. The hostess led them to a table adjacent to a bar crafted from rough-hewn wood.

Seated, Orchid looked around. This was far from the elegant restaurant she thought Phoenix preferred. She appreciated the rustic décor, and the wood floor announcing perhaps a century of wear.

They scanned the menu. Orchid was drawn to an extravagant concoction. "Truffle oil and artisan sea salt over a marinated and twice-grilled Portobello," she read, happy that she had been handed a menu in English. "I might try making that at home. But not for dinner. I prefer something light."

"Would you like that scotch now?" he asked.

"Surprise me," she said.

He ordered in French, sounding like a native to her American ear.

"Is the entire week going to be this much fun?"

"Wait'll you see Cannes."

"I want to see more of Paris first."

A member of the wait-staff placed martini glasses on the cocktail table erected in front of them and prepared their drinks. They gave him their order and settled back to take in the room.

Orchid took a sip. It flowed glacier-cold over her tongue.

The waiter returned and delivered their order. There was a porcelain server filled with dark grapes, a plate with Port Salut cheese, almond-stuffed olives in a smaller bowl, a basket filled with miniature ovals of pain grillé, toasted to perfection, and a plate of cheese. He rushed off and returned moments later with the grilled mushrooms, still hot.

"You ordered all vegetarian?" she said. "That was so thoughtful of you."

"You're a good influence on me," he replied, placing a slice of cheese on the pain grillé.

She sampled an olive. "What's the story behind this place?"

"It's an underground market from the eleventh century. It created so much traffic that, in the 1960's, the city moved it to the outskirts of town. That is, until some architects revived the original place."

"I love it here," she said, aware that perhaps something else was fueling her emotion.

"You're a marketing exec for a French company. You

should finagle more trips to France," he suggested, popping into his mouth another crust of bread, this one with a smear of cheese.

"Sure. And maybe you could open counterAgency's next office in Paris." She pictured a life for them among the streets and boulevards of this magnificent city, enjoying hot chocolate for breakfast, and crusty bread and French table wine spread out on a picnic blanket in the Bois de Boulogne at the end of each workday.

"I've often wondered about expanding. But French labor laws are intense, making it almost impossible to fire anyone."

"Did you know they're guaranteed at least five weeks of vacation a year?" Orchid asked.

"The country shuts down in August. It's a lost cause setting up a meeting then."

"Forget China," she said, a morsel of mushroom waiting on her fork. "I'm going to transfer here."

"I'll join you," he said.

They shared the moment, laughing together, heads thrown back in the dim light, bellies full. Orchid's brain effervesced lighter than champagne bubbles. Never mind his comfortable upbringing; their bond transcended class.

When they'd finished eating, Phoenix pointed towards the bar. "Want another drink? I've heard that alcohol is the antidote to jet lag."

"That's BS, but sure."

He led her to one side of the curved bar and they chatted with the bartender. The foreign tongue flowed quickly and she did her best to follow along. Now that they were standing, she had a clear view of the dance floor through a curtained opening. Music and pulsing lights issued from the space.

Phoenix handed her a shot glass and a lime.

She arched a brow. "Tequila…in Paris? Is there anything less French?"

He leaned towards the bartender and ordered something that Orchid couldn't hear over the din of the crowd.

"Cheers," Phoenix offered, and clinked her miniature glass. They downed the burning liquid and sucked on the tart citrus, temporarily turning their grins into puckering mouths.

The bartender pushed two bottles towards them. Orchid placed her empty shot glass onto the bar and eyed the chasers. "Beer?"

Phoenix handed her a Budweiser.

She laughed. "Okay, so you actually found something less French than tequila." She took a long draw from the bottle. The cool brew washed away the tequila burn.

She glanced towards the dancing club-goers and tapped out the rhythm as the percussive bass beckoned. "Want to check it out?" she asked.

He nodded. The beat grew louder as they neared.

She picked an open space on the dance floor. Her body moved to the compelling beat. Phoenix had no trouble keeping up. Not only did he move well, but his steps were sharp, then slow, capturing the pulse of the music.

She couldn't believe it when he said it was time to return to the hotel.

"It's not easy to find a cab around here," he said. "We could wait quite a while in one of the cab queues. How do you feel about taking the Metro? There are several lines that run through Les Halles, and even this late, there's hardly a wait."

They walked toward the line taking them back to the Marais. "Where do you want to go tomorrow?" he asked.

"What time does that market open?"

"Ha, we've created a monster."

"Just a fan. You're the monster, spoiling me with all this fun!"

"The closer we hold to French time, the faster you'll adjust to the time change. You're going to want to be on French time in Cannes, believe me."

He bought a carnet from one of the machines. "These are for getting through the turnstile and onto the train. Don't lose it. The Metro police often ask for proof that you paid, and most stations require that you put your ticket into a machine before you can pass through the exit turnstile."

"You know what I'm afraid of more than anything?" she asked, taking in the station around them.

He ticked off each item on his fingers. "Doctors? Military ads? Is this a trick question?"

"Maybe, but I'm actually referring to fear." She tried to infuse a teasing note in her tone. "I'm afraid of getting too close to the tracks." She gestured towards the dark pit.

He stepped closer. It rewarded her with his scent of soap and spice, but she was certain he did this to make her feel safer. It was only a few minutes before a train entered the station, its loud rumble, and then the ear-splitting sound of brakes, causing her to grab his arm.

"You okay?" he asked.

It took her a moment to be able to answer. "The noise reminds me of my parents' accident."

She felt his cocoon of protection even in the distance between them. "I'm sorry," he said. "Such a tough thing to go through as a kid."

They stepped onto the train and slipped into the seats. "The worst part is, I can't remember much of them. And I'm an only child, so I'm their legacy. If not me, who's going to vouch for the way they danced together in the kitchen? And told silly inside jokes? Their willingness to play Apples to Apples with me over and over because we lived in a remote location with no neighbors?"

"It sounds like you remember their legacy quite clearly."

She looked at the other passengers. A few young couples,

many others on phones, or tapping out messages. Despite the late hour, it seemed that nearly everyone was either carrying a book or reading one.

"Sometimes I think there's no reason to be good. Because who's keeping track? No one would even know."

"I don't believe you," he said. "That's not you. *You* would know."

"That means a lot, coming from you."

Phoenix studied her. "The worst time for me is during the holidays."

"Yeah, holidays are tough."

"I avoid Hallmark stores before Father's Day."

"I was such a selfish kid, I don't think I even wished my mom a happy Mother's Day the last time I could've."

"I bet she knew how you felt, even without a card."

"Your dad, too."

"I think he'd be impressed with you."

"You do?"

"He saw a lot of kids come through court after a tough life, and not everyone took such a positive path."

She groaned. "Next, you're going to call me an inspiration."

"Definitely not. Your vibe is more like desperation." Playfulness scampered across his lips.

"Shut it," she parried back.

Despite his teasing tone, it filled her with pleasure. To be known. To have her enigma understood. And with flaws and all, to still be cherished. Her parents gave her that. Perhaps one day someone else would, too.

She thought about the kindness he showed her. On the one hand, it was soothing. On the other, it was her nature to wonder if, after making a commitment, he would abandon her, too. Sitting beside him, she didn't want to acknowledge the risk of getting in too deep… too fast.

As if apropos of nothing, he casually said "You should come to our Fourth of July event."

Her eyes narrowed, as if clearer vision could interpret his motivation. "Because…"

"Because Tammy asked."

"Tammy?"

"I think her exact words were that she wouldn't come unless you were there."

"I thought you didn't want me there."

He turned to face her. "I'm sorry if I gave you that impression. I think Caleb's being there threw me off."

"I'll come, sure, if you need Tammy there."

"You know we do."

"As long as I don't have to wade out in the water."

"Deal," he said.

Mandy always said that fate repays childhood injustice with good fortune in adulthood. Orchid hoped her best friend was right.

Fate, are you listening?

CHAPTER 16

CURSE OR CURE

Orchid

Within the hotel lobby, Orchid's vision landed on Phoenix as if he were the Swarovski-studded centerpiece of a holiday display. He was seated in a leather lounger, a folded newspaper in his hand. Even from afar, she could detect the way his eyes scanned the headlines. The polyglot was probably reading in French.

As she crossed the room, she told herself to be honest. She'd been smitten with this man since they'd first met in the men's room. These travel days together were a conundrum of pleasure and longing, with a promise of goodbye nearing like a speeding train… that was about to derail.

When his eyes shifted from the newspaper to her face, a smile broke across his face, reminding her of her eleventh Christmas, when ballet shoes and a fine linen sketchpad sat under the tree. With Phoenix, she had been gifted with what she dared not hope for even in her dreams. He was warm, funny, and intelligent. His soul shone deep. And it had to be all business.

With one fluid motion, Phoenix stood, tossed the paper onto the leather chaise, and strode towards her. Each step sparked her imagination, from the movement of his muscular build to picturing his fingers grazing her skin. That was too much, too far. She had to keep herself in the moment, in reality.

"Bonne matin, hungry bird," he said, standing so close that she caught a whiff of milky coffee.

"Isn't it early to be cheery?" She aimed for snark, an antidote for her enamored heart.

"Nope. Don't even think of New York time. It's ten-thirty and don't tell me otherwise," he advised.

"Aye aye, captain. So… where to?"

"Have you eaten?" he checked, thoughtful as always.

"French bread and hot chocolate. You?"

"Here, we could probably just call it bread. Seems redundant. Like everything could be French. French water. French carrots."

"French pains in the asses," she pointed at him.

"Okay, I asked for that." He smiled broadly, with a seemingly unending reserve of good humor. "How about French sightseeing. What would you like to do?"

Her view of the bustling room included the concierge desk. Beside it, a wall of brochures beckoned. She headed toward the rack, feeling him close behind her.

"Have you seen that random game on Tiktok? Close your eyes and pick a brochure."

Phoenix grinned. "Feeling spontaneous?" he teased her.

"I see your cheeriness, and raise you spontaneity," she said, then added. "Don't look. When I say stop, just pick a brochure and we'll go do that."

Phoenix stifled an eye roll and sailed over to the start of the rack.

"Okay. Go," she said.

Curiosity played across his lips. He sauntered past the options, his right arm raking over the sightseeing photos.

This industry icon doing as she asked filled her with a sense of playfulness.

A woman with bright red lips scored Phoenix with a look of want, then moved on. His gorgeous elegance made even the most ordinary undertaking look appealing.

A secret hope ballooned inside Orchid. This weekend, Phoenix was hers. Neither knew anyone else here. The hours of the day stretched before them, filled with the potential of anything and everything. She tossed aside caution. Screw mentorship, and the etiquette of business. Today, they were simply two people in Paris.

"Stop," she ordered. *Never stop*, she wished.

His long fingers plucked a glossy trifold from the high shelves where his reach had paused. She joined him, and he angled the find towards her. The photo featured a flat black expanse scrawled with white markings, set against a stone wall, surrounded by trees.

"Le Mur des Je t'aime," she sounded out.

His hand pushed through his hair in alarm, as her high school French caught up with the meaning. "The something of I love you?" she asked, then felt heat rising in her cheeks.

"The wall. Le Mur is the wall," he replied.

"The Wall of I Love You?" she repeated, understanding dawning. Not really appropriate for coworkers.

He cast his gaze at the description. "Eighteenth arrondissement. In Montmartre, very close to Sacre Coeur. Want to visit the basilica?"

She looked at the photos showing angles of the church, the water tower nearby, and the steep drop from the church down a hill. Some people were walking the steps, others were riding the tram. "It looks pleasant," she said. "Like a lovely Parisian stroll."

"Whatever your wishes, madame. Sunlight will help reset our inner clocks."

"Pick another one too," she said.

He closed his eyes and grasped a slick pamphlet.

They looked together at the cover. "Catacombes? I've never heard of that," she said.

He hesitated. "We can do better. I'll pick again."

She slid the paper from his fingers and slipped both glossy brochures into her bag. "Let's go to our love wall!" she announced.

"You're fun," he declared.

Together, they crossed the lobby and emerged in the time-adjusting sunshine.

They rode the Metro to Montmartre, exiting at Metro Abbesses, and then taking a large elevator up to the street. The place hummed with pedestrians. Greenery scraped the blue sky. They traversed the busy sidewalk and then ascended a staircase that delivered them to a plaza near the church. The place was filled with artists selling their work, others doing chalk drawings of tourists. It seemed to Orchid that everyone, adult and child, had a camera and was snapping photos.

"Where have you traveled?" Orchid asked as they walked through the cluster of easels and tourists.

"Work has taken me all over the U.S., and Asia recently. I've seen a lot of Western Europe. Central America's nice. Canada, too."

"Moon landing next?"

"Mars."

"Venus for me," she joked, and then they were laughing together.

It wasn't until he placed a hand under her elbow that she noticed a tree's root and how it lifted the sidewalk into a tripping hazard. His hand was warm, stealing her voice. She nodded her appreciation.

"How about you?" he asked. "I know you want to visit China, and this is your first trip to France. Are there other places you want to see?" He phrased his question thoughtfully, as if to avoid assuming she'd seen the world as he had.

Orchid looked around at the awnings giving shade to a few little cafes. This place was quaint, historic, and yet filled with the art and energy of the present.

Phoenix steered them through the crowd and down the steps leading to the mural. Ahead of them, near the Metro station, they came to a wall covered with black tiles. Painted on them was "I love you" in hundreds of languages.

Tourists milled before the unassuming structure, pointing at phrases along the dark tiles, excited when they recognized their language.

Orchid and Phoenix strolled nearer to the installation. The cheerful markings infused the area with a sense of joy.

"So pretty," she said, as they walked along the wall.

"There are more than two hundred and fifty languages here," Phoenix told her. "Hundreds of ways to say…the same thing." His hesitation underscored this as one the most awkward tourist destinations for a pair who'd agreed not to cross a romantic line.

Orchid pulled out the information sheet from her bag, seeking facts as the antidote to her quickened pulse. "It says here that there are 612 tiles. They're made from volcanic rock, to protect the messages from the weather." She continued reading to hide the heat she felt rise in her cheeks. "There's a crew that cleans them every night."

He looked over her shoulder and pointed at a caption under a photo. "You see those red shapes? Those are the pieces of a broken heart scattered over the wall."

"They represent the broken pieces of humanity," she read aloud. "How sad." She looked up at the splashes of crimson dotted across the tiles. Crisp-white Arabic, Romanic and Asian phrases danced before her view. And so many languages she had never seen.

Two young women paused beside them. They were holding hands, and sporting matching yellow scarves, one shining luminescent against a pale neckline, the other beaming brightly against dark skin. The taller woman pointed, and the second one exclaimed with delight.

Orchid and Phoenix glanced towards the direction of their interest. They'd found a French phrase on the Parisian wall.

"Je t'aime," Orchid recited aloud. Phoenix caught her eye just as the words fell from her lips.

"You promise?" he joked lightly.

Her cheeks tingled with embarrassment, and then the warmth of wishing. *Je t'aime.* "What happens in the city of love..." she began.

"Stays in the city of love," he said, guessing the ending to her thought.

The tall woman gave Orchid a wave of her hand. "Would you please to take our photo?" she asked.

"A film camera!" Orchid exclaimed.

She handed the metal box to Orchid. "Press here," she explained.

The duo put their arms around each other and faced Orchid. She looked through the viewfinder and saw their joy.

The women hammed it up for the pictures, posing with fingers giving the peace sign, then arms high in the air, and finally, with their cheeks pressed together, smiling broadly. For the last shot, they turned and puckered their mouths for a kiss.

"Aww," Orchid said.

"Merci," they said, retrieving the camera.

Phoenix looked at Orchid. "How about us?" he asked.

"Us?" *What a beautiful concept.*

"Would you like a picture together?" he clarified.

She nodded, and offered her cell phone to her newfound friend. "Would you kindly return the favor?"

Orchid tucked beside her Adonis and faced the French couple.

The woman took a few shots... and then paused. She gestured for them to reduce their distance.

Phoenix leaned towards Orchid and she slipped an arm around his torso. She felt her body tingle.

The photographer smiled at the image on the phone screen, and then urged, "Closer!" until they were practically embracing.

It struck Orchid that they could've been performing the tango, with Phoenix about to dip her. The woman snapped a few more shots, then commanded, "Kiss."

Startled, Orchid peered up to assess Phoenix's reaction. At the same time, he leaned down to meet her cheek. Her movement made him miss his target, and land at the corner of her mouth.

His lips were tender.

A feeling coursed through her until her knees wobbled. This close, any conscious thoughts were eviscerated by the golden flecks swimming in his blue eyes.

The woman stepped closer and returned the phone. Orchid stared at it, but hardly saw it. Her brain was processing what had just happened. *He loves me*, she thought. "We're just friends," Orchid quickly announced, as if clarifying as much for herself as for him.

The women tittered, then rushed off, arm in arm with her partner.

"They seemed nice," Phoenix said. Orchid nodded. She scrolled through their pictures, aware that his head was close to hers, so he could view them as well. His breath warmed her collar bone. In each pose—whether they were smiling, hugging, or near-kissing—their faces emanated pure joy.

"I guess she assumed that people at the Wall of I Love You would be a couple," she said.

His lips compressed, as he seemed to try to quell an expression of pleasure. "Have you seen enough? Want to head out? Grab a bite?"

"I'm ready to go, but I'm not hungry yet. How about you?"

"I'm okay, too."

They retraced their path, passing tourists heading towards the mural.

"That wall's such a great concept. Have you been here before? With… a girlfriend?"

"You're the first woman I've toured Paris with," he replied.

"Would your girlfriend be jealous, knowing we're here this weekend?" As soon as she asked the question, she wished she hadn't. She and Phoenix were not a couple, they were business associates. Business associates who just happened to share a bit of mutual attraction.

"No idea. Completely theoretical question, since there's no girlfriend."

"You mean… since Tish?"

"Yup. Since Tish. How about you, Ms. Twenty Questions?"

"Me? I'm single as pie. Bad breakup last year."

"Sorry to hear that." The lightness in his voice didn't sound sorry.

"Thanks," she said.

Prancing down this Parisian path with Phoenix, Orchid didn't feel sorry either. Not one whit.

"Your expression makes no sense by the way, why would pie be single?" he continued.

"That's me. I get my aphorisms mixed up. Or is it cliches? Sayings. I get my sayings mixed up."

He grinned. "The copywriter in me is dying over here."

"Single as a pringle!" She called out, giving the correct expression.

He fake-groaned. "That's awful."

"Not my fault if you like pie better than Pringles," she tossed back.

Phoenix's tone stayed nonchalant as he steered back to their earlier conversation. "So, who would your ideal be, if you had to pick someone for a lifetime?" He asked as if they were discussing what brand shampoo the hotel carried.

She thought about this as they sauntered past benches and weathered trees, and wondered why he was asking. A loaded question, to be sure. "Intelligence is a must-have, otherwise the conversations fall short. Funny is nice. And kind. He has to be a good person. Most important is that our values match. Like… I'm big on social justice."

"And sustainability."

"Right. You?"

"Well, I dunno if it's recency bias, but as you were talking, I was like, yup, me too."

"Okay, so if you find a funny, smart, nice activist, let me know," she summarized.

"Same here," he agreed with a chuckle.

Her heart felt buoyed, full of unfounded optimism.

They reached the street and descended the steps into the metro station. There was a crowd there, everyone awaiting the huge elevator that would take them down to the train.

"Do you know how to get to the catacombs?" she asked.

This time, his groan sounded genuine. "The Catacombs are morbid. The French moved remains from cemeteries there. We can go anywhere else in Paris. Back to the underground market. Arc de Triomphe, the Louvre, the Eiffel Tower. "

"Fine. Let's do those things. First, we'll go there, then you can choose the next thing."

They took the train to the Metro Pasteur, then waited for the train leading to the catacombs.

"This one's ours," he said, as the train slowed to a stop.

He waited for her to board first. She slid onto a bench and he sat beside her, warming her arm where they touched, and lighting a different kind of warmth somewhere deep inside.

"Are you having fun?" she asked.

"We're in Paris for the weekend, heading to Cannes tomorrow. It's just awful. No fun at all."

She elbowed him in the ribs. "Ugly American," she teased.

"Hideous," he agreed.

An idea suddenly surged through her. She could spend the rest of her days with this man.

Her fingers pulled out their brochure. The front photo showed a cavern, its limestone walls and columns lit to a caramel yellow. "Cemetery, huh? That does sound dark," she said.

His mouth compressed. "Orchid, they moved six million bodies into this underground space hundreds of years ago.

Into an old storm drain. It's pretty gruesome."

She saw his expression. "You're worried about me," she deduced.

"This place isn't getting five-star reviews from people who don't like medical stuff," he said lightly. "Or dead bodies."

The train stopped at several stations before they reached their destination and disembarked.

"You do know that people fall on subway tracks every year," she stated.

"Perfect, you're getting in the right mood for a visit to six million corpses."

When they arrived at the entrance to the catacombs, she insisted on paying for their tickets. "My treat," she said.

The somber stone exterior started giving her second thoughts. They were in Paris, a metropolis known for food, fashion, and art. Despite all the options, her stubbornness had led them to one of the most macabre sights in the city.

A trio of teenaged schoolgirls horsed around the entrance. If they could take the tour, so could Orchid.

She descended the stairs, with Phoenix close behind. The brochures said there were 131 steps, but it seemed much more. Jet lag was taking hold of her.

Phoenix leaned forward and whispered into her ear. "You did see those were bones in the pictures, right?"

Orchid stopped, turned, and looked at him, startled. "Bones?" she repeated. She paused to pull out the brochure. "Like patterns of bones on the walls?"

"Like actual human bones," he clarified.

They'd reached the bottom landing and stood before the mouth of the cavern. Orchid shone her phone light on the cover and leaned closer. What she'd thought was a decorative herringbone pattern were piles of femurs. She gasped. Inside the trifold, an image showed ancient tibias piled floor to ceiling. The next photo flashed neatly arranged skulls, two of them turned out to greet onlookers with gaping eye sockets and bared teeth. Orchid dropped the pamphlet. The horror floated to the dirt floor, abandoned, a pariah. Her knees nearly followed its path to the ground.

Phoenix's arm was around her when she hadn't remembered him beginning to comfort her. "To be honest, hungry bird, this isn't really my thing," he said. He'd gifted her the kindest untruth.

Orchid glanced up to meet his eyes. He looked stricken, reflecting whatever he saw in hers. Over his head, black letters were carved into the arch above the doorway leading into the Catacombs. Like a warning, they were stenciled in all capitals.

"Arrete! C'est ici L'Empire de la Mort" *Stop! This is the empire of the dead.*

She gulped breaths. Slick ice. Crumpled metal. Hissing pipes. The smell of gas. Blood, and exploded bits of…*No, make it stop.*

"It's okay, Orchid, this way." His voice was deep and soft, a rumble devoid of meaning, yet one that tethered her to safety. Phoenix held the pieces of her together, her jagged limbs and sack of organs. His ribcage pressed against hers. His arm wrapped around her shoulders like he'd never let her go. He guided her up one step, then the next.

"Pardon," he said to those descending.

That was then. This is now, she recalled.

"My fault," Phoenix murmured, sounding wrecked himself.

Inhales came easier as they reached street level, twenty meters up. The sky vaulted blue towards the sun, disinterested in the petty drama of its citizens.

Not then, now, she chanted to herself. Breathe in for four, hold, exhale for four, hold.

Phoenix nudged them towards a sunflower-bright awning, café tables and chairs scattered beneath the shade. A sweet smell wafted towards them. The thought of something as mundane as a snack brought her back to the moment.

"I could use some coffee. What would you say to a pastry?" he asked.

"Bonjour?"

His relief came out as a low chuckle. His hold on her loosened from ACE-bandage-tight to a gentle embrace.

He navigated them into a bakery. Inside, the air was scented with buttery baked goods and café au lait. That, mingled with the sight of worried blue eyes, thawed Orchid's freeze.

"Chocolate croissant?" he asked her.

"Yes, please," she said, and dropped into the chair he'd pulled out.

Phoenix departed, then returned with plates of fat croissants. A server delivered two steaming white mugs. Bit by bit, Orchid returned to earth, to Europe, to their little square table, and lost herself in Phoenix's azure gaze.

"You okay?" he checked.

"Yeah," she said. "And thank you."

She broke off a piece of flaky pastry. The dough was delightful, even more so when dipped in the coffee. It'd been hours since they'd eaten. "What do you want to do next?" she asked.

He peered at her from below dark lashes. "Maybe let's not pick randomly," he suggested.

The edge eased from her hunger, feeling cared for, she laughed. He joined her.

He proposed options for their remaining free time… before they had to pack for tomorrow's flight to Nice.

"The underground market tonight," she requested. When he nodded, she relaxed even more. And why not? She'd survived! Breathing exercises and her mantra had helped. Phoenix had filled her with empathy and care.

She wasn't ready to admit her biggest realization, not even to herself.

She had fallen head-over-heels for this kind and handsome entrepreneur.

CHAPTER 17
AZURE COAST

Phoenix

NICE, FRANCE

"D'accord," Phoenix assented, when the flight attendant asked him to straighten his seatback and store his tray table. They would soon land in Nice. He absorbed the engines' hum through the soles of his shoes. Orchid was asleep beside him.

This trip wasn't like the others.

He and Orchid had spent the last few days together, including two dinners at the underground market. It was as if they were magnetized together, through the sheer force of their circumstances. He knew that even strangers could act like chums, especially when they're traveling and find someone with a connection to home.

Here in France, Orchid was his link to New York, to the agency world, and to the ad campaign they'd worked on together. Their shared experiences made him feel like she understood him best. When they were no longer tied by proximity, would their thread dissipate, like gossamer, something fragile and only glimpsed in dreams?

He knew that Orchid protected secrets behind an invisible veil. Her mystique didn't frighten him. Perhaps that was because, as he unraveled each clue, her true nature revealed itself, pure and beautiful.

The plane braked, skidding against momentum along the tarmac. Phoenix braced his thighs against the force that hurled them forward. There were no such brakes for his emotions.

She woke as he pulled their bags down from the overhead compartment.

"Hey." She slipped on oversized sunglasses, and followed him onto the jet plank.

He felt his face widen in joy, of its own accord. "Are you incognito?" he asked.

She laughed, then started walking towards the signs for public transportation. "My disguise, for when the paparazzi spot you."

He strode beside her, his pace well-matched to her long legs. "Paparazzi? Hate to break it to you, but there are no fans for agency founders."

"Maybe one," she muttered, as if to herself.

He didn't have time to ask what she meant. Orchid had stopped to look at a map on the wall. Her chin notched up, silver earrings swinging.

"Which line do we take?" she asked.

"Follow me," he said with a big smile.

He led the way as they took the tram from the terminal into Nice, and then the train for the short trip to Cannes.

On the train, he observed Orchid. Her face was turned, her attention riveted to the scenery rolling by.

"Oh," she said, as the blue sky revealed itself, without the hazy filter of unwashed station windows.

Tenements, untended shrubbery, and graffiti-covered apartment buildings swept by. A darkened tunnel, telephone wires, and streetlamps dotted their view. Then, the city gave way to more ordered vegetation interspersed with suburban homes, wide avenues and, at one point, trees shaped to resemble giant mushroom caps.

"What makes this feel different from home?" Orchid wondered aloud. She shifted her to Phoenix, as if checking that he was paying attention.

He was.

She turned back towards the view.

He watched how the curve of her cheek was lit by sunshine, and then darkened by shade, each image like a frame in an old-time film.

"It's subtle stuff," he said. "The flat line of the roofs, the proportions of the windows, the different plants...not Manhattan, that's for sure."

She nodded, then squinted, as if sharpening her observation powers. "

Before long, the vista opened up to a blue sky faded to pale hues, its color in contrast to the deeper azure of the Ligurian Sea.

"Wow," she breathed, her shoulders relaxing a notch.

Phoenix watched her. The intimacy of their shared space, and this enclosed car, everything cocooned this moment, as if it were just for the two of them.

The rhythmic clack of wheels grinding against metal tracks reminded Phoenix of all the ways this could go awry. Everything seemed placid at the surface, as if there were never ocean winds howling, or riptides churning up beaches.

Phoenix wondered if this was his predicament. That, like the nearby sea, passersby might mark them as a calm couple, and not recognize the churning under the surface.

There was a linen-clad man seated beside a dark-haired woman, a beauty who was bejeweled with dangling earrings. If they looked at Phoenix, would they know that underneath his tranquil demeanor was a heart that kicked and bucked, debating whether he could maintain his decorum, only to find each inhale suffused with Orchid's scent of honey and roses.

The train sped towards their destination. They entered a tunnel and emerged inside the concrete fortress of the Cannes station.

"Bienvenue à Cannes," Phoenix said as they stepped off the train.

"Do you remember your first time here?" Orchid asked, as they rolled their bags towards the taxi line.

"Yeah, during my first job out of ad school. That agency probably regretted sending me," he laughed, recalling the innocence of his twenty-something-year-old self. "Our senior guy got sick and couldn't go, so they sent me in to pinch hit, to schmooze with clients. I fell in love with the idea of award-winning creative. I just kept thinking that I could do this. What would I make that would be fresh and different? My old agency had teamed me with Dex. I went back to New York afterwards, and kept talking to him about starting our own shop. Every day… until he was sick of me. I think he said yes to shut me up."

Orchid smiled. "You're very persistent."

"When it matters, yes," he responded, gazing into her eyes.

"To a fault," she accused.

He didn't disagree.

They took their place at the end of the queue, along with the dozen other weary travelers awaiting taxis.

"Maybe you'll come to some epiphany after this week, too," he predicted, noticing how her hair waved in the breeze.

"I doubt I'll be starting an agency."

"But you might find a company you want to work for."

"Or a cause," she mused.

"If it's a lost cause you're seeking, look no further," He jabbed a thumb towards his chest.

"Oh pul-leez," she muttered. "Mr. Perfect? A lost cause? At what?"

They moved forward a few feet, as travelers were loaded into taxis.

"You don't know the half of it," he said, and then wondered what had made him utter those words. A light joke? Perhaps. Or not. Whatever his motive, he was learning that Orchid was inspiring some new honesty in him.

Phoenix Walker had long worn the veneer of success. But it came at a price. Always striving; never allowing himself to rest; never being satisfied with himself. Each time he weighed the payment for pushing himself at any cost, it had seemed worth the tradeoff for this enviable career, and what he considered to be a satisfying life. Even Tish's break-up hadn't made him waver. He had let her go with no regret, except her accusation that he had hurt her.

And yet, in three short months, Orchid had changed him. With her, he didn't need to be perfect. She could see his vulnerabilities. She understood his loss. With her, he could be fully present.

That concept of being present hadn't made sense to him. That is, until they met. Before then, he saw no point in *being in the moment*. Why bother, when he could be planning for the future? And the faster it came, the better.

It was different with Orchid. She slowed time, showing him how to savor vegan eggplant, or translate sustainability values into action. She taught him how unadulterated kindness can sway even the toughest veterans... like Tammy.

This trip was like entering unknown territory. When was the last time he'd observed the scenery through a train window without succumbing to the pressure to generate conversation, or have a need for pretense? He could just be. Nothing was more freeing.

A triangle of sunshine broke through the clouds and lit Orchid's face. He felt as if he could watch her all day.

The taxi dispatcher interrupted his thoughts. "Deux?" the man asked, and grasped Orchid's luggage handle. She nodded and they followed him.

The cabbie tipped his head towards a car whose trunk was already popped open.

Phoenix lifted his bag in with one hand, and they sat next to each other in the back seat.

"Are you presenting this week?" she asked, as they rolled towards their hotel.

"Yeah I'm heading up one session," Phoenix told her. "What are your plans?"

"I'm planning to focus on the marketing and strategy tracks."

"The evening stuff is fun too," he said.

"I can't believe fifteen-thousand people show up for this!"

"Biggest ad awards show in the world."

They pulled up to the white-washed front of a hotel. Phoenix paid the cabbie, and trailed Orchid into the hotel lobby. A clerk was already handing her a room key.

She waved a hand at him as she headed to the elevator bank. "Thanks for traveling with me!"

"Have a good time," he said, the words tinged with melancholy, sounding like the beginning of goodbye.

A little stitch caught in Phoenix's chest. He watched her sail through the lobby with confidence. There was no need to worry about Orchid; she was fine. More than fine. She was resilient, and smart. She'd earned her place here. And she certainly wasn't seeking some protector to shield her.

Orchid didn't need him. Smart, capable Orchid was just fine without him.

He tried to think it through. Was it chance that their worlds had collided at a time when she could benefit from an agency founder? Had she used this opportunity to gild her resume and then move on?

A concept from college chemistry popped into his mind. Collision theory. It postulates that most reactant molecules can't change another's path.

Phoenix and Orchid: their orbits had collided for a few months. Chances were low for a resultant change in their trajectory.

Soon, there'd be little left to mark their interaction at all.

Like a rehabilitated songbird, Orchid was ready to return to the wild.

CHAPTER 18
FATE FETES, FATE FREES

Orchid

Only one day in Cannes, and Orchid believed she could live here very happily. Every experience felt new. Fresh. Shiny. Exciting. The elegant hotels, boutiques, and golden sands of the Cote D'Azur hinted at generations of luxury.

In the morning, she enjoyed a breakfast of fresh-baked croissants and espresso, and headed out. It was the first day of the conference. She slipped on a chic blazer and asymmetrical dress that filled her with confidence.

It was a short stroll to the conference center along this jewel of the French Riviera. She walked past buildings that ran the gamut from Moroccan to funky-beach architecture, many of the painted in that salmon shade so typical of this area. There were palm trees everywhere, trimmed and stately.

She joined the throngs registering at the event hall. She saw at once that her unique sense of couture style didn't mark her as *other*. Mixed in with polo shirts and summer wear, the attendees wore unabashedly unique clothing, from fedoras to bowler hats. There were man buns, shirts in wild color blocks, scarves doubling as halter tops, even bustiers! And, in one case—and how she wanted to know the backstory!—someone was wearing a football jersey over a knee-length kilt.

Orchid fit right in.

Uplifted by the beautiful surroundings and bustle of creative energy, she greeted the couple ahead of her in line.

"Hullo, doll," said the man, a portly fellow sporting a

flamboyant suit that was adorned with sequined lapels.

"Where you from?" asked the other man, who was wearing a graphic tee, skinny jeans, and cowboy boots.

"New York, unless you mean where I'm *really* from," Orchid replied.

"Gawd, if anyone asks you that," said Mr. Skinny. "I mean, where you're *really* from—sic me on them!"

The chubby guy leaned over and kissed his beau. "I love when you get on your high horse."

"High? Did someone say high?" said his partner. "I'm ready. Right now."

"Tonight, doll. Be patient."

Orchid watched this banter with amusement. "Have you been here before? I don't even know what the night's events are." Chubby fingers clasped her bejeweled ones. "Girlfriend, you stick with us, and you'll know where they ALL are. Get 'ur party shoes ready."

Orchid laughed. "We'll see."

They picked up their badges and filed into the opening session, a rousing presentation about the power of messaging, and how it needs to be human-centered.

Before Orchid knew it, half the day had passed. She exchanged numbers with her new friends, and then bade them farewell. "Don't forget to disco nap," one of them called out in parting.

Orchid entered the dining hall. An agency executive she knew from home rushed over to greet her. "I was hoping to see you. Join me for lunch!" her friend nearly shouted over the din of conversations and clinking silverware. Orchid wished the volume could be turned down a few decibels.

They joined the buffet line, and then found two seats at an almost-filled table for ten. Orchid pulled out the program and studied the offerings.

"You have to come to this next session," said the woman, between bites of her buttered roll. "It's for young execs in advertising. And I've heard the presenters are the best speakers."

"Sure," Orchid agreed. She closed her program, trusting her friend's judgment.

After eating, they traipsed to what was billed as the *Under-30 Young Lion Learning Academy*. Orchid sank into a back-row seat beside her friend.

The room quieted when the emcee began the introductions. Orchid glanced towards the front of the room, expecting a gray-haired lecturer, similar to the morning's passionate speaker.

Instead, a good-looking young man ran a hand through waves of brown hair. A navy linen shirt stretched against his well-developed body. Phoenix's presence scrambled her ability to blink. What were the odds he'd be here, teaching this workshop... with her in the audience?

Her friend expelled a low whistle. "Hot damn. This is why I chose this session. Am I right or am I right?"

"counterAgency," Orchid uttered, and then remembered his mentioning that he was scheduled for a *small speaking role* at this conference. Orchid didn't want to give him the impression that she was stalking him, so she hadn't scoured the schedule for his name. Instead, her plan was to play it cool and stick to sessions on strategy, marketing and business development.

Now here she was. What would he think if he saw her? She calculated that chances were nil he'd even notice her, since she was in the last row.

"Is your camera any good? We're so far back," her friend whispered, pointing her camera at the stage.

"It's just meh," she replied, showing her phone as evidence. On the screen was a selfie she had taken... with Phoenix.

Her friend sucked a breath. "Are you messing with me? Isn't that the same hunk?"

She glanced at the photo. "Yeah, in Paris," she said, as if that could clarify it all.

"You got some 'splaining to do," her friend muttered, then gave up trying to snap a pic.

Orchid tuned into the moderator's introduction. He listed Phoenix's awards and public speaking credentials, some of which she already knew. Like AdAge dubbing him "A Small Agency to Watch."

Her attention was piqued when he continued with, "When he was a kid, our speaker attended his first parade featuring combat-wounded vets. Ever since, he's wanted to help military personnel. We're lucky to have him here today to share how purpose can drive creativity. Please join me in welcoming Phoenix Walker."

Phoenix bounded onto the elevated platform, accompanied by a lengthy applause.

The room fell silent, as if everyone present wanted to hear him speak.

His opening story elicited warm humor from the audience, yet Orchid absorbed none of his meaning. Her hearing buzzed with a fresh insight: Phoenix Walker was like a hero to this crowd. An industry magnate. A towering force.

Something churned in her stomach. By giving her this creative work, was he simply being charitable? Like his contributions to help military veterans.

Her imagination had wanted to attach meaning to what they had been sharing. Hadn't his kindness indicated a special connection? She wanted to believe in their kismet, but today was proving this to be wrong. He was a selfless, giving person. Everyone around him knew it. And she was one of his recipients.

It wasn't that she was special to him.

It was that this unattainable bachelor had become special to her.

Her plans for the week had to change. She wouldn't bother him. She had watched advertising superstars flock to greet him. He was here for work. He was busy. He'd probably already forgotten that she was here.

Orchid exhaled, in gratitude that they wouldn't be traveling back to the States together after her epiphany.

She needed to think this through. When they returned to New York, she would attend their agreed-upon final meeting. She would go down to the shore for the July Fourth meeting with Tammy. She'd leave before the fireworks, which meant she wouldn't have to explain why the booming noises frightened her.

After that, she will have delivered all her commitments.

And then? As much as she didn't want it, all that was left was to say goodbye to Phoenix.

CHAPTER 19
GOODBYE SHORE

Orchid

Was today goodbye?

There'd been little contact since they'd returned from Cannes, and returned to work.

Until today.

Phoenix picked up Orchid in his car, with old-school Renegade Soundwave pulsing from the speakers.

"It's a party in here," she said.

"Always," he agreed. He looked fit in patriotic navy shorts and a white polo. They escaped city traffic and headed towards the diner in New Jersey, where Tammy would join them to discuss the final plans for the advertising shoot. "How was the rest of your trip to Cannes?" he asked.

"It was good. I saw you speak." She recalled his command of the stage.

"You did? I was surprised that I didn't see during the week. Except from afar on the last day of the conference."

"That place was packed."

"Any word on the China assignment?" he asked.

"Nope, but thank you for this opportunity. Joan told me she'd gotten a great recommendation from your client on my work."

"You're welcome. You deserved it. Your work was fabulous."

Past tense. One more meeting and their collaboration would be finished. Goodbye to texts or poring over briefs. Au revoir to reasons for them to see each other.

Tammy was waiting for them in the parking lot. She greeted Orchid with an admonition. "No beach, and no water for you."

Orchid laughed. "Don't worry, I'm prepared this time." She pointed to thick-soled combat boots. "We're staying on dry land."

"I like your get-up," Tammy noted. "Beats hell out of my military khakis!"

Orchid glanced down at her camouflage jumper with a zipper running down the middle. "I wore this to honor your service."

"Probably not military issue," Tammy said with a snort.

The women linked arms and walked into the restaurant. Late in the afternoon, the place was half-empty.

As they stood inside the entrance, Tammy pointed to a folder Phoenix was carrying. "Always working, heh?"

Before he could respond, the hostess approached them and escorted them to a small booth. Phoenix and Orchid scooted onto one vinyl bench and Tammy took the one facing them. He placed the folder on the corner of the table.

Orchid was keenly aware of his presence, her upper arm warmed by his.

"Veggie burger, no fries," Tammy ordered, when the waitress returned.

"I'll take a veggie burger on a whole wheat roll, and no fries here, either," Orchid said. The women exchanged grins. Synchronicity, even in their orders.

The server turned to Phoenix.

"Eggplant parm sandwich. And I'll have *double* fries, please," he asserted with mock defiance.

"Good choice. I'll give you theirs," the waitress nodded, and left with the menus.

"You're going to want those fries, believe me," he predicted. "I grew up eating here, lots of summers with my cousins. You'll be begging to share mine!"

The food arrived quickly, and the three of them dove in,

chewing accompanied by the 90's hits playing over speakers.

Phoenix nudged his plate towards the center of the table. "Try some," he offered, gesturing towards his fries.

Tammy snuck one off Phoenix's plate and popped it into her mouth. "These are addictive," she said.

"As long as we're together, we should go over plans for the shoot," he said to Tammy. "We're proud of the final script; it covers all your main feedback."

He pulled a page from a manila folder. Tammy read the script quietly.

Orchid had written this based on input from several sources. She knew that it was a moving piece, one in which Tammy would share her first-hand experiences during combat. It related her journey, after being wounded from denial to anger… and worse. And then, ultimately, how she had benefitted from PTSD counseling.

Tammy finally looked up. "Wow, that's powerful stuff."

"That's you," Orchid assured her.

Looking into Tammy's face, understanding the impact this film would have, Orchid inhaled with pride.

"It even sounds like me. How'd you do that?" Tammy asked.

"The creative team did a great job. You'll love them on set," Orchid replied. "And when—"

Phoenix interrupted. "What Miss Humble isn't saying is that she wrote a manifesto, in addition to the brief. That is, she set the stage for this entire project. And then she created the video montage of your experiences. She's also leaving out the part about delivering it all with heart."

Tammy nodded her gratitude at these two people who were seated like a couple. "Will I see you guys at the shoot?"

"My producer and creative director will be there, but not me," he said.

Tammy turned to Orchid.

"Nope. My job was just the brief," she said.

Phoenix leaned closer to Tammy, as if reassuring her. "You've met my team, and you'll have a chance to go over everything with the director. You'll be fine."

"Okay. If it sucks, I know who to blame," Tammy said with a mischievous grin.

Orchid waved away her comment. "No way is it going to suck. Phoenix wouldn't have gone to all this trouble of making you his main talent if you weren't absolutely perfect. And think about it, Tammy. You're going to help so many people."

The waitress tented a green slip of paper onto their table and lifted their empty plates. Before she could stack them, Orchid grabbed a fry.

"They're better hot," he said.

"This is perfect timing," she announced. "Before I'm tempted to have more."

Tammy snorted. "You skinny thing. You could eat a hundred of those and it wouldn't show on you!"

She watched Phoenix check the bill and then cover it with his credit card.

The waitress appeared, took his payment, and returned moments later. He signed the receipt and they stood to leave.

"Sorry to eat and run. I've got plans," said Tammy.

Orchid took a deep breath. "Maybe I should go too, and let you spend time with your family."

Phoenix looked at her. Was that disappointment on his face? "Come say hi to Caleb, and meet my cousins. Save us all from ourselves."

The trio emerged into the afternoon heat undulating against a blue sky. Orchid tilted her head toward the sunshine, this beautiful man's hopefulness coaxing a smile from her. "If you like, but I'll be heading out before the fireworks." Before he could respond, she quickly added, "And I can find my own way back to the city. You should stay with your family." She wouldn't outstay her welcome. Their assignment was officially over.

"If this is goodbye, let's take a photo." Tammy pulled out her phone. The three of them crowded together to fit inside the virtual edges of the lens.

"I hope it's not goodbye," Phoenix said, looking at the picture.

Orchid scanned the happy image. They looked like they belonged together.

"I'll send you the best ones," Tammy said, and eyed the folder in Phoenix's hand. "Do you mind if I have that?"

Orchid's mouth widened as Phoenix handed her the script. "All yours."

Tammy hopped onto a low-slung motorbike, secured the papers into her saddlebag, and made a wide arc out of the parking lot, leaving them with a wave.

Orchid stood with Phoenix. She felt the air shifting between them. He was so close. Their connection was invisible yet strong.

She turned to face him, holding out her phone. "Take one with me. Tammy's right, this is goodbye for us, too."

Before he could say anything, she faced her camera towards them. The screen was vertical, so they moved closer, their faces filling the screen. The thought of no longer seeing him, no more texts, no reason to contact each other... caused a knot to tighten inside her.

In the photo, they looked ebullient.

They walked to his car. A breeze ruffled her hair as she walked to the passenger side.

He opened her door. "Have you given up your corporate guise?" He gestured towards her outfit.

She slid into her seat. "My guess is that Joan's going to announce the decision on Tuesday... you know, about China...so my look doesn't matter anymore."

Phoenix slipped into the driver's seat. "I doubt your look was a bane before."

Orchid smiled at the compliment.

They drove on side streets leading to where his aunt and uncle's house faced the sea. He kept within the speed limit, which told her that he remembered her white knuckles during their last trip.

"This is where I used to lifeguard," Phoenix gestured at the beach. "It's where I spent my summers."

She nodded and watched the beach go by. "It's beautiful."

"What'd you do over summers, when you were growing up?" he asked.

She simplified a complicated childhood with a well-practiced wave of her hand. "I worked. Mostly babysitting. You know."

The car glided to a stop in front of the house. When he turned towards her, she felt her heart squeeze. She flashed back to his care after the triathlon. Her skin tingled with the memory of the two of them tucked close in Paris. The truth was that she had fallen for Phoenix. Completely. Irrevocably.

She met his eyes. Was he feeling the same?

The walked up to the front door. Caleb swung it open and nodded a chin towards her boots. "Hey. No blood?"

"Blood?" She looked down, too.

"I hear there was helluva commotion last time you were here," Caleb grunted.

Orchid smiled brightly. "Oh, the cut! All better now," she assured him with a grin.

Two young men bounded down the stairs to greet them. The younger one swung his dirty blond hair off his forehead. "Stew. I'm the handsome one." He winked, and Caleb groaned.

"Orchid, and it's nice to meet you." She leaned forward and shook his hand.

The older cousin straightened his preppy shirt, which could have been snatched from a Ralph Lauren ad. "I'm Harry. You're Phoenix's friend," he stated with a wave.

"Coworker. Mentee," she corrected. "We came down for a

meeting." She glanced at Phoenix and reminded herself that their relationship was *business, all business.*

Stew checked out her outfit. "Work makes me think corporate. You seem too cool for school."

For the second time in minutes, Orchid laughed.

"You, too." Her gesture indicated Harry's sun-bleached hair and faded beach attire.

"Let's get you drinks and a tour around the house," Harry said, leading the way towards the large kitchen.

"I don't need a full tour," she told him. "Let's see, your family room's on the other side, there's a baby-blue powder room, and I love the photos of you guys on the slopes."

"What the bejeezers, are you psychic?" Harry spewed.

Caleb butted in. "You don't know? She practically bled out on the sofa."

Bled out. Orchid felt her eyes cast down for a millisecond, a flash that the others probably didn't notice. Phoenix brushed her sleeve, a gentle motion offering comfort. After all these months working side by side, it was as if he could read her telltale signs.

He saved her, by giving his family a quick recap of her sliced foot, and then reminding them about getting drinks.

Stew produced a six-pack from the fridge.

"Cheers," said Stew. "To Orchid, for brightening our Fourth."

"How could *I* brighten it? I thought this was a highlight of your year." She took a sip of beer.

"We've grown a little too old for the parade. So, all that's left is drinking." Harry clinked his brew against hers.

"Are you going to the parade?" she asked Caleb. "Nope, my vote's on drinking," he replied, and demonstrated with a sizable gulp.

"How 'bout you, Phoenix? Since that parade inspired your work with combat-wounded vets," Stew snickered.

"Nothing against vets." He raised both hands.

Orchid noticed how Phoenix's lips compressed.

"This family doesn't let you live anything down," he said. "No, I'm not going to the parade." He turned to Orchid. "But I bet Stew here would accompany you, if you'd like."

"Why not you?" she asked, almost as a tease, and then regretted having asked.

Stew answered for him. "Baby Phoenix went the first time hoping to see animals."

Harry and Caleb guffawed in anticipation of the punchline.

"Cause he thought vets were doctors for pets."

Orchid tried to hide her giggle behind her hand.

Phoenix feigned hurt. "I did eventually figure it out, but—"

Stew cut him off, as if on a roll. "Then he comes back and is like, *where were the vets? All I saw were gwandpas in wheelie chairs.*"

Caleb slapped the countertop. Harry doubled over, holding his side.

Phoenix opened his mouth to playfully respond, as if trying to be a good sport while his family embarrassed him.

Her phone vibrated. She pulled it from her bag and glanced at it. "Sorry, it's my boss," she explained, then returned the phone to her bag. She looked up at the cousins, who seemed to be vying for her attention.

"What did Joan say?" Phoenix asked.

"She said to call her next week."

"Could be good news," Phoenix said encouragingly.

Harry pointed at their starfish wall clock. "It's after five on the Fourth—bosses can wait."

Orchid glanced at the kitschy timepiece and grinned. "I love the beach theme here. It suits this house."

"We have starfish everything," Stew chimed in.

"It's half past the third leg," she read the time.

"Third leg?" Caleb grunted.

Phoenix redirected the tone of the conversation, as if Caleb might devolve into something inappropriate. "I always thought it was cool that starfish can regenerate limbs. Only a handful of animals can do that."

"Scientists found the genes for regeneration in us, too," said Caleb. "They were able to regrow a frog's leg."

Orchid felt the bridge of her nose wrinkle. "Not something I want to picture," she said.

"Come for that tour," Stew insisted. He hooked one arm in Orchid's and turned her toward the staircase.

Caleb slunk towards the family room with his beer. "I'm going to see if there's a game on."

She saw Phoenix follow his brother, and then sink into the other end of the sofa.

Upstairs, her feet sank into thick carpeting. The bedrooms were outfitted in soothing lavender. She listened to Stew prattle and thought of Phoenix.

Last time they'd been at this shore house, he'd cared for her. The lavishness of the place, its sumptuous status, wasn't a barrier between them. Gratitude swelled inside her chest. "Thanks for the tour," she said to Stew and headed downstairs.

From outside of the family room, she overheard Phoenix's voice.

"I'm tired of holding onto secrets," he said. "I know how it looks—our relationship—but it's more complicated than I can explain. Believe it or not," he said, "Dad had a hand in this."

A chill ran up her back, freezing her in place. Our relationship; was he talking about her? And what about his father? She stilled an urge to run in and ask. Caleb did it for her.

"Dad? What are you talking about?"

There was silence before Phoenix spoke. "He asked me to do a favor for him."

"Geez, what kind of favor?"

"He wanted me to look her up. She was part of an old court case."

"That makes no sense," Caleb said.

"Well, we can't ask him now, can we?" Phoenix retorted. "You might say it was his final wish to me before he died. He said to tell no one."

Orchid felt sick, light-headed. *Court case* took her back to being twelve. Nothing made sense. She could make out the back of Phoenix outlined against the flickering TV screen. He always was too good to be true.

"Hey, I wanted to say goodbye and thank you," she called, and then opened the front door. Fresh air would help her think.

Phoenix got to his feet and rushed after her. "You're leaving already?"

"I want to get back to the city before dark, but you stay."

Hearing the conversation, Stew came down the stairs. Harry emerged from the kitchen. "Just a few more hours until fireworks," the younger brother cajoled.

"I'm not a fan of fireworks." Her brow bunched, and she stepped outside.

"Actually, heading out before traffic is a good idea," said Phoenix. He waved to his brother and cousins, grabbed his keys, and followed Orchid out onto the porch.

"Stay. Hang out with your fam." Her voice caught on the last word. After all her success, the one thing she didn't have was family. And now the trust Phoenix had earned was evaporating. She jogged down the steps.

"Orchid, I'll drive you," he said. "There's no public transportation around here and you'll wait forever for an Uber. If you can even get one."

He followed her to the curb where she was tapping on her phone.

"Shit. No car service."

He pressed the fob to unlock the door, then held it open for her.

She tilted her face up from her phone and stared at him, tension throbbing through her head, judging him, questioning his intention.

"C'mon. Let me drive you. You can text Joan from the car."
He looked at her with care.

"Joan," she nodded, remembering. "Fine," she finally conceded.

She slid into the seat, her mind swirling with confusion. They sped along the quiet streets towards the highway, *I'm a favor? A last wish?*

Like a volcano under pressure, she exploded. "Your dad had you look me up? What does that even mean?"

"Oh, God," he said. "I'm so sorry you heard that. You were never meant to know. He didn't want me to tell anyone."

"I don't understand any of this," she said, wishing she were miles away from him.

"He said that being a judge weighed on him. He asked me for a good Samaritan deed. Your case was special to him. he wanted me to do a kindness for you."

"Was the kindness to mess with my brain?"

"I didn't mess with you."

"You let me think that we met by chance, and that I earned that creative work because I was talented. So, well, yeah, you screwed with me. How the hell did you find me anyway? How'd you know what I needed?"

He gripped the steering wheel. "I can hear you're upset."

"Upset? Everything between us has been based on pretense. How can I trust you?"

"You've known me all these months. Have I done one thing that's not in your best interest?"

"Dishonesty is not in my best interest. Everything between us was a ruse. A handout. I'm one of your damn charities."

"Nothing was a handout. Dad told me about you, but–"

She interrupted. "You think you're some prince. Makes you feel good, to take pity on poor me, doesn't it?"

"I don't pity you."

"You think I'm just some charity case. Everything you did. That's unethical."

"I don't think so."

All her thoughts were pouring out now. None of his protestations mattered.

"I thought I was lucky to meet you. I thought I earned that assignment. I thought I'd done a good job."

"You deserved it, you earned it."

"It was a lie. It was a handout. You think I need that? You didn't respect me. You felt sorry for me."

"I did respect you. I do respect you."

"Everything was a lie from the start, wasn't it? Even meeting at the Pyramid Club." Her hysteria cooled to detachment.

"Okay, I'll tell you everything. Let me explain," he said.

She was a statue. Her hard stare could have crumbled the road for miles ahead of them.

"I did come to the Pyramid Club to see you. I just wanted to know that you were okay. Dad wanted me to see if I could do something for you, and I didn't know what you needed."

"How the hell did you even know where to go?"

"This might sound bad, but I was really busy, so I outsourced."

"Outsourced? What does that mean?"

"I hired a PI. She overheard your conversation. When you were talking to Mandy. She told me where to meet you."

Orchid swiveled like an automaton. The force of her astonishment was immeasurable.

The car lurched and Phoenix had to adjust, in order to keep from heading into a ditch.

"PI? As in private investigator? You had a detective trailing me?" she shrieked.

"Months ago, but not anymore. Dad wanted me to do something nice for you, and I didn't know what it could be. I didn't have time to figure it out, so I hired someone."

Orchid felt her face screw up with renewed rage.

"Hire someone? I was followed?" She wanted to strike him,

cause him pain. His deception went straight to her bones, painful and unrelenting.

"It wasn't supposed to come to this, I swear. It was supposed to be one good Samaritan deed, then move on. For Dad."

"Your whole family is a piece of work. They think they can play God? Just because I didn't grow up with money and a family? Seriously, who do you think you are?" She took a deep breath. "I feel like I'm going to throw up. Or punch you."

He extended arm. "I'd prefer the punch."

She rubbed her forehead. "You think it's a joke. You don't even get how horrific this is. Who else have you done this with? Played with them like a pawn?"

"No one. Dad said this was like a good deed for all the kids who came through his court. He didn't want you to know the source of the good will."

"Of course not. Because it makes no sense." She put her hands on the dashboard. "Never mind the ride—let me out. I'd rather walk than take another favor from you." She reached for the door handle as if that could make him pull over.

Phoenix put a hand on her forearm. "Orchid Kai Lan Paige. You're misunderstanding, I promise. I didn't know about you until Dad told me. But everything else, you've earned it. I didn't give you the ad work out of pity. You had the skills to do it, and you helped me out. You did an amazing job. I should've let you go before now. I should've had someone else mentor you. But I was selfish. I wanted to spend time with you. I—"

Orchid felt her face pinch. She pulled her arm out of his reach and let go of the door handle. "Now I'm your outlet for some savior fantasy."

"Not at all. You amaze me. With your smarts, and savvy, your ability to never give up."

"Yeah, that's what people do when they don't have any safety net. You know what's so sick about what you did? I've battled for everything I have. I worked my way through school, I fought for this job, and earned everything, including my shoebox apartment, my transit card, my gym membership. But now, if I get this assignment, I won't have that satisfaction. You've soiled it."

She watched him drive, his face a study in anguish. He must see how manipulative it looked from her perspective. Their whole relationship had been built on a falsehood.

"My intentions weren't bad. But I'm still a shit." His self-recrimination sounded genuine.

"You're not a shit. What you did was shitty," she corrected, her fury mollified a touch.

"So, what did Joan say after all?" he asked, now that her voice was calmer.

"Do you have any right to ask? For all I know, you paid her off. Money can buy anything, can't it? What does she know about us, anyway?"

"She doesn't know about Dad's last wishes. No one does."

"Except Caleb."

"Not until now."

"At least one of you isn't a liar."

"I'm sorry, Orchid. But the truth is, no matter how it all started, now we're in each other's lives. I can't undo that. And I don't want to."

"What a novelty it must be, meeting someone who didn't summer on the Riviera."

"You're going too far. You know me. You've known me these months. Do you really think I'm elitist? That I'm getting a kick out of saving someone? Think about it, does that make any sense?"

"I don't know," she admitted, "Knowing that your dead father made you do a good deed for me recolors everything you did. You could've been doing it out of guilt, or obligation. I'm your way to feel better about yourself. Why else would you go out of the way?"

Phoenix glanced at her. "You know why else? Because I believed in you. Because you earned it."

She suddenly realized that she wanted him to say, *Because I've fallen for you.* If he did, then what? She'd sensed that his heart was pure. Despite her anger, she knew he was a good person.

As they approached the tunnel, the sun already well below the horizon, they could see faraway bursts of sparkly lights. Fourth of July. Celebrations. Happy families.

She heard her phone vibrate. It was from Joan. She read the text, then felt her eyes grow wide. "Joan just gave me the China assignment." She sat in shock.

"That's great!" he said.

"She says we'll talk about details next week. I guess I really do need to practice my Chinese." The thought of language school reminded her of Peter, so she texted him the good news. Someone honest, who'd never betrayed her.

She looked at her phone again, as the news sunk in. "I can't believe I got it," she said, hearing the tinge of wonder in her tone.

"You deserve it."

Another thought struck her. "How do I know if you rigged the race?"

"No," he insisted. "You can think I'm a cad, but don't doubt yourself."

She heard the phone vibrate again. Reluctantly, she retrieved it. "Peter says congrats. It's nice to know normal people."

"Who's Peter?" he asked.

"My study partner from my Chinese class. He's also teaching me guitar."

"How is guitar related to Mandarin?"

"It isn't. He's taking me out for drinks to celebrate."

They arrived in front of her apartment building. Phoenix turned to face her. "This doesn't have to be goodbye, you know. Screw Peter. Come out with me tonight. Please. Give me a chance to explain. I'd like to talk."

She opened her passenger door. "You've fulfilled your dad's wishes. What's there to talk about?"

And then she was gone, as if fleeing into the night air.

She wiped her eyes as she slipped past the doorman and into her building.

Goodbye, Phoenix.

CHAPTER 20
TRUST FALL

Orchid

Screw Peter. Come out with me tonight.

Orchid's heart pounded as she hoofed across the foyer to get ready for the evening.

She'd wanted these words, right? Waited for them.

Yet her insides were calcifying with anger. She stormed through her apartment to change her outfit.

Every interaction with Phoenix replayed in her mind, and each one cast with a new shadow. How could she trust someone who lied to her? Who maintained subterfuge over so many meals, during all those days and nights traveling together, working together in offices, cafes, at conferences? Even while entertaining her in his own home?

And yet, beyond Phoenix, her scorn had found another target.

Judge John Walker. He'd dealt a blow to her self-respect, to her free will.

Orchid's life had been lived in darkness for too long. Finally, after mountains of effort, she'd secured the basics, the fundamentals that those with privilege took for granted. She had a job, an apartment, friends. Now, she felt like a cog in some judge's whim.

Judge John Walker. His name hadn't registered. But, looking back, she recalled how his court made her feel. At the age of twelve, her hair plaited down her back, and wearing her aunt's oversized cardigan to "look more somber," she had choked out the details of the worst moments of her life. Even though the couple who had served her parents alcohol were being judged, Orchid could not stop reliving the shame of her guilt. In that massive courtroom, standing below the judge's elevated altar, she had a sense of how insignificant her life was.

Her biggest loss was a blip in a ledger of tragedies.

A new thought struck her. Judge Walker had also turned Phoenix into his pawn. How must he be feeling? She paused fixing her makeup, her blush brush frozen midair, to consider this.

Her attempt to hold onto her anger started to wane, replaced by a new and unexpected compassion for Phoenix. As hard as it had been for her to grow up without parents, perhaps it had been just as hard to live under the watchful eye of a powerful father. So powerful he could continue to exert his influence after death.

Her head was spinning in this whirl of contradictions. She put down her makeup brush.

Beautiful, powerful, thoughtful Phoenix guarding her from the swirl of club goers. His concern over her sensitivity to images of wounded veterans. His care for her injured foot. Were his actions motivated by fealty to his father? And if she'd known the source of their meeting earlier, would pride have made her walk away from the opportunity?

She began to feel uncomfortable, embarrassed. She was the one who'd requested work on an ad campaign. Who'd asked to attend the Effies. She had accompanied Phoenix to the triathlon, even when it wasn't clear if he wanted her there. And she was the one who chose to drive down on the Fourth of July, even when he'd resisted Caleb's invitation.

If Judge Walker had dictated that Phoenix look after some Joe Smith from Bayonne, would Phoenix have sought out the guy to grant his father's wishes?

Paris. Cannes. She was a fool. She could've been anyone and

he would've done the same. It wasn't her. She'd simply won the lottery of one judge's memories.

What would she have done, if her own father had left a last wish? As long as it didn't contradict her values, she'd fulfill it, of course.

She finished applying her lipstick and vowed to revert to self-protection. She'd been abandoned enough. Hell, she couldn't even count on family. Dad's little brother had promised at her parents' funeral that he'd come visit. He never did. Last she knew, he lived in California. After fifteen years, they probably wouldn't even recognize each other.

Memories of family soured her mood even further.

Now dressed and ready, she slouched downstairs when the doorman called to say Peter had arrived.

"Hey," she offered in greeting.

Luckily, Peter's freakish energy made up for her sullenness.

"Alright, there's this new song you have to learn," he said, the words coming fast. "We can work on it when you get back. And don't forget, we have to practice Zhong wen before you go!"

She continued to nod as he babbled on during their short walk to a local bar. And then through two beers. He was speaking mainly in Mandarin. Orchid figured he was practicing enough Chinese for the two of them, telling story after story.

"Pee-duh, pee-duh," he cackled at some joke he'd just cracked, nearly slipping off his bar stool.

Orchid tried to coax her cheeks into a semblance of a smile, and do so without grimacing, but she could manage little more than a lopsided grimace. What the freak was wrong with her emotions? Hadn't she gotten everything she wanted? The list ran through her head: creative work to prove her worth, Mandarin skills that her boss had praised, the plum assignment no one thought she could win. So why did she feel tears prickling her eyes?

Peter had moved to hard liquor, and was tossing back his second Lemon Drop.

"Do guys drink that stuff?" she asked. She was still nursing her first beer. She motioned to the bartender for the check.

"Shure," he swaggered. "Want one?"

"No, I'm good." She handed the waitress a credit card, without even checking the bill.

"You are better than good," he said, his words slightly slurred. "You are fire. You and me, we could be a thing."

Orchid stared at his chubby-cheeked grin. Twice in one night? Had some fairy dusted her with a powder that attracted men?

The bartender saved her, arriving with her receipt, and she half-expected a hand-scribbled heart, with a phone number. She added the tip and signed the receipt.

"You're a good friend, Peter. Time to go," she said, and stood.

He stumbled to his feet. "Aww, already?"

"It's been a long day," she admitted, and led the way outside.

The street was thankfully quiet, compared to the bar's hubbub.

"You're not driving, right?" she checked.

"Subway." He produced his pass.

"Great. Get home safe."

She could see an idea fighting its way through the fog of Peter's brain to his lips, so she started walking away before he could speak.

She didn't look back as she trudged towards her building. Grief simmered in her chest. Along with anger. And... confusion. She knew her emotions, including disappointment, weren't entirely deserved. Memories of her day at the shore were heavy with the weight of loss. She'd never have family like Caleb, Harry and Stew.

Goodbye, Phoenix.

Orchid locked her apartment door and texted Mandy. Are you up?

An immediate response. *Unfortunately yes!*

Being the mother to a small child seemed to result in sleeplessness. Before she could reply, her phone buzzed.

"Matty's teething," she said. "He'll be fine. Not sure about Mom."

Orchid pictured Mandy cradling her son. She heard the soft sound of baby hiccups in the background. "You're the best mom ever, you know that?"

"Aww thanks, hon. What's up with you?" asked Mandy.

She lay down on her sofa and blew a sigh. "I am so ridiculous. I know that there are people worse off all over the world, and that I'm lucky to have my little shoebox apartment and a job that college kids would kill for. So... my stupid self-pity is undeserved. Because today! The nerve of Phoenix."

"Uh-oh, what now?" asked her friend.

Indignation spilled out faster than her brain could process. "Everything about Phoenix is a lie. Even how we met. It wasn't just luck. His dad made him come look for me. Like a charity case. I can't trust anyone!"

There it was, the ugly truth laid bare. *I can't trust anyone.* Not Peter, not Phoenix. Certainly not haughty Princeton. Only her longtime friend Mandy.

"Hold on," said Mandy. "Slow down. Do you mean Phoenix was stalking you? Did he do something to you? Because I'm not above punching that pretty face."

Orchid laughed through her gulps of air. Goddammit. The inequity of all the ways people had let her down. Life was a lie. Getting everything she wanted still left her empty. What was the point of striving? Who even cared? Thoughts, not words. She couldn't speak them... not yet.

"Aww, hon, you know you have me. I wish I could come over. Except you definitely don't want baby drool all over your stuff."

Orchid swiped at her eyes. A chuckle escaped over the thought of slobber on her velvet couch. "Thanks for offering. I totally don't deserve this pity party. Here's the scoop." She went on to explain about the judge, and how they really met. "All I want to do is scream at him for lying this whole time. I thought we'd be celebrating."

"Whoa, you're like a freight train. Celebrate what?"

"I got the assignment: I'm going to China."

"What? Oh my god. How did you forget to tell me?"

Orchid's mood began to rally. She suddenly imagined seeing her mom's features on the faces of strangers. China. "I just found out today."

"And Phoenix is a jerk because?"

"He didn't tell me the truth. You know, about meeting me…"

"Why would he lie?"

"His dad did swore him to secrecy."

"What do you want to do, sue him? File a restraining order?"

"Nah. He did give me an opportunity. He was always a gentleman." She inhaled a soft breath. The image of the way he'd guided her through France floated into her consciousness. He'd given her his seat on the plane and squeezed into an economy seat. "And he says even though he found me because of his dad, he stayed because he wanted to."

"Would I be a romantic if I said that was sweet?"

"He really is… I'm in so deep."

"You know what, you need space between you two. Too much drama."

"We'll have plenty of miles between us soon."

"I'll miss you, hon."

"Yeah, likewise." Orchid felt the weight of the day's emotions. "It's late. I'll let you go. Kiss Matty for me."

"Honestly, that's the only guy I'd trust in your life. The cute, toothless types. Forget Phoenix."

Orchid laughed. "Love you," she said.

Too much drama. Time to move on.

CHAPTER 21
YOU FIRST

Phoenix

Phoenix had scared Orchid away. Terrified her by not protecting her. He'd promised his dad to do one good deed, and keep it confidential. He'd promised himself never to hurt her. And yet, in one night, he'd screwed up both those commitments. How to make it right? *Leave her alone.*

Now he was grieving, and missing her already. What would he do without her, this woman who brought vegan meals to hungry ad execs? Who listened with an ocean of empathy? The woman who now believed that all of his actions were calculated.

But what hurt him most was how learning the truth had caused Orchid to question her own worth. He wanted to right that hurt. If he could.

He had taken out his phone and entered a text. "I know this must all seem like a shock. I'm sorry. We can talk anytime you'd like."

The lack of a response over the next days had left him wondering if she'd blocked his number.

This silence had now gone on for weeks. Their lack of communication had become a painful buzz. She was leaving for Beijing in a few days. Despite his heavy workload, including helping his creative team prep for their REBBL pitch, she never left his mind.

What was she working on? How did her coworkers take the news? Was she prepping for the trip? Celebrating? Was there some way he could help her get ready?

In his mind, these were legitimate reasons to contact her. Yet, his high road was to aim for what was best for her.

He didn't want to cause her any pain. He wanted to express his sorrow, and then he'd leave her alone.

The flower shop near his apartment beckoned. His trip to the airport for his early morning flight could wait.

The florist came out of a back room. She was wearing a green smock with large pockets. Potting tools protruded from one of them. "What's the occasion?" she asked. "Birthday? Congratulations?"

"A little of all of that… but mostly an apology."

"Ah, then perhaps a potted plant… or cut flowers."

He looked over at the plants displayed on floor-to-ceiling shelves. "Orchids? Or would that not go over well?"

"They're not as fragile as they appear," she said.

"You can say that again," he declared. When she looked confused, he added, "Her name's Orchid, and she feels it's cliché for someone to buy orchids for her. Plus, she's leaving for a trip soon, so I think she'd enjoy cut flowers."

"Roses? They're always classic."

"I'm not sure it's that kind of relationship."

The woman arched a brow, reminding him that she'd probably heard every possible reason for flowers.

He suddenly remembered Orchid standing before his aunt and uncle's photos. "Peonies. Her favorite are peonies."

She nodded. "Wonderful choice, I'll make a bouquet. She can have them as early as tomorrow." She pointed to a stack of cards on the counter. "Would you like to write a card?" There was an ornate bowl at his elbow. It was filled with pens.

He picked up one of the cards. There was more to say than could fit on a small space.

He recalled how Orchid had intrigued him that first night at the club, this gorgeous apparition who'd barged into the bathroom and then connected with him over Mandarin. He should be teaching her Chinese, not this Peter guy. And she'd looked like a rock star skating into the Lauder conference room. Those blue streaks in her hair, rings on every finger. The refined features of an empress cast into modern times. He knew the grace of her movements, the selfless ways she considered everyone's feelings. And the depth of her empathy when she was comforting him about the loss of his father.

The florist returned with an armful of pink and white flowers, nestled inside fuchsia paper. They were beautiful enough to be an oversized wedding bouquet. He inhaled deeply, at his mind's image of Orchid, her delicate features as she took in the scented blooms.

"Jot down her address and a delivery date, and we're all set." She handed him an iPad Always the adman, he wondered how they'd personalize their marketing? Would the florist forevermore send him photos of peonies? Could they train Artificial Intelligence to play off the idea of flowers for Orchid? Or that bouquets from a phoenix would first have to burn, and then rise from ashes? His creativity had no OFF button. Perhaps it was time to understand why.

He wrote down Orchid's business address and swiped his credit card.

While the florist rang up the total, he edited his whirlwind of thoughts down to those phrases appropriate for a mentor. He picked up a pen and scrawled, *I'm truly sorry for hurting you. You've earned the assignment and more. Congratulations! P*

Not "*Call me. And never I've missed you.*

CHAPTER 22
FLOWERS FOR ORCHID

Orchid

Another world awaited Orchid. Beckoned her across geographies and time. In four days, she'd be jetting to Beijing. Her Mandarin dreams come to fruition.

She was walking back to her office, trying to make a list of the to-dos that needed to get done. She toted a bottle of sparkling water in one hand and a mug of hot coffee in the other, while making a silent plea to the gods that these drinks wouldn't send her to the loo. Not, that is, until lunchtime. She was too busy for a break.

The travel department had secured her work visa, flight reservations and a dodgy-looking hotel that met her daily stipend. She still needed to select outfits that would look professional in a sweltering August, complete her pre-assignment interview calls, and finish transitioning her workload to Violet.

"I'm going to be swamped," Violet had complained.

"I'll be reachable, if you need me. Anyway," she added, her voice almost lilting, "you won the pool!"

"I only picked July 4th because no one else thought you'd get the call over the holiday!"

Orchid pushed aside the office pool, Violet, and even the need to pack. She had Peter coming through her earbuds, drilling her as she strode through the corridor.

"Ni xiang qu nar?" he asked, playing the part of a Chinese taxi driver.

She thought of his drunken offer, and was relieved that it was never mentioned.

"Where do I want to go? Lidu fan guanr," she replied, proud that she'd internalized the guttural "r" ending that Beijingers favored.

"Lidu fan dian," he corrected her. "That's restaurant, not hotel."

"Oh my god," she uttered, frozen in her tracks at her office door. A shock of pink sprouted from her desk like a veritable botanical garden.

"That's not so bad of a mistake," he joked. "They won't take you to a Timbuktu."

"It's not that. It's just… flowers. Huge. Peonies. My favorite," she stuttered. "I'll call you later, alright?"

She hung up before he could add a farewell.

She put the drinks on her desk and stared at the flowers. Leaning closer, she inhaled their citrus-sweet scent.

Who had sent these? Mandy?

At that moment, Violet peeked her head into the office.

"Everyone saw the delivery guy," she said with a big smile. "Someone dropped a mint on them!"

"For something that I'll enjoy for a few days," Orchid replied.

"I can give them a good home, if you'd like," Violet offered.

"No way." Orchid plucked the card from between the blooms. She read the note, registering the handwriting before absorbing the words. A whoosh of longing and forgiveness sent a shiver across her skin.

Violet peeked over her shoulder. "P? Princeton sent you flowers?"

Orchid looked over at her friend. She hadn't yet shared the way that Princeton had redeemed himself last week. "Princeton ended up taking the high road," she said.

"What do you mean? Are we talking about the same Princeton?"

"People change. He came to congratulate me after he found out that Joan had awarded me the assignment."

Violet's wide-eyed gawk sparked a new, terrible thought.

"You don't think he felt bad for me and talked Joan into giving it to me, do you?" Orchid asked.

Her friend recovered her composure and straightened. "Honey, you deserve that assignment. That's why I put most of my money on you."

"Most?"

Violet shrugged and gave a little grin. "Hey, a girl's gotta diversify her holdings."

"Besides, I don't think P is Princeton," Orchid mused.

"Who do you think it is?"

"I just got off the phone with Peter. He's almost as eager for this trip as I am."

"What would he be apologizing for?"

"He was a drunken mess, and he hit on me."

"You *are* Miss Popularity," Violet said. "Could it be anyone else?"

Orchid opened her mouth. No sound emerged.

Violet glanced at her phone, shrieked "I'm going to be late for my next meeting!" and rushed out.

Later that day, Orchid picked up her phone and called counterAgency. She'd been busy these last three weeks, since she'd seen Phoenix. Questions still remained about his father's wishes. Why had Phoenix agreed? Why had his dad picked her? Had Phoenix ever considered being honest and telling her? And how much had he swayed Joan's decision to send her to China?

She called Phoenix. Not for him. For her. There remained too many questions.

He answered on the second ring. "Orchid, you okay?" He puffed air, like he was finishing the last sprint of a marathon.

"Yeah, how about you? You sound like you're dying. Not that I'd care," she added.

"At least I know where I stand," he said. "Sorry, I left a client meeting to take your call, and now I'm walking around trying to find a quiet spot."

"Take the client meeting. I just called because I got some flowers."

"Oh, good, I hope you like them. And the message, too," he added.

"I'll let you go," she said.

"No, it's okay. I'm in the stairwell. The door just clicked shut, so I hope I can get back in."

She pictured him crouched in the staircase and she chuckled, despite her residual ire. "I'd guess the prez should be able to get back into his own agency," she remarked.

"I'm not at counterAgency, I'm at REBBL."

"You're pitching REBBL… right now?"

"That's okay. How are you?"

"But this is the account you're trying to win!"

"Never mind work. Are you ok?"

"I am, but I have some questions for you."

"Shoot."

"It's complicated."

"Want to meet somewhere?'

Was that what she wanted? She had called him. "Yes," she said, surprising herself. Maybe this was the best route, to restore her peace of mind. To make sure, once and for all, that he hadn't meddled in Joan's decision-making. Or that he had. In either case, she needed to know.

"I get back from California tomorrow afternoon," he said. "You name the time."

"I'm free tomorrow night. I'll text you. Now go pitch your client."

"Gotcha. We're representing your ideas in there, too, you know."

"Don't be boring," she reminded him, and hung up.

She tried to push away thoughts of Phoenix. For now, there were her commitments at work. She needed to prep for a call, plan for transition meetings, plus a list of other preparations that would consume her attention until the end of the business day.

No longer able to concentrate, she ordered a ride service. She didn't want to take the subway with an armload of posies. She had fifteen minutes before the car arrived, so she called Mandy while waiting on the street.

"Phoenix sent me flowers."

"Is he trying to buy you?"

"His note said he was sorry."

"Are they nice at least?"

Orchid laughed. "They're stunning. How are you? I want to see Matty soon."

"Come by before your trip. You can have diaper duty. Or diaper doody, as the case may be."

"Gross. Whoever said only guys have potty humor?"

"It's my whole life now."

"Better you than me!"

"So, what are you going to do about your rich suitor whose dad set him up from the grave."

"It's really twisted when you sum it up that way."

"No more twisted than meeting guys on an app."

"I don't know about that. But I just called him and asked him to meet me."

Mandy paused. "The plot thickens."

"The thing is, I keep wondering about stuff that only he can answer."

"Plus, you're nursing a massive crush on the guy."

Orchid smelled the flowers in her arms. The truth freed her tongue. "It's not about his looks, though that doesn't hurt. He's charming with this funny sarcastic humor, and he's open-minded about all kinds of things. He never makes me feel bad about my sensitivities, and sometimes I think he'd do anything to protect me. I just wonder about his motives."

Mandy laughed. "I'm not even single and I can read the guy. Sure, maybe coming to see you the first time was out of obligation. But don't you think he satisfied his dad's promise just giving you the campaign to work on? Everything else—the trip to Paris, the invitation to his apartment, that fancy awards show, even your first coffee—was icing on the cake. That wasn't for his dad. That was for him... and you."

Before meeting him, she'd dated all types. She'd attracted badass bikers, studious prep schoolboys, artists, and architects. Phoenix orbited a sphere that defied easy classification. There'd been attraction for sure, and then mutual admiration, shared values and interests, matched intellect. One thing was certain. Phoenix had imprinted a space in her that was indelible.

"I may be a mom," said Mandy, cutting into her thoughts. "But I still have eyes. And that guy is—"

"A living god?" Orchid answered.

"Exactly, so you gotta decide: you want a mere mortal, or are you ready to level up?"

Orchid burbled a laugh. "You sound more boy hungry than you were in college... which is saying a lot."

"You know that I'm on your side. If you wanna say hasta la vista, I'm behind you. But I wouldn't blame you if you went batty every time you're with him."

Orchid leaned back. "Actually? I do have feelings."

"Boom!" Mandy sounded victorious.

"I'm seeing him tomorrow. I'll ask my questions, and then I'm afraid it's goodbye for good."

"Oh that's kinda sad."

"Thanks for making me question my sanity."

"All I know is you better call me from China. I already miss you, hon!" Mandy said.

"We can still talk or text from China," Orchid assured her friend.

"Promise?"

"Of course."

Orchid waltzed in a fog up to her apartment, propelled by a new dilemma. She placed the flowers on her little breakfast table, but decided on the coffee table. The peonies matched her décor. Her mind and heart battled.

After she changed out of her work clothes, she texted Phoenix. It was best to meet at the coffee shop near their offices. It seemed like a smart, neutral choice. He agreed.

The moment she arrived at the coffee shop, she realized her mistake. Nostalgia overcame her as she crossed the threshold.

Phoenix stood up and took a step towards her. And then, as if thinking better of it, awaited her approach. Her drink steamed beside his espresso.

He pulled out her chair and then sat down.

"You're early," she accused.

He opened his mouth, and she held her breath for his snarky comeback. Instead, he pressed his lips together.

"Sorry," he said, in his low rumble. He looked sad, a faint shadow of unshaved scruff darkening his cheeks and jaw.

She recalled his ravenous appetite that evening at the agency, him spooning vegan eggplant into his mouth and wrinkling his nose at the concept of nutritional yeast.

She spoke, but only to blot out her true emotions. "How was REBBL?" The way he looked at her made her wonder. He'd just flown across the country. He'd met her as requested. And she was asking him about work?

He answered gamely. "I think it went well. The client liked your sustainability suggestions."

She nodded and sipped her beverage. "Caramel macchiato?" she asked.

"Frappuccino. Same as the first time we met here. Same table, too. And I brought something else." He pointed at the manila envelope next to his drink and then, before she could ask, said, "It's my father's letter. With his last wishes. You're welcome to read it. Or not. I'll answer anything you want. You deserve complete honesty. Even if this is the last time we see each other. Which is completely up to you." She noted how his sadness deepened, the creases beside his mouth, his cheeks unable to lift. He hadn't smiled since she'd arrived. His somber attitude conveyed farewell. For a moment, relief relaxed her shoulders. Then she pictured leaving this place, never to see Phoenix again, and she began to miss him. She needed to regain control, of her emotions, and of this meeting. "I want to know if you swayed Joan to give me this assignment," she began, naming her first fear.

"She doesn't even know that I know you. That is, outside the one presentation at your office," he stated.

Orchid looked at the cover note and read a portion of it aloud. "To be read six months *after my death*. It really must've meant something to him, that he wrote this down."

He unsealed the envelope and handed it to her. "It must've."

She slipped out the single page and scanned Judge Walker's words.

> *I never fully shared how much it weighed on me, the gap between your privileged life and those who came through my court...it would ease my soul if you could sprinkle one more good deed into the world on my behalf.*
>
> *With complete discretion, and without revealing the source of the request, could you please find and*

bestow a good Samaritan deed on one of my long-ago cases? If there's anything she needs, provide a little nudge in the right direction.

Perhaps I'll rest easy, knowing that you might be able to help this girl, and knowing that you'll keep this confidential. Please don't tell even your brother or mom. Her name is Orchid Paige.

God bless you in this endeavor. Dad

He remembered her. For all those years. He cared about righting wrongs. She felt moved, then angry and, finally, emotional.

"You did tell your brother. Against your dad's wishes," she noted.

"Caleb was goading me about you. I guess the secret was too much to hold in," he said.

"Your dad saw me at the lowest point in my life. My aunt was trying to win money against the people who'd served my parents alcohol before their accident. I testified in your dad's court. In the end, the case didn't amount to much."

"He'd be happy to see you doing well," Phoenix predicted.

"I think he meant well," she said at last. "At least his letter's not maudlin or pitying."

"You made an impression on him. After all the cases he'd seen, that was really saying something."

"Did you consider doing nothing?" she asked.

He nodded. "I did, yes, but maybe not long enough. At the time, I couldn't see a downside. I do now. I can see from your perspective how manipulative this whole thing must feel."

She studied his face and saw honesty, sincerity. "Walk me through what you did. After you got the letter."

"I will," he agreed. "But first, I want to say that you've helped me see him in a new light. Not necessarily a good one. I was blinded by being Judge Walker's son, and I took his counsel as gold. It's making me realize that the way he pushed us boys wasn't all good. I'm going to be honest here." He paused for a long moment. "He's the reason why I turned into a perfectionist who's never satisfied."

Honesty rippled his chin for a moment. She remained silent, seeing pain on his face. Clearly, he was trying to understand how all this happened.

"My brother grew up thinking he could never be good enough."

Orchid nodded. "I've been thinking that I've been selfish. You know, just thinking of me. But you had it tough, too, in a different way. I had no father, and yours had such high expectations."

"I'm sorry for what you missed," he said.

"Don't be sorry for me," she declared, and then heard the edge in her voice. "I hate pity," she added, her tone softer. "My life, and what I was lacking, has made me stronger."

Phoenix smiled. "I can see that, and I respect that. Just remember that it's okay to need other people, too."

His words landed close to home. She shivered, and hid it with a sip of coffee. "Okay, so walk me through what you did. That is, to fulfill your father's wishes." She wanted to know... and she didn't. And yet, without understanding, how could she move forward? She looked him squarely in the eyes. In that moment, he wasn't a proud athlete, an agency founder, or even a mentor. Just a man with a heavy heart. No artifice. No subterfuge.

"I promised my father that I would find a good Samaritan deed. I Googled your name and... voilà. Orchid Paige is a unique name. I didn't know how to figure out what you'd need, so I called a private investigator."

Orchid flinched. "How weird that I was tailed and didn't even know it."

"If it makes you feel better, she put me through the paces, pressed me on my motives before she'd take the job. She even suggested just sending you money and being done with it. But, I don't know, there was something about your picture, your LinkedIn profile. I could see that you were successful. You didn't need a handout. So, I asked her to find out what you did need. She called to say she'd found what you wanted, but you thought there was little chance you'd get it."

Orchid's eyebrow lifted. "China? So, you thought you'd win me the assignment?"

"I didn't even know what you wanted then. She didn't either. She just had the name of some club that you liked. I talked my brother into going with me."

She thought about this for a moment. "So, your plan was to run into me, and talk to me as if we were strangers bumping into each other?"

Phoenix shook his head. "Honestly, I had no plan. This was all new to me. I naively thought I might overhear what you wanted. Or at least get a sense if you were okay. And maybe that'd be it. When I saw you looked fine, I finished my beer and was about to leave. I told Caleb that we could skip out after I used the bathroom."

"And then I ran into you."

Phoenix leaned closer, his forearm nudging away his drink. His intensity tempted her to look away. His magnetic power won.

"Exactly," he said. "And here's the thing. I've been thinking about us. I get how it looks bad, and I'm not denying my responsibility or my actions. But... do you believe in destiny?"

"Destiny? Like fate?"

"Yeah."

Orchid searched her mind for a moment. "When my parents died, people talked about God's destiny, and they said it was their time. Even then, I didn't buy it."

Phoenix nodded. "Sometimes there are senseless accidents. And I'm sorry about that." His palm turned like he wanted to reach for her hand.

"I believe in free will," she said.

"Me, too. I don't think every minute of our lives is preordained. It's just that, do you ever wonder, maybe some people were meant to meet?"

She filled her lungs with air, and then said, "Sometimes I tell myself that I picked my parents in another lifetime—even knowing how little time I'd have with them."

When he spoke, his voice was deeper. "I haven't felt it often, but I wonder if sometimes the people we meet… it's kismet."

She nodded. "I guess anything's possible."

"Think about it: my dad kicked off my search for you, but then actually you found me when you came to the bathroom. That was your doing. Still: destiny."

She'd wondered the same thing. Now, this path of thinking was leaving her vulnerable. She had more questions. "Destiny? But you could've left well enough alone after that."

"Except you wanted to go to China, and you wanted to learn Mandarin, and I could actually help with that."

"I see that, but how'd you end up at my office?"

"The same time I hired the PI, I saw where you worked. So, I called Joan, because we'd worked together in another job. She checked in with me a few weeks later and asked me to present my ideas. I hoped you'd be there, and—"

"You're not going to believe this," she said, interrupting him, "I went to Joan with the idea to have agencies come pitch, because I was looking to work on a campaign. And she said she'd call some people she knew."

"She must've called me because you asked. So, it looks like half of it was luck."

"Or destiny," she said, her insides warming with the idea.

"Yes. Like, you staying after the presentation and walking me to the elevator."

Orchid measured the candor in his face as she sipped her drink. "I can't help but think it must've affected how you saw me, because of your dad."

Phoenix stared down into his cup, then lifted his eyes to meet hers. "I don't know. But couldn't I ask you the same thing? How much of your view of me is informed by my being able to help you? Could it be misplaced gratitude?"

She considered this. From his view, she could be another hanger-on, using him for his brains and connections, like his fellow classmates had in high school. "Or worse," she said, her perspective shifting. "It could even look like selfishness. Taking advantage of."

Phoenix nodded once, a terse conservation of motion. "Not to take away from my culpability in not telling you, but you see how things can look bad... even when intentions are good?"

She nodded, and could feel her defenses melting.

"My dad set things in motion, that's true. But what I did afterwards was my choice. Please believe me," he said.

Again, she was struck by the sincerity in his voice.

She looked at his hand, and the freckle that winked from under his left shirt cuff. He had abandoned a client pitch to take her call, and then he'd come directly from the airport to see her. "I believe you," she said.

His shoulders relaxed, and a low breath left him. "Thank you."

"But... here's what I want to know. Were you ever going to tell me the truth?"

His eyebrows pulled together; his answer was revealed slowly, as if he were mining his mind for the answer. "I did think about telling you. But dad's letter was clear about keeping it confidential. And then after a while, it seemed too late to come clean."

She searched her emotions. Her anger had dissipated. The power of what lay underneath had not yet been released. She wasn't ready to admit what she felt about his affection for her. In truth, she wasn't sure she knew. "Well," she said, gathering her things. "I better go home and pack."

He sat there watching her. Even though she'd asked all her questions, she wasn't ready to say goodbye. He hadn't requested anything from her. He was leaving the ball in her court. She was in total control.

Then, an idea began to percolate.

She told herself to remain silent, to think about the consequences first. The words came spouting out before she knew it. "Would you like to have dinner before I go? I'd like to thank you for helping me with the assignment. It really was kind of you."

The way his mouth stretched into an enormous smile radiated such joy that her heart thudded.

"I'd love to," he said.

"Saturday's free, but dinner'll have to be early. My train to JFK leaves at an obscene hour. Tell me what you'd like and I'll make reservations."

He spoke in such a low voice, as if he didn't want to frighten away her offer. "I appreciate it, really I do. But do you have time to think about making reservations?"

She scoured her brain for restaurants. "There's a Shake Shack near my place. Or we can do Circ take-out."

"May I be honest?" he asked.

She grinned. Her chest felt lighter than it had in weeks. "Honest is what you've been tonight, so go ahead."

He granted her a small smile. "Let me make reservations. We'll celebrate your assignment. And forget the train, I'll take you to the airport. Are you on the ten a.m. flight?"

"Yeah. You sure about the ride? Ten a.m. means I'm outta here by six."

"*We're* outta here by six," he corrected her.

"That's really nice of you." She pictured seeing him in the wee morning hours, riding in his sports car. Maybe he'd walk her into the airport. It'd be a fitting start to her trip to China.

"Besides, having plans might take my mind off my dad's anniversary," he said.

That did it. All her defenses gone, she said, "Thank you." Standing up, she stuck out her hand. "Friends?"

He considered her, then met her palm in his warm grasp. "Dagger to my heart," he said. When he stood, he pretended to stagger, his fist against his chest.

She felt the corners of her mouth twitch. He'd been completely vulnerable and she'd given him nothing. Not even her own feelings. She pointed at the letter. Her last request. "Let's never discuss this again. We met at a bar. We met at work. Any answer closer to the truth takes me back to being poor orphan Orchid."

He frowned. "It's a deal. But to be clear, I see nothing poor about you." And then, right in front of her, he ripped the letter in two, then continued until it was nothing but shreds. After dropping the fragments into a nearby recycle bin, he turned to face her. "What letter?" he asked.

She almost laughed with joy. His action felt as if he had just chosen her over his father. "I totally forgive you," she said with honesty. And then she sauntered out of the café, her steps light with a new beginning. She did not glance back.

She had promised they were just friends. She had lied

CHAPTER 23

HALF YET WHOLE

Orchid

Orchid flung open her closet door and fingered each item, seeking inspiration for this final night out. A shimmery organza minidress, low cut and edgy, suited her mood. She paired it with summer spiked booties, the contrasting styles mirroring her mood.

Dressed, freshly made-up, she stepped into the elevator. As it descended, she checked her bag. Lipstick, keys, phone. Check. A Houdini-worthy cage around her heart. Check.

Phoenix had suggested the most exclusive eatery in her neighborhood, one with enough plush perfection to cause her to peek inside whenever she passed it.

"What?" she had asked that morning, when he had texted to tell her where they were going. "The place with truffles that cost an arm and a leg?"

"Yes, and whatever you wear will be uniquely Orchid, as always!"

They met in her lobby. She saw how his eyes grew wide, sending a jolt through her. The Art Deco lamp near the entry cast a yellow glow around him. He ran his hand through his hair, a move she'd seen many times. And yet that simple gesture caused her chest to well, as if she were drowning in this man. Even if her eyes were closed, she could only see Phoenix. A hundred echoes of Phoenix in every corner.

From him, she had learned about grace under pressure, and

that leadership meant doing the right thing, even if it cost you. This man, the one who waited for her with cheeks that couldn't stop grinning, filled the room with his presence.

A woman he didn't heed stuttered her gait over the sight of him as she pushed out onto the street. His gaze never wavered from Orchid's.

He took two long strides towards her and said her name.

They walked to the door and he held it open for her, while keeping his distance.

Outside, she tried to shake off the chill, the fabric of her dress suddenly thin for nighttime temperatures.

"Would you like my jacket?" He began to shrug out of his blazer until she waved off his efforts.

She knew that her willpower would crumble under the scent of his coat. The heady mixture of musk, spice and Phoenix might unravel the ribbons threading her dress. She imagined the fabric pooling at her feet. Right there on the sidewalk.

A cold wind shoved them towards the brown brick buildings that lined the sidewalk. Her teeth clacked from the shiver that ran through her.

She saw how a corner of his mouth twitched at her fib.

"Okay, fine, you can block the wind, but keep your jacket, no sense in both of us freezing," she said, edging closer to him.

He smelled even better than she'd imagined, like freshly laundered linens sun-dried in a field of blackberries and vanilla.

There was no sense of time as they walked. She never wanted this to end.

Inside, Phoenix answered the hostess' greeting. "Reservations for two, under Kai Lan."

Orchid convulsed with merriment. He attempted to maintain a straight face.

Those two words were the golden ticket that unlocked a little round table, one with a view to the outside.

They were handed menus.

"So many choices," she said. And then, "Wait, is this place vegetarian?" She looked up at Phoenix.

His eyes glistened with delight.

"I don't understand," she said. "I've walked by here dozens of times. I knew I could never afford it, but even so… I thought I knew every vegetarian place within ten blocks of my place."

"It isn't normally," he said simply. "Vegetarian, that is."

Orchid felt her jaw fall open. He not only had wanted to celebrate her success, he'd convinced a Michelin-starred restaurant to produce a meatless menu.

"This is the best day ever," she said, the sentiment traveling from her heart to her lips.

"You deserve it," he told her.

She looked at the menu. No one had ever done such a thoughtful thing for her. Memories wound through her teenage years, where the frozen end of a Sara Lee pound cake marked her special occasions. Those were the days when it was easier to pretend she didn't matter. Today, she did.

Their waiter approached. He was an older gentleman whose dark eyebrows and kindly manner resembled her dad. That is, her dad who had been filtered through an aging app. As if she needed more nostalgia to push her emotions over the edge. She dabbed a finger under each eye.

"Bonsoir, I am Edward. I hope the chef's choices are to your liking. Do you have any questions?"

Orchid smiled at him. "I'm having a hard time choosing. What do you recommend?" She handed him the menu.

"Everything is fresh from today's market," he said, and went on to describe the goat cheese-topped crepes, fresh burrata with Roma tomatoes, aubergine with truffle aioli, and garlic drizzled portobello mushrooms.

Orchid stopped him. "I can't even listen to the desserts," she laughed. "You're making it harder, not easier." Her stomach rumbled.

"What would you say to one of everything, hungry bird?" asked Phoenix.

"You're spoiling me," she said, and nodded her agreement to the waiter.

After the server left, Phoenix joshed with her. "Your payment is to write a hundred briefs on the flight."

"Oh, the flight, don't remind me. No business class for me this time."

"I prefer center seats."

She shook her head. "So you say! And by the way," she added. "I haven't finished packing. I still can't believe you talked me into coming out tonight."

"Oh, I understand," teased Phoenix. "A microwaved burrito would've been preferable to this." He waved a hand to indicate the place that was both grand and intimate.

Gratitude welled inside her as she scanned the weathered tapestries hanging around them. She returned the gaze of this man whose presence dwarfed everyone and everything around them.

A young woman arrived at their table, a dark green bottle in her hands. "Good evening. It's lovely to have you celebrating with us tonight. Is this what you've ordered?"

Phoenix turned to Orchid. "Would you like this, or something else?"

She recognized the label and drew a breath. Then she tried on Mr. Princeton's haughty tone. "I suppose Dom will do."

Phoenix chuckled.

The cork exited with a soft pop, releasing a little of the pressure in her heart. With no assignment to bring them together, this could be their last night. She didn't want it to be.

Liquid gold filled their slender flutes. The sommelier placed the bottle on the table and walked away.

"A toast to your talent." Phoenix raised his glass to touch hers.

"And mentors."

The bubbles broke bright like night stars across her tongue. "How's the champagne?" he asked.

She touched fingertips to her lips and set free an invisible kiss to express her pleasure. "Hen hao." *Very good.*

Edward returned, pronounced the names of the two appetizers, and settled the plates between them. Orchid flashed to how they must appear to this doppelganger for her dad, the handsome couple in a suit and evening dress who arrived laughing, enjoying each other's company. A thought flashed through her mind: Her parents would've loved Phoenix.

Between the exquisite champagne and cuisine, Orchid found that she couldn't stop talking. She commented on every flavor combination, on ads she'd seen, even questions about Phoenix's family.

When the entrees were consumed, she asked, "You're not missing meat?" "I'm not missing a thing." He looked into her eyes.

The bottle, now empty, was a truth serum. "Phoenix, I wish you were coming with me. To China. For all six weeks. We'd have so much fun. Like Paris."

He paused, as if measuring the meaning in her eyes. "You're probably teasing me, but I wish I were, too."

"Then come. We only live once. Get a ticket and meet me there. It'll be an adventure. I could use your Chinese skills.."

"Your Chinese has improved a lot. You're going to be more than fine."

Edward and the sommelier approached, but she hardly saw them. Instead, words rushed into her head, a revelation that hit her hard: *We're meant for each other.*

Her heart stuttered, and then bloomed, blossoming infinite petals to envelop both of them, even the diners in this restaurant, and every living being. Unconditional love. It welled up, so abundant that it might have taken her to her knees, were she not seated. Pure joy. Enough to fill the universe.

She wanted to tell someone. Anyone. The world. Maybe the server who looked even more like her father after several glasses of Dom Perignon.

Phoenix was smiling at her, as if words of shared joy were spilling from his lips. Yes, her mother would've liked him. Her father, too. Three words floated into her consciousness that startled her with their gravity. *I'm in love.*

The servers saved her descent into sentimentality with dessert.

Orchid returned to earth and thanked the waiter for the crème brûlée topped with blueberries. He smiled and walked away.

Then, it was just the two of them. Pale light shone down, cocooning Orchid and Phoenix in this moment filled with enough joy for a lifetime.

He pointed a spoon at her custard. "Acceptable?"

She scooped a taste onto her tongue. Sweetness spread. "More than acceptable." He was asking about the confection. Orchid could only see Phoenix.

Her phone buzzed. She checked the screen. It was Mandy, asking how dinner was. The message caused her to notice the hour and she startled. "I don't want this night to end but I have to finish packing."

"I'm your expert at China trips. Don't forget your adaptors. And your passport! Work visa? A copy of your hotel address in Chinese?"

She groaned. "I have a feeling I'm going to forget half the important stuff."

"No way am I letting you feel stressed. Let me come up to help."

What could she say? She didn't want any more risk to her heart. And she didn't want to let him go, either. Phoenix had saved her all these months.

He studied the worry on her face.

She tried to unpucker her brow.

"The check's taken care of; want to go?"

"Are you sure you don't want to split the bill?" When she saw his face, she quickly added, "Thank you for dinner."

His expression softened. "No, thank *you.*"

"For?"

"For one last night. For forgiving me."

The evidence of his dad's wishes had ended in shreds. Tearing up that letter had unified them. "Nothing to forgive." Bubbly melting away her barriers, she thought about grasping his extended hand.

Was Mandy right? Do childhood travesties earn adult contentment? Maybe. She was more than content.

They walked into the chilled night air. A round moon filled the sky, brighter than the lights of the nearby bodegas. Her view blurred. Everything she'd wanted a few months ago was just ahead of her. The Beijing assignment. Her first trip to China. And this unexpected gift.

Her shoulders relaxed, her body's confirmation that she could trust Phoenix.

As they walked, he slipped off his blazer. "It's getting cold," he said.

She draped it over her shoulders, the oversized jacket reducing her to a child's proportions.

They walked together, bodies close, Phoenix's pace in step with hers. Her arm brushed his as they sidestepped uneven pavement and dark puddles. Deep inside her, a barrier continued to drop, like water breaking against the sand.

Emboldened by a dark stretch before the lights of the next block, Orchid turned to face Phoenix. Without thinking it through, she tucked herself into his arms.

He pressed his lips lightly to her hair.

His breath warmed her scalp. Her legs felt like jelly.

He wrapped his arms even more tightly around her. It felt as if their strength, and the power of his caring for her, could carry through anything.

They separated slowly, then turned towards her building.

When they arrived, she paused, key card in hand. "It's late. You don't have to stay," Her words faltered over the mismatch with her true feelings. She didn't want to let him go. Ever.

"There's nowhere I'd rather be," he said.

Something in his voice urged her to look up. The lighting illuminated his expression.

She used the card and they walked through the empty vestibule to the elevator.

In the lift, she shrugged off the blue blazer and smoothed it with one hand.

The door parted and she led the way through the hallway to her apartment. She opened the door and saw the place afresh, as if through his eyes. The pale pink décor cast a feminine hue, in sharp contrast to his masculinity. Piles of clothes were scattered about. She was glad she'd cleaned the mail off the breakfast table. On the ground, an opened suitcase awaited her attention.

Orchid kicked off her high heels with a groan of relief. "That was the best dinner. Would you like a nightcap?"

"Only if you have something to slow time?"

"I wish." She scooped some folded garments into the valise, clearing a space on the sofa.

"Ah, the flowers." He nodded towards the vase on her coffee table, and then settled into the couch. His muscular form made the only seating in her living room seem even smaller than normal.

"They're really beautiful, thank you. They're not even drooping yet." She looked at them and thought how they filled her with such pleasure. "There's a superstition that wilted peonies are a sign of impending disaster. So, I'm going to hang them to dry while I'm away." She ran a thumb over the pinkest of blooms, and it bobbed as if in bashful agreement.

"I can send you more."

Orchid chuckled. "I had to win a coveted assignment for these. What will I have to do for more? Cure cancer?"

"I'm sure there will be many more accomplishments to celebrate."

She met his eyes. *Will you be here to celebrate whatever is to come?*

"Do you want a hand with packing?" he asked.

She pictured him happening upon her lacy undergarments. "Maybe you can just run through your list of stuff I might forget."

"Power adaptors," he began, counting off on one hand. She snagged the black velvet pouch from the sofa and plopped it into her luggage.

"Passport?"

"It's in my carry-on."

"Chinese currency?"

"I'll change money at the airport."

"You won't need much cash as long as you've downloaded one of their digital apps. Next time, I'll bring you some of my renminbi," referring to Chinese currency.

Next time. Her hope rose that they would see each other again, even after the assignment had ended. "Speaking of next time, would you like to pick me up from the airport?"

"I'm taking you, so I don't see why not."

She didn't revisit her request that he join her. "The details are on my itinerary."

One suitcase was already packed, and the second would stay open until she'd brushed her teeth in the morning and could secure her toiletries into the bag.

She deposited stacks of blouses into the last few spaces, then joined Phoenix on the couch. "I think I have everything, including your book on Asian culture."

His mouth widened with pleasure. "I'm glad it was helpful. I'd hoped you'd like it."

"So thoughtful. And we barely even knew each other then," she said.

"I knew enough to see what was important to you."

"How is it fair, you always giving to me?" she wondered aloud.

"You've given to me too, more than you know."

Orchid waited, feeling the disbelief plain on her face.

"You woke me. I didn't know it when we met but I was sleepwalking through every day, working, going to the gym, attending social events. Instead of staying present in the moment."

She saw the honesty in his admission. "Ditto." Buoyed by the certainty of seeing Phoenix again, in six weeks, she suddenly wanted to tell him the truth.

"You know, tonight was the best day ever. You thought of everything."

"I'm glad."

"But tonight? It reminded me of my dad."

His full lips compressed. He leaned towards her. Like a lioness with her mate, Orchid nestled into his warmth. His muscular embrace could unlock secrets to Bronze age cave paintings. She could live in this one spot until the end of days, magical fairies spiriting berries and sparkling water to them for sustenance.

"The waiter looked like him."

"Are you okay?"

The thought of his dad and their shared grief gave her encouragement to continue.

"You called it my kryptonite, that night at the Effies." She checked his expression for courage. He was calm, and kind. "I don't really talk about it. But my parents' car crash?"

He nodded, and offered his hand. For the second time that night, she slipped her palm into his left hand. The comfort of his scent, and warmth, lifted her courage enough to share what had weighed forever heavy in her memories, paining her by pounding at the cage bars that had reinstated themselves around her heart. She looked down. His thigh skimmed hers.

"I saw it. That cold night. In my pajamas." He already knew this, yet she couldn't help talking about what she never told anyone, buoyed by the safety of this man who accepted even the damaged parts of herself.

"Right, when you were twelve," he encouraged her.

"Yeah. I don't even know anymore what I saw, or what I've imagined since then. But these images come to me, when I see someone who's been hurt. Like waking nightmares."

"PTSD."

"Ironic to have me work on that campaign."

His lids lowered for a beat. "Sorry if that was hard for you. I didn't know when I'd first offered it."

"I think it was good for me. I feel like I've come a long way."

He breathed a sigh. "That's good."

He deserved to know. She would feel better for sharing the burden of her memories. Beyond the icy driveway, she was haunted by other images. "At the funeral, they had a half-open casket for my dad. I wanted to see him, all of him. Like mom. But when I asked, the adults turned away. My uncle just hugged me. No one would tell me but the way they reacted when I asked, I think the crash crushed his legs. I don't think he even had legs anymore. And it's not like he could use them if he did. He was dead after all. But in my nightmares, there's just blood, and an empty space where his legs were. And sometimes stuff triggers me. I'm going to shut up now, before I make things worse for me."

"Oh god, I'm so sorry. That's terrible for anyone to go through. And as a kid, it's like, you wouldn't even know how to process it."

"That's why I was a mess at the triathlon. And seeing the injured veterans."

"Now you're doing better?"

"Yeah. You know meeting Tammy helped. And you."

"Me?"

"You saw me. You didn't make me feel less than," Orchid explained.

"You have nothing to be ashamed about."

"My ego thanks you for understanding."

"Your ego has nothing to fear from me, I'm not judging. Or if I am, I see nothing lacking."

His grip cupped hers. She caressed the soft pad of his thumb then traced a finger up the lifeline along his palm, to the faint pulse in his wrist. The intimacy of crossing the boundary beneath his shirt cuff shifted their intimacy from comfort to electrifying.

Something barely perceptible passed over his face. Light as a feather. She searched his expression, and the softness around his eyes. A look of longing. Maybe more.

He paused, weighing something in his mind. "I should let you go. Get some rest before tomorrow. I'll swing by with the car at six." He shifted to the edge of the couch, as if intending to stand.

She could foresee the inches between them expanding to the length of this room, and then the city blocks between their apartments. And after tomorrow, six thousand miles from here to Beijing.

"Don't go. There's one more thing." She took his hand.

He paused and turned. There was confusion on his face.

Their time since April had filled her with a lifetime of joy, and she wanted more. She leaned closer.

There was a furrow across his brow. "I made a promise to myself that I'd never hurt you." His voice was a murmur, low and hoarse.

Courage filled her. Swelled up from her heart and radiated into every part of her body. She felt as if she were growing beyond her stature... to meet the giant that was this man. Then, the force of all that had transpired between them, the magnitude of the love he had bestowed upon her—this expansive, unconditional love—suddenly burst through. The scaffolds around her heart, structures that had protected the young Orchid, and continued their grip until this day, suddenly splintered. His care had begun her journey, but the rest of this change was her doing. She, Orchid Paige, was more than enough. What she'd been through didn't make her less. Not less than those with trust funds and Ivy League pedigrees, not less than those with parents and loving families. Her right to rise above her past came from within, from her reserves of strength. With Phoenix, that power glowed, like a thousand ancestral warriors. She could barely catch her breath.

In this moment, she had shared her gift with the one person who had helped her see it.

She studied his face, then tilted her head. "This won't hurt. Either of us. I promise."

His confusion seemed to fade with understanding. Matching the delicacy of her barely perceptible motion, he narrowed the gap between them.

"You've been extraordinary. And I made a mistake... in the ground rules, from the start," she said.

"It was no mistake," he replied. "Trying to adhere to your ground rules, and failing every time we were together, that's how I knew this is the real thing. You are amazing. Everything about you."

She touched his face. "How I've wanted this," she said.

All those wasted months, adhering to propriety.

His look of desire touched her heart. What if she let whatever happened... happen? Without assumptions.

She leaned closer and their lips met with a tender touch. His embrace was full and warm, like the man she'd known him to be. She felt desire... and urgency.

Every late night of want, tipping towards reality, exploded in her.

He mirrored her tenderness, fingers through her hair. The contours of his lips fit hers, impressing care and want in every caress.

A ragged edge of their shared histories suddenly softened.

The kiss was unforgettable. Soft. Hot. Too short. Yet...like falling into eternity. Vulnerability splayed open her heart, as if he'd unlocked a secret in her core. In truth, he had.

They pulled back, their breathing rough.

He glanced at her, studying her expression. "If it makes you uncomfortable, we can forget that kiss."

"I hope I never forget it," she said, not meaning to sound so earnest and vulnerable.

He smiled. "We aim to please. Did you know LUSH has a new line?" he asked. "It's like those plaster imprints of baby footprints only you use their natural beeswax to capture the imprint of lips. It's a kiss-print."

"You made that up."

"Yeah, I did but it's a damned good idea."

She threw her head back in appreciation.

This was his gift to her, not the dinner. Not Nice or Cannes. She had thought she wanted nothing more than to unearth her ancestry with a ticket to China, and that this opportunity, along with Mandarin, was what she was missing. She was wrong. Looking back at her pleas to Joan, her hijinks with Peter, her jealousy over Princeton, and Violet winning the office pool, all seemed so trite. The reality was that she'd changed these last months. She'd helped wounded warriors, was learning a language, and was about to explore China. Her world had grown.

The biggest gift of all was that she had learned to trust. She trusted Phoenix. More than that, she'd fallen in love with a man for his compassion, his humor, his impossible standards... everything.

Theirs was the deepest relationship she'd experienced in her adult life.

Phoenix murmured something that she didn't hear. She saw him press his fingers to his lips and then touch her cheek. He slung his jacket over his shoulder and walked out her front door.

His kiss told her that he felt the same about her.

Tomorrow would be *Goodbye, New York*. And not *Goodbye, Phoenix*.

Her heart had healed. She had learned to trust. Most of all, she could now trust herself.

She admired the peonies bowing over the lip of the ceramic vase. She touched a petal and a leaf tumbled to the table. Her aunt might say this was a sign of bad luck. *Pshaw.*

She found a scrap of paper and scrawled:

I'm going to miss you more than you know.

She'd slip it to Phoenix tomorrow, in case they didn't have an opportunity to put words to all that had transpired between them. On a whim, she pressed her lips to the bottom of the page, imparting a talisman to keep their hearts tethered over the next six weeks. Her lipstick left a smudge, a personalized kiss-print.

She was ready for this trip. Not just logistically. Emotionally.

Pursuing this assignment had inspired her to grow.

Her pulse, persistent and steady, marched along as evidence of her strength.

Her family might not be here, on earth, but they were still inside her.

No matter the broken pieces of her past, she was more than whole.

Not a thing missing.

NOTE TO READERS

Dear reader,

You've been immersed in the worlds of Orchid and Phoenix. Research shows that readers' brains when reading activate in the same places as the author's brain when writing. So, thank you for sharing this brain-to-brain connection. I hope you were touched by Orchid's heartache and growth, and Phoenix's kindness and dilemma, as I was when penning their stories.

Most of all, here's a request for a kindness. Please help others find the healing in these journeys by telling friends, and leaving a rating or review – on Amazon, Goodreads, Barnes & Noble, Target, BookBub, Kobo, bookshop or anywhere else. Links to these sites and more are available at

www.linktr.ee/cvdh

I'll look forward to meeting you again in the pages of Goodbye, Orchid and subsequent novels.

Wishing you days filled with joy, orchids and more,

Carol

Carol

MEET CAROL

CAROL VAN DEN HENDE is an award-winning author who pens stories of resilience and hope. Her *Goodbye, Orchid* series is inspired by wounded veterans. Her debut novel won 16 literary awards, including the American Fiction Award, IAN Outstanding Fiction First Novel Award, and 2020 Royal Dragonfly for Disability Awareness.

Buzzfeed, Parade, and Travel+Leisure named "heartwarming, heartbreaking" *Goodbye, Orchid* a most anticipated read. Glamour Magazine recommended this "modern, important take on the power of love." The International Pulpwood Queens selected *Goodbye, Orchid* as a 2022 Bonus Book-of-the-Month.

Carol's mission is unlocking optimism as a writer, speaker, strategist, Board member and Climate Reality Leader. One secret to her good fortune? Her humorous husband and teenaged twins, who prove that love really does conquer all.

ACKNOWLEDGMENTS

Many readers wonder about the inspiration behind the *Goodbye, Orchid* series. I'm honored to say that the stories are inspired by wounded warriors. Even though the main characters aren't military personnel, the work pays homage to their experiences. Out of respect for their real-life trauma, much research went into these books.

In *Orchid Blooming*, Orchid Paige comes to realize that her symptoms match those of veterans with PTSD. By seeking treatment, Orchid's character aims to impart hope to those with Post Traumatic Stress Disorder.

While each person's experience with PTSD is unique, I extend gratitude to those who helped anchor Orchid's world in reality. Sgt Aaron Michael Grant (author of *Taking Baghdad: Victory in Iraq with the US Marines*) shared his personal challenges to help make Orchid's reactions and fears even more authentic.

I'm grateful for the professional guidance from Joe Dennis MA, LCMHC, the Clinical Director at Mindful Counseling. He taught me how a professional like Todd Head would approach a client. Appreciation to Jennifer Ambis LCSW for sensitivity reading, and Murray Klayman Esquire for my legal questions on behalf of character Judge Walker (more to come in the sequel!)

Professionals' attention to detail honed the final experience. Many thanks to Caroline Leavitt for her encouragement and ʳervations in the developmental editing process. She ʳed me to have Orchid write about her trauma to help her

Victoria Zackheim is an editor extraordinaire. She slimmed the narrative to its most powerful form, while pointing out aspects that were missing. Special thanks to editor Ellie Maas Davis, the brilliance of cover designer Sarah Baumann-Flood and the formatting expertise of Nina Pierce, and advice from NJRW writers. Any flaws are my responsibility.

Early readers gave generous amounts of time to review draft manuscripts. They provided both feedback and encouragement for the strength and beauty of the characters' experiences. Thanks to Christine Tsai for her focus on character agency, Rachel Mack's finely tuned emotional intelligence, Colleen Tucciarone's keen observations, Lisa Wetzel and Robin Batterson for radiating pure excitement for the work, Corrie Viola (the chapter in Cannes is for you!), Dot Lagg for her smart comments, Tina Levine for her speedy turnaround and trademark enthusiasm, my supportive Women Who Write critique group (Mary, Pat, Michelle M, Michelle S, and MaryLee), and Melody Moser, who was the impetus for the chapter in Paris!

Endless thanks to my humorous hubby and twins for granting me the time to lose myself in my heart's work.

I'll end where I started – what really gives my writing meaning is the way in which it touches people. Readers' enthusiasm for Phoenix and Orchid's story fueled the creation of *Orchid Blooming*. Gratitude to every person who rated, reviewed and told friends about my award-winning work. Thanks to the many groups who helped get the *Goodbye, Orchid* series into the hands of readers, including Kathy L. Murphy and Mandy Haynes, the founder and executive director of The Pulpwood Queens, Susan McBeth and Debbie Harpham of Novel Network, Crystal Patriarche and her team at BookSparks, book advisor Larry Kirshbaum, publisher John Koehler, bookseller

Shari Stauch, REBBL CEO Michele Kessler, Authentically American CEO Dean Wegner, USA Cares CEO Trace Chesser, Heather Abbott Foundation, bookstagrammers, podcasters, DIYMFA, WABC Radio Host Joan Hamburg, award contests, my street team, and many more.

Thanks to every reader for your reviews, middle-of-the-night emails gushing about my book's ending, and invitations to book clubs, libraries, bookstores, festivals, and conferences. We're all on this spinning rock together, and literature brings us even closer. I'm looking forward to hearing from you, and joining together for our next fictional adventure.

DISCUSSION QUESTIONS

Readers and book clubs love discussing Phoenix and Orchid's relationship. Contact Carol at https://novelnetwork.com to schedule a virtual visit with your book club!

1. During Orchid Blooming's opening, Orchid tells her best friend Mandy that she wants to win an assignment to China. Why does she want to go there? What place holds a special personal connection for you?

2. Phoenix offers to help Orchid get the work experience she needs; what's his initial reason for helping her? How do his motivations change over time?

3. Orchid sets ground rules for their professional relationship, that they must keep to business, all business. When do you first sense that this will be hard for her to adhere to? How about Phoenix?

4. On the surface, Phoenix appears to have everything going for him, yet on the inside, he harbors insecurity. How does his feeling he can never live up to his dad drive his actions?

5. Orchid faced trauma in her childhood. Phoenix lost his father a year ago. How does their shared grief shape their relationship?

6. Phoenix and Orchid both strive to be good people, yet their struggles cause angst. Which parts of Phoenix and Orchid's experiences touch you? Which can you relate to? Do any remind you of personal experiences?

7. In the opening chapter, Orchid describes being multi-racial. "Beautiful, dark-haired Mom was the artist in the family, the woman who amused young Orchid with

drawings of dogs in tutus, and cat soirees. When she was little, Orchid thought her Chinese half was connected to her creative side. Her analytical brain was from her dad's side, his long English ancestry stamped with stories of tradesmen and entrepreneurs." What are the varied or paradoxical ways that Orchid experiences being half Chinese?

8. Phoenix is an agency founder. Orchid is successful in the beauty industry. What do they have in common that draws them together? In your experience, how do shared professional interests develop into mutual respect?

9. What leads Phoenix to feel protective towards Orchid? How might his honorable intentions cause conflict for them later?

10. Which portions of Phoenix and Orchid's experiences or beliefs foreshadow difficulties that they'll experience later in their relationship?

11. How do both Phoenix and Orchid grow when the secret of how they met is revealed? Have you ever forgiven someone for keeping a secret?

12. At the beginning of the story, Orchid believes that going to China will bring her closer to her mother. By the end of the story, does she still need this trip to connect with her mom?

Please turn the page
to enjoy this excerpt from

Goodbye, Orchid

CHAPTER 1
TEMPORARY GROUND

Phoenix

SUNDAY JULY 29, MANHATTAN

Phoenix never believed today was goodbye. Even though hellos come with goodbyes. Like black holes and Stephen Hawking. Like doughnuts and donut holes.

But today's goodbye wasn't the end of something.

Orchid's kiss, petal-soft, had changed everything. That was last night. Today, she stood before him, in a leather-edged tunic layered over tights. "It's not too late to come with me," she said, her laugh tinkling like the metal bangles on her arm. She and Phoenix stood at the mouth of the TSA pre-check line before airport security, parting a stream of passengers. Lodged like two boulders in a brook. Her flight was boarding in minutes.

"I'm not going to spoil your moment in the spotlight," he replied.

She reached up for a hug. Her slender frame made Phoenix feel even taller than six-foot. Yet, there was tenderness too. *Mentor, I'm her mentor,* he recalled, slipping from her embrace.

"Spoil my moment? You know I wouldn't be going to China if it weren't for you. You always encouraged me." Her voice rose above the hum of conversations around them. Her lashes were ringed kohl black. Pale skin and ebony hair framed her dark eyes.

"Who, me? You did all the hard work. Stop giving me the credit you deserve. You're going to be awesome," Phoenix said.

"Thank you. Thanks for seeing me off."

"How else was I going to get rid of you?" he asked, his voice oddly gruff.

"Shut up. I have abandonment issues, you know that." She blinked, then her left cheek dimpled. He knew better than to think that she was joking. He wasn't going to tell her but if it came to it he'd protect her from a 787 Dreamliner crashing through the windows of their terminal.

Orchid tiptoed up to kiss his cheek. The edges of their mouths brushed. Crap. He stepped back and her hopeful expression came into focus.

"You better get going or there won't be any China," he said and released her elbow. It struck him that their stance mimicked Michelangelo's Creation of Adam, their hands nearly touching, as if heaven was in those millimeters between.

"I don't want to leave you," she said.

"You have to. You have exactly ten minutes to get through security."

She held his glance for a beat too long and opened her mouth. "This thing between us—"

He shook his head to stop her words before it was too late.

"Don't go all dramatic on me," he said. What he really meant was, Don't screw up our magic, the thing that keeps it real.

So real that she'd comforted him when he confessed it was too late to live up to Dad's expectations. Gone one year today. That had led Orchid to trust him with memories of the accident that had killed her parents. The one thing they shouldn't talk about was them. Phoenix's ex, tough mouthy Tish, had said it best. You break women until there's nothing left, Tish had said as tears fell down her face. And she never cried.

"You better go," he said, distancing himself from Orchid's reach.

She looked at him as he soft-pedaled back, keeping the attraction between them at arm's length.

Her mouth opened and closed. "Do you want to talk about last night?"

The previous evening validated every feeling Phoenix had suppressed since starting work with Orchid on a pro bono project months earlier.

Standing in the airport he recalled what his brother, Caleb, had said the first time he'd seen them together. "You two are hot for each other."

"You're going to miss your flight. We'll talk when you're back," Phoenix said.

She sighed and ran a hand with rings on every finger through her silken hair. "You're a piece of work, Walker."

She used his surname when she was pissed.

"And you are a magnificent marketer about to wow the world of beauty. Now go," he said, and watched as she passed through security to board her overseas flight.

Tish's accusation rattled his brain. Orchid is not a woman I want to break.

Later that morning, after working out and showering, Phoenix pulled on a white button-down, and tailored slacks. He was leaving his apartment to see Mom. She was in town for some flower show. Or a color seminar. And most of all, to be with her sons on the anniversary of their dad's death.

Phoenix held the elevator door for Mrs. V, and her dog. They chatted until the lift descended to the lobby.

"How's Elton feeling today?" he inquired about her panting little terrier.

She told him about the pup's joint issues. They walked out into the sunshine together. She bent to lift Elton's paw in a miniature wave. He waved back, then turned left towards the subway station.

As he strode, he couldn't stop thinking about Orchid. What

makes her so different? Did something shift when she confessed her secrets? She had worked so damned hard to raise money for military vets; even when she couldn't bear to see their injuries, It was like she felt their pain as if it were her own.

At the 86th Street station, he descended the steps two at a time. Energy buzzed to his fingertips. Down below, the cavernous space echoed empty except for a homeless man seated on the ground. This guy looked worse off than most. Phoenix fished for a rumpled bill. The vagabond scowled over his bulbous nose at the lone single. Phoenix was distracted by a square of paper that tumbled out with the money. He walked towards the track, and unfolded the note. It read, I'm going to miss you more than you know. Orchid had pressed a lip-shaped kiss print into the blank spot below the words.

He'd miss her too, until her return in six weeks.

At the edge of the platform, he punched up a song from Orchid's playlist and plugged in his AirPods.

"Where have you been, all my life?" wailed Rihanna. Indeed.

He stood without noticing his physical surroundings, lost in thought about Orchid. Sleek hair; slender; smart; strong. Orchid sparked tenderness and more. Like no one else he'd ever known. On a whim, he texted Caleb both thumbs a blur.

You were right about Orchid.

Eighty thousand pounds of solid mass squealed towards the station. Phoenix stepped forward. Rihanna belted out a ballad over the sound of metal on metal, "Are you hiding from me, yeah? Somewhere in the crowd—"

In his peripheral vision, he noticed a figure swaying towards the gaping hole in the ground. "Hey!" Phoenix shouted, turning as the beggar stumbled right for the open track.

Without thinking, Phoenix dropped his phone and bounded forward. He grabbed the guy's coat to pull him away from the blurred train speeding towards them. The man jerked back. His bearded face screamed with fury. For a moment, they swung with wild centrifugal force. Suddenly, the guy yanked himself free. Phoenix tripped backwards. His feet scrambled to find purchase. Until there was just air over the edge of the platform.

With a split-second to grasp at nothing, Phoenix crashed through the empty space to thud onto the track. He could feel the train's screech judder. The sickening crush of steel slicing bone. Fuck! He could barely breathe. The air filled with screams. He attempted to lift his head. Except he couldn't move. Broken until there's nothing left, he wanted to say.

To continue reading award-winning Goodbye, Orchid, *purchase your copy through this link and remember to leave a rating or review:*
linktr.ee/cvdh